THE GIRL BEFORE EVE

BY

LISA J HOBMAN

This is a fictional work. The names, characters, incidents, places, and locations are solely the concepts and products of the author's imagination or are used to create a fictitious story and should not be construed as real.

5 PRINCE PUBLISHING AND BOOKS, LLC
PO Box 16507
Denver, CO 80216
www.5PrinceBooks.com

ISBN 13: 978-1-939217-96-7   ISBN 10: 1-939217-96-2

The Girl Before Eve
Lisa J. Hobman
Copyright Lisa J. Hobman 2014
Published by 5 Prince Publishing

Front Cover Viola Estrella
Author Photo: Craig@craigphotographystudio.com

First Edition/First Printing January 2014Printed U.S.A.

5 PRINCE PUBLISHING AND BOOKS, LLC.

Dedication

For Rich

We have over twenty years of history together and there are so many songs that eloquently put into words how I feel about you...too many to fit onto one CD. But "Somersault" by Zero 7 is one of my favourites.

Acknowledgements

I would like to say a huge thank you to my wonderful family, especially Rich, Grace, Mum and Dad for supporting me, advising me and putting up with me since this writing journey began. As always, you are the stars in my sky and I love you with all of my heart.

A huge hug to all of my friends, old and new, who have happily taken this roller coaster ride with me and have put up with my incessant talking about books, plot lines and rankings. I adore you all.

To my wonderful beta reading team – it's been such a busy year and I can't express how much I appreciate you taking time out of your busy lives to read my books and give your valued opinions.

I've made so many new friends through Facebook, authors and readers alike, and so a massive thank you to the abso-flippin-lutely faberoo gang from my Facebook page and to my wonderful street team. You've stuck with me and have encouraged me to keep going. Thank you for helping me to fulfil this dream. The Happy Hobman Dancers rock!

To all of the blogs and pages who have supported me, helped spread the word about my books and shared my news, you and everything you do are very much appreciated.

Thank you also to my wonderful 5 Prince family, including my amazing editor Linda. It's wonderful to be a part of such a positive, friendly team. Long may it continue.

THE GIRL BEFORE EVE

Prologue

Friends Will Be Friends (Queen)

The Beginning of Lily and Adam - Primary School 1986

"She is *my* friend, Stewart Campbell, and if I see you pinch anything from her ever, ever again or try to push her over, I will punch you on the nose, and then I'll tell Mrs. Craven and she'll tell your mum, and then you'll be grounded...*forever*!" Adam yelled as he towered over the snivelling little blonde-haired boy whose T-shirt he was grasping.

"I'm going to tell my dad on you, and he'll come to your house and kick your dad's arse, and he's lots bigger than your dad, you smelly pig!" Stewart retorted through his tears and threw the packet of crisps he'd stolen on the playground, the contents spilling out. He stamped on the crisps, crumbling them under his feet.

Adam laughed in the other boy's face. "Oh no, he isn't, and now I'm going to tell Mrs. Craven that you said a swear word! Don't you ever hurt her again, do you hear me? She's a girl and you should never, *ever* hit girls or pinch their snack. And now you've dropped it on the floor and she hasn't got one. You're just mean and nasty, Stewart Campbell. And that's why nobody likes you!" Adam released the blonde boy's T-shirt and pushed him away. The boy ran off to the other side of the playground just as the lunchtime supervisor came around the corner. She must have noticed the gathered crowd of children.

"Everything alright over here, Adam?" the tall, red-haired lady asked with a sour look on her face.

"Yes, Mrs. Craven. Stewart Campbell said a rude word though, so I told him off and said I was going to tell."

"Oh did he now? That boy needs to learn some manners. I think I'll tell his teacher. Perhaps a quick call home might be in order." Mrs. Craven glanced toward Adam's friend just as Lily wiped the tears from her eyes and pushed the mass of wild, dark curls from her damp face. "Lily? Have you been crying?"

Lily nodded.

"What happened?" Mrs. Craven asked, narrowing her eyes.

Lily worriedly looked to Adam.

"It's okay, Mrs. Craven. Stewart was being mean and he took her snack and threw it on the floor and stamped on it. But I told him off for that, too."

Mrs. Craven smiled and ruffled Adam's scruffy, dark hair. "Eeeh, for nothing but a six-year-old boy you do look after her well, don't you, son? You keep that up." She patted his head lightly and then turned to walk over to where Stewart had run off to sulk.

Once Mrs. Craven was out of sight and the crowd of children had dispersed, Adam turned to Lily. "Here, you can have the rest of my crisps if you like." He held out the blue crinkly packet to her.

"Thank you, Adders," she croaked, almost in a whisper. "You're my bestest friend."

"Aye, I know that and you're my bestest friend too, Lil, and Stewart Campbell is just a big meanie. You need to stay away from him. I'll make sure he isn't nasty to you again though. Don't worry." The two children walked over to the grass and sat down side by side.

"Are you coming to my house for tea on Saturday? My papa says we can have the paddling pool out if it's sunny?" Lily asked munching on the salt and vinegar crisps.

Adam nodded. "Yep...I can't wait. I've got one of those big water pistols that soak you through, so you'd better watch out." He nudged her with a wide grin fixed in place.

She giggled. "Yeah, well I'm going to make sure I get my big sand castle bucket out then, and it holds about ten gallons of water, so *you'd* better watch out." She nudged him back.

He snorted. "It *does* not! And anyway I'm a faster runner than you, so *you'd* better watch out." He chuckled.

"It does, too! And you're not faster than me...*you* run like a girl!" Lily jumped to her feet and set off at a sprint, her musical laughter echoing behind her.

"I'll get you Lily Macrae! Just you wait!" Adam laughed heartily as he sprang up from the grass and set off in pursuit.

And there began the soundtrack to Adam and Lily's lives...

Chapter One

Eve, The Apple of My Eye (Bell X1)
Many Years Later - July 2009
"She simply lit up every room she walked into... Her beautiful smile was contagious...and her eyes...she showed every emotion in those beautiful blue eyes. My life...sorry...my life will be a whole lot darker without her in it. She had this amazing ability to make everyone she encountered feel cared for...loved even. She would have been an amazing mother... I just...I just *know* she would. She had that way about her. Always worried about others...never herself. She was one of a kind...my Eve...my beautiful, *beautiful* Evie. She was supposed to be my happy ever after...my forever...and she was taken...stolen... I'm so sorry...I can't..." Adam's breath caught in his throat and his legs weakened. With clenched eyes, he gripped the lectern for support.

The congregation sat silently as he spoke his heartfelt words. Tears trailed down each and every face. The forlorn and lost expressions of his closest family and friends told him their hearts were aching and broken, just like his own. The loss was too much. Too sudden. With a pain inside him that no one could even *begin* to understand, Adam Langton returned to his seat, placed his head in his hands and let the pent-up emotion break free. His shoulders shuddered and the tears flowed unabashedly from his stinging, sore eyes. Arms came around him offering what little comfort they could, but nothing...*no one* could do anything to quell the ache in his chest. She was *gone*.

Nothing could bring her back.

All the *if onlys* and *what ifs* swirled around his head like a carousel spinning out of control, but what was the point? What was the point of anything anymore? His bright, wonderful future had been snatched away. The prospect of having children with her and watching them grow up, of growing old with her beside him, was gone.

Jeff Buckley's *Hallelujah* echoed around the vast space of the eighteenth century church as Adam's friends and family left the building with obviously heavy hearts.

♥♥♥

Back at the house Lily walked into the kitchen where she found Adam staring out of the window over the pretty cottage garden. The glass of whiskey in his hand remained untouched. People talked in hushed voices in the lounge, but it appeared they had seen fit to leave him alone with his grief for a while.

Walking over to where he stood, she placed her arm around him, her hand on his left shoulder, her head on his right. She heaved a sigh. "How are you holding up, Adders?"

"Oh…you know…fair to *utterly* crap…you?"

"About the same I'd say." She wiped her eyes and he hugged her to his side. "Your eulogy was just so…beautiful. I know it's a stupid thing to say, but she would have loved what you said about her."

"Thanks, Lil. That means a lot." His lip quivered, and he placed his glass on the worktop before rubbing his eyes. "It doesn't feel real. I keep expecting her to shout down and tell me off for not replacing the loo roll, or to climb into bed beside me and stick her freezing cold feet on my legs to warm them up. Or snuggle up to me on the sofa whilst she pretends not to cry at some soppy ad on TV. But…that won't ever happen again. I'll *never* kiss her again…I'll *never* hold her again." He shook his head and whispered, "I'll…I'll never make love to her again. It's all gone…she's *gone*." A deep sob broke free from his body.

Lily buried her head into his neck and held on tight as her best friend let his anguish and sadness pour out onto her.

Adam's mother walked through from the lounge. "Adam, darling. Some of the...gosh what do you call them? Guests? Anyway...some people are leaving and I think maybe you should come and say goodbye." Adam nodded and left the room.

His mother shook her head. "Goodness, what do you call people at something like this? *Guests* sound so...*happy*. It seems wrong." Confusion and salt water clouded her eyes.

Lily thought for a moment. "Friends. I think you simply call them friends. They all loved her after all, Gwen," she said before standing and putting her arm around Gwen's shoulders.

Gwen slid her arm around Lily's waist. "Are you okay, dear? I know it must have been quite a shock for you. And I can tell you're trying to stay strong for Adam...but she was your friend too."

Lily's lip quivered so she bit it. Her eyes stung with unshed tears. "Yes...she was...the best. But Adam is in bits right now. I'll grieve in my own time. He needs me."

Gwen kissed her cheek. "Lily, you are *such* a good friend. You always have been. I'm so glad he has you." Her voice wavered.

Lily tried to smile. "He would do exactly the same for me."

Gwen squeezed her hand again, nodding. "He would, dear. He would." Gwen turned to go to her son.

♥♥♥

In the lounge, family and friends surrounded Adam, patting his arm, hugging him and smiling sadly. It was all just too much. He wanted everyone to leave now. He needed to be alone. He had always hated being the centre of attention. That was always Eve's place. She deserved it and handled it so well. She was interesting and fun. He enjoyed watching her from the sidelines, watching her work her magic, watching with adoration as others inadvertently fell in love with her, too.

Eventually, everyone apart from Lily left the house he had shared with the love of his life. Before the accident it had been a home filled with love, lust, and laughter. Now, however, being here with his best friend just wasn't the same.

♥♥♥

Lily leaned against the doorframe and watched Adam as his six-foot-plus frame slumped onto the sofa. He huffed out a long, hard breath and loosened his black tie, undoing the first two buttons of his crisp white shirt.

He scraped a shaking hand through his thick, dark brown hair and ran the same hand over his face. "Well…that's it, then. It's official. I'm a widower." He glanced up at Lily, his bloodshot eyes still glistening. Her heart ached for him. "What the hell do I do now?"

She walked over and sat beside him, nudging his shoulder with her own. "You carry on, Adders. You take a deep breath and you carry on. You're twenty-nine. You *have* to move forward."

Adam took a faltering breath. "I know. I do know… It's just—"

"Hey, no one expects you to get over this in a week. There is no time limit on grief, but just know that you have a long life ahead of you and you *have* to live it. Don't disappear into your own head and never come out, okay?"

"No…I'll try not to." He turned to face her. "Thank you for everything. I mean it, Lil. Having you here…it's just… I mean…just…thank you."

"Hey, I've told you before; we're family, you and me. You need me and I come running. You'd do the same... Mind you...I have to find someone to love who actually loves me back first." She blushed.

"You will. How could you not? Who could *not* love you, eh?" He nudged her now.

Lily forced a smile. "Hmmm, no one worthy of my time up to now, but I never give up hope."

Adam looked thoughtful for a while. "The thing is...you'll go back to working abroad for the TV station...and I'll...I'll be here on my own." Tears escaped again and his bottom lip trembled.

It killed Lily to see him like this. Why did this have to happen? It seemed so *unfair*.

Taking his face in both hands, she stared into his eyes. "Look, I'm here for the next week. Then I'll be here for Christmas. And in between that, I'm at the end of a phone or at the end of an email. I'm not *leaving* you. I'll *always* be here for you, Adam. And if it all gets too much, then you just ask and I *will* come home."

He covered her hands with his own. "Thank you." He pulled her to him in a tight embrace and sobbed again.

Adam and Lily had been friends since...well...forever. They met at primary school, and from long before he told off Stewart Campbell for pushing her and pinching her snack, they had been inseparable. He defended her at every given opportunity. They were two halves of the same whole. Two peas in a pod. They were the couple most likely to *become* a couple at high school, but had never actually made the transition from friends to something more than that. Always together but...never *together*.

And here she sat by his side on the day of his wife's funeral. Offering whatever she could of her time and closeness—anything to ease his pain and suffering. Taking time away from her job was not something she did lightly. But she would cross the fires of hell if he needed her and she knew he would do the same.

Chapter Two

Wicked Game (Chris Isaak)
Many Years Earlier –1998

Adam and Lily had always been there for each other. It was just how things were and everybody knew it. Primary school was fine. Everyone thought it was sweet that they were best friends. It didn't matter to anyone. They never suffered teasing because it was just *the norm*.

As they grew up, Adam was always the one to oversee the potential boyfriends Lily had chosen. If he didn't think they were good enough, he would tell her straight. More often than not she agreed and the boy was rapidly kicked to the curb. Likewise, Lily had very strong opinions when it came to potentially sacrificing time with her best friend to another girl. She didn't beat about the bush making her feelings known.

High school had been a nightmare for Lily. She developed quickly and got a lot of attention—very positive attention from boys, but jealousy, spitefulness, and negativity from the girls. She earned a reputation not at all befitting her, learning very quickly that teenage girls can be very cruel. She made no female friends, and so her reliance on Adam was further compounded. He tried on so many occasions to stop the wretched rumour mill from turning. But his efforts were futile. Regardless of what he said, people would believe what they wanted to believe. She appreciated his efforts and told him so frequently.

Her Spanish heritage, womanly curves, bright blue eyes, and dark unruly curls gave her a combination of being both exotic and a little wild, rather like the character Cathy from *Wuthering Heights*. She already had the personality, and all the boys wanted to take her out. Looking back on it, she knew Adam had done his best to wheedle out the wheat from the chaff, but there came a point where he had to grow up and realise there were only so many times he could butt in. Playing the big brother was hard work.

Adam was there for Lily through every bad boyfriend, through every heartache. He came running when she needed a shoulder to cry on. He was such a *good friend*. Aside from her parents, he was the one constant in her life.

During the summer of 1998, after they had both turned eighteen, however, there was one heartbreak he couldn't help her through. Why could he offer no solace? Because he could never know about it.

The summer break prior to starting university had been a fateful one for Lily. One that in some ways broke her, but in many more ways she couldn't possibly regret. It was the year she realised she was in love with Adam. She didn't *mean* to fall for him. It was a complete accident. But fall for him she did.

Hard.

She didn't *want* to be in love with him at all, but as she discovered the hard way, you simply cannot help who you fall for nor can you help *when* it happens. She knew Adam simply didn't see her that way. He never would. He had always been her big brother, her protector, and her guardian angel.

He was tall and had dark floppy hair back then. His chocolate brown eyes sparkled when he spoke and his full lips were so kissable. He had saved up and bought a set of weights, which he used religiously. She used to laugh at him and call him vain. At first. But other girls started to notice.

Looking back, she couldn't quite put her finger on when she *actually* fell for him, but she could remember the day she *realised* that it had happened. It was the day they had played tennis at the local outdoor courts. He had overheated and removed his T-shirt...

♥♥♥

July 1998 – Jedburgh

"Forty thirty!" Adam huffed as he pulled his black Pearl Jam T-shirt over his head and tucked it into his belt. In doing so, he exposed a broad chest and shapely biceps. His abdomen was sculpted and almost every muscle was visible under his tight, olive skin. He bent to rest his hands on his knees.

Lily may have been losing, but she was putting up a good fight. She was thankful that she'd put her shorts and a tank top on, as the summer heat was almost unbearable. Sweat ran down her spine, and she pulled up her hair into a scruffy knot on top of her head, securing it with a band she carried around her wrist.

Lily panted. "Well, that last ball was out as far as I'm concerned."

"It was *not!*" Adam's voice rose an octave. "You're just a sore loser."

"Ha! Says the man who emptied a bag of cheese puffs over my head when I beat him at gin-rummy!"

Adam straightened and pointed his racket at her. "That was an accident and you know it."

Lily huffed. "Accident-schmaccident. You don't *accidentally* do something like empty a *whole* bag of snacks on someone's head! If it's an accident you stop when you realise! I wouldn't mind but I'd only just washed my hair and the crumbs made it all greasy." She pretended to sulk.

Adam bent double again but this time it was through laughing. "Yeah…you smelled pretty bad too. You came close to getting a new nickname from that incident. Well…I say *pretty* close…*Cheesy.*"

That was it. She decided to seek revenge and there was no time like the present. Dropping her racket, she set off running toward him at full pelt, and before he could protest or get out of the way, she launched herself onto his back.

"Time to pay, Adders." She clung onto his body with her thighs.

"What are you doing?" He gasped in between loud guffaws. Spinning around, he tried to release himself from her grasp. His laughter caused him the weakness she needed to finish him off and so the struggle ensued. "God, you have the thighs of bloody She-Ra!"

"And don't you forget it. Maybe you'll think twice about pouring snacks on my head in future, eh?" She squeezed him, making him cough.

"Gerroff me, you loony!" He struggled, still laughing, but she was relentless in her attack, and he stumbled toward the grass at the edge of the court. He slumped to his knees and then onto his stomach. Lily fell flat on top of his back still holding on.

It was then she began the tickling. "Do you surrender?" she asked as her fingers dug into his sensitive ribs.

He squealed in a high-pitched, girly voice. "Never!" And so she continued her revenge assault. "Get off, Lily! Pleeeease! I'll pee in my boxers!"

Out of breath, she finally stopped, and he rolled onto his back. His chest heaved as she laid half on and half off of him, her hands flat on his toned, bare, glistening chest. She locked her eyes on his and suddenly felt trapped in his melted chocolate gaze. Her smile disappeared. His smile faded too as he stared up at her and his hold on her upper arm tightened slightly. His heart pounded underneath her fingertips. His cologne, mixed with the manly scent from his damp body, infused her nostrils and her heart rate accelerated. God, he was stunning. She inhaled sharply at the realisation, and heat rose in her cheeks. He frowned and opened his mouth to speak, but she broke the spell.

Clambering to her feet and turning away from him, she spoke as breezily as she could. "Come on. We need to get going. I think we can safely say that you won." She turned to where Adam still laid on his back, propped up on his elbows, brow furrowed and looking confused. "Adders! Come on!" She feigned frustration and made her way out of the tennis court.

Back at home, after they had parted at the end of her street, neither willing to discuss the moment they had shared, Lily went straight to her room and sat on her bed. With her head in her hands, she recalled his toned body and his smell. *Oh shit. Not Adam. Please not Adam.* She sent up a silent prayer to God, willing her feelings to revert back to the norm she was used to.

She had never really had a first love—until now—she'd had several boyfriends but none of the heartbreaks had been *that* serious. She always made them out to be worse than they were simply because she liked the attention she got when Adam thought she had been wronged in some way. *Now* the pieces had clicked into place. *Now* she understood *why* his attention had always meant so much. *He* was the reason. *He* was the one she was in love with. *Please let it be a phase. Please. Just a phase…please?*

Neither broached the subject after that. Things did go back to normal, whatever normal was. It turns out that God had more pressing issues to deal with, and so to Lily, normal became loving Adam from afar.

It seemed that Adam's normal was playing tennis and dating girls, *lots* of girls. How different one person's normal can be from another's.

Chapter Three

Adam and Eve (Paul Anka)
October 1998 - Edinburgh University

Unwilling to be apart from each other, Adam and Lily had applied to the same universities and when they had both been accepted at Edinburgh—Journalism for Lily and English for Adam—they had been overjoyed and had gotten a little drunk to celebrate. It was just a continuation of life as they knew it. Always together, *never* apart.

Edinburgh University had been the first choice for both Adam and Lily for several reasons. First of all, it wasn't a million miles away from home in the Scottish Borders. Second of all, it was the most amazingly bright and culturally varied place making it exciting to spend time there. The atmosphere was electric and the history was enough to keep even the most enquiring minds sated. The multi-coloured buildings of Grassmarket's curved street brought a smile even on a dull day, and the multitude of bars and restaurants meant that even a student's meagre purse was not negated.

Another attraction for the pair was The Fringe Festival that took place annually in the month of August right in the city centre. It was such a blast with comedians and street performers taking over every available inch of the Royal Mile and every venue with a room to spare. The place came alive with laughter, fancy costumes, and vivid colours. Myriad aromas wafted through the air from vending carts, tantalising the taste buds, and a wide variety of music vied for the attention of each person's auditory senses. A person could walk down the street and be accosted by all manner of characters, wielding leaflets and free tickets, trying to entice you in to see their shows. Both Adam and Lily made the trip up to the capital every year, together. When they were younger they would travel to the festival with their parents, but once they got older, they would travel by themselves, feeling very grown up and independent.

Although they had spent many Christmas shopping trips in Scotland's capital, both Lily and Adam never failed to be overwhelmed by the stunning stonework as they gazed upward. The Scott monument stood in its proud position overlooking the main shopping thoroughfare of Princes Street. The imposing castle, high on its rocky precipice, peered out over the city below. History and hidden stories from days past oozed from the very mortar of the churches and tenements in the Old Town area. Edinburgh truly was a spectacular city and the decision to study there had been made with very little trepidation.

Their first day on campus had the butterflies on edge for every new student. Lily and Adam were no different. First day nerves were a certainty. But the excitement was what got the adrenalin pumping. This was the start of life as an adult; the first day of the rest of their lives.

"I can't believe we're finally here, Adders!" Lily twirled around, arms spread, and head back with her long chocolate waves following like streamers, as they took in the centre quadrangle of the Old College. They had been taking the self-guided tour of the campus and had stopped on the grass to take a break and grab a quick drink of water. The sun was surprisingly warm for the time of year, and its presence, hung low in the autumn sky, cast a golden glow over everything, giving an ethereal quality to the old architecture.

"Yup, it's pretty spectacular, eh?" Adam laughed watching his best friend collapse dizzily in a heap next to him. "Bit of a change from high school that's for sure."

Lily stood again. "You're not kidding. I'm looking forward to being treated like an adult," she stated as she began to spin around again with her eyes closed.

Adam burst out laughing. "Yeah...because that's what you are, eh? An adult!"

Lily stuck her tongue out at him and plopped herself down beside him again. "Durrr, I'm officially over eighteen, so yes. Are you happy you decided to live in halls for the first year?" They had several options, from renting a place, to driving in every day, to living in halls. They had both chosen the latter.

"Yeah. I think it will be much better to get the whole university experience," Adam replied thoughtfully, pulling at blades of grass and throwing them at her.

"Yeah right, that's the reason." Lily rolled her eyes. "I think what you mean is that we're out from under our parents scrutinising gaze, and what they don't know can't hurt them." She pulled a chunk of grass, and threw it back at Adam in retaliation.

He laughed heartily. "Oh yeah, that's what I meant. Seriously though, I think it'll be cool."

"I reckon so. And we're close enough by so that if you need me for anything—"

"If I need *you* for anything? Don't you mean that the other way around? You're the one who's always forgetting shit. I can see it now. *Ooh Adders, I've run out of coffee...ooh Adders, I can't find my textbook on the Principals and Practises of Investigative Journalism... Oooh Adders, my boyfriend has dumped me because I'm still in love with Chris Cornell from Soundgarden.* If *I* need *you*, pah!"

She hit him playfully with her satchel. "Bloody cheek. The only part of that likely to come true is the last part. I only have eyes for Chris Cornell. God, he's *so* sexy." She threw herself backwards onto the grass swooning and feigning a black out.

He smirked. "Yeah, well you ain't likely to bump into him here, so get over it…Cheesy."

At that, she sat bolt upright and pursed her lips. He readied himself in case she decided to launch another attack, but instead she stood up, huffed and stormed off.

"Oy! Lil! Come back, you muppet!" He ran after her. And so was laid the foundation of their time at university…

October 2000 – Edinburgh University

The first two years at university had Lily and Adam forging many new friendships and making the most of the social aspects of the wonderful city of Edinburgh. Both had found part time jobs in local bars and still managed to spend time together in between. Summers and Christmas holidays were spent at home with their families, and two years on, half way through their respective courses, things were going well. The summer of 2000 had seen a group holiday to the Spanish resort of Magaluf, where they had over indulged in alcohol and raising hell like normal twenty-years-olds. But as always, the time was coming around for uni to be back in session again.

The two friends had moved into a shared house after their first year in halls, and they arrived back just before their next term was due to start. The first week of lectures came around quickly. They had met up to walk in together, and had made plans to meet for lunch so they could regale each other with tales of their first encounters with new lecturers. Lily had talked non-stop about the fact that one of her lecturers for this year had worked all over the world for *The Times* and she was so excited to meet him.

The refectory was buzzing with the hum of myriad conversations going on simultaneously. Adam arrived first and grabbed himself a bacon, lettuce, and tomato sandwich and a coffee. He bought a coffee for Lily, knowing she would no doubt be too excited to eat—as was usually the case when she was enthusiastic about something. He found an empty table, and whilst he waited, he went over his notes from his first lecture of the day. He had thoroughly enjoyed listening to Marcus Foreman, his knowledgeable tutor, and knew from the start this was going to be his favourite lesson of the academic year. He glanced up just as Lily approached his table. A big, mischievous grin spread over her face. He knew that look all too well. She was closely followed by someone he couldn't quite see, as whomever it was hung back.

Lily was finding something very amusing. "Adders! You're not going to believe this!" She pulled the person who had been walking with her around to her side. "Adam...this is Eve! Ha ha! Adam and Eve." She playfully gestured back and forth between the two.

He smirked as his gaze moved up to meet the person in question. He swallowed hard and stared. Just stared. Eventually when he snapped out of his stupor he realised the girl, whom he had been informed was called *Eve*, was blushing profusely.

"Sorry...sorry...I...I was just eating my sandwich." *Smooth, Adam, very smooth.* He stood, wiped his hand down his jeans, and held it toward her. The whole situation had seemed to take forever, and he felt very, *very* stupid. "Ahem...I'm Adam... Oh, but Lil already said that." His cheeks heated as the girl took his hand to shake it.

"Hi, Adam. I'm Eve...obviously." She giggled. "For some reason that's a sentence I never thought I would be saying."

He decided then and there that she had the most beautiful smile he had ever seen. Her hair was long, thick, and golden blonde, and her eyes were a vivid sky blue. She had a lovely figure, curvy like a girl should be, not skinny. Her skin was flawless. He lost the ability to speak again and had reverted back to staring.

"Good grief, Adders, put your tongue away." Lily snorted derisively.

Realising he had been staring again, he sat. "Are you girls going to join me? Lil, I got you a coffee."

Eve nodded and sat in the seat next to him. "Thanks Adam, that'd be great. I've only just transferred in, and it's all a bit strange right now. Lily is the first person I've really spoken to."

Lily grabbed her coffee from him. "Cheers, Adders." She slumped into the seat next to Eve.

"It's a nice friendly place, so you should find you settle in quickly," he reassured Eve. She smiled warmly and nodded. "So what brings you to Forrest Hill?"

"Oh, I was studying down in England, but my Dad has been ill, and so I applied for a transfer nearer to home. I can get back easier from here...not easy...but easier, at least."

"Oh right... Sorry, I must seem really nosey." His cheeks heated.

"No, no that's fine." She smiled.

They chatted through lunch about their respective courses and the lecturers they had all experienced that morning. It turned out they were all free for the rest of the afternoon, which pleased Adam to no end. "Hey, Lil, seeing as she missed it, we could take Eve on the tour that we did when we started here," Adam suggested eagerly.

Lily shook her head. "Oh, I can't...I have to...go...and get some books... Yes, there's a book I need, and I need to go get it today."

Eve turned to Lily. "Isn't there a book shop on campus? I'm sure I saw a sign—"

"Oh yes," Lily interrupted. "I've tried there. I really need to go into town to Blackwell's. You two go on the tour though."

"Nah, we'll go when you get back. It's fine," Adam said.

"No, don't be daft. You should go. Show Eve the delights of Forrest Hill." She smiled. Adam knew there was no way Lily could have missed his reaction to their new friend. She appeared to be giving him an opportunity to get to know Eve alone. He'd have to thank her later. Seriously, he owed her one for this.

"Okay, great. What do you say, Eve?"

A blush spread from Eve's neck up to her cheeks, and she nodded shyly. "Thanks, Adam. That would be great." His heart swelled in his chest. She was so sweet.

❤❤❤

After waving Lily off, Adam and Eve set off on the tour. Adam thought Lily had seemed distracted by something. Perhaps her concerns about not finding the right book were playing on her mind. He would make a point of chatting to her about it later.

"So, where are you from, Eve?" he asked as they strolled around the large campus, weaving in and out of the other students.

"I'm from Skye. I was born and brought up in a village north of Portree."

"Oh it's a beautiful place, Skye. I went there on holiday with my parents and my brother when I was little."

"Yes it's stunning. It's completely different to here though. I've been living down in England for two academic years, but even after all this time living away from home, I still feel a little like a fish out of water when I come back to uni...a country girl in the big city and all that." A wistful look washed over her face. "The views from home are stunning. I can see the tops of the Old Man of Storr from my bedroom if I stand on my tiptoes. I kind of miss that already."

"Oh yes, I remember that place. It's quite spectacular. Out of interest, why is it called the *Old Man* of Storr?"

She smiled. "It's simply because people think that the rock formation looks like an old man." She giggled.

"Really? Oh, I'd never really thought about that to be honest. I'll have to look it up and see."

She looked down to her feet. "I feel quite homesick… Well, I did until I met Lily and you." She tucked a golden strand of hair behind her ear and the pink hue rose in her cheeks again.

"I think it's hard moving away from home as it is, but…well, if your Dad is ill it must be compounded for you. I only moved up from Jedburgh, but even now, a couple of years on, I still miss my mum's cooking, right from the first week back after summer." He chuckled.

"I've never been to Jedburgh. What's it like?"

"It's not a huge place. But we do get a bit of tourism. Mainly people stopping off on their way to Highland though. There's an abbey and an old jail. Oh and it's where Mary Queen of Scots stayed, too. Lots of history for a wee town."

She smiled as he spoke. "I'd like to visit, maybe one day."

"Yeah, well one day is probably all you'd need." He laughed. "Nah, it's a lovely town. I lived there all my life until I moved here to halls." A comfortable silence settled on the pair as they strolled the campus. She glanced up and around as he watched her from the corner of his eye.

He turned so that he was walking backwards right in front of the gorgeous blonde girl. "So, Eve, what's your ambition for when we're done at this place?"

Eve pursed her lips and glanced skyward again. "Hmmm, I'd like to maybe go into reporting. You know interviews with celebs, reporting on all the gossip. Maybe have my own column one day."

He cringed. "Wow…my ambition kind of pales into insignificance against that."

She giggled. "I doubt that. What is it you want to do?"

He grinned. "You'll probably think I'm mad."

She stopped in her tracks. "Go on?"

He took a deep breath before he admitted his seemingly small dreams. "I really want to teach English at high school level." His words came out in a rush.

She laughed. "Why do you think that pales? I think teaching is a wonderful and very noble thing. I just couldn't cope with someone else's kids all day."

He loved the musical sound of her laughter. "Well, yeah…I understand that."

"What made you decide on that career path, then?"

"I helped out during my last summer at the high school I used to attend. They were doing a summer school and I was working with some of the younger kids. I was helping some of the kids with learning difficulties and some of the kids who are…how do I put it? A little disaffected. They responded well to how I taught them and I just loved it. The feeling of…oh I don't know…pride…was immense…It pretty much cemented in my mind what I wanted to do. Does that sound pathetic and corny?"

She shook her head vigorously. "No…no, not at all… Wow, when you put it like that it sounds really fulfilling. I'm full of admiration for anyone who chooses teaching. I'm sure it's very hard work."

"I'm sure it will be, too, but rewarding all the same."

The pair talked easily as they walked around the impressive campus, with its arched windows and chiselled stonework. The multitude of windows, set into the aged buildings, glistened as the autumn sun bounced from their surfaces. The imposing domed foyer of the old college appeared almost cathedral-like in its austerity, giving an appearance of old world grandeur to the place where so many learned scholars had studied in years past. Every so often, Adam pointed out the features he and Lily had noticed when they'd done the same tour, the ornate balustrades, the carvings above the entrances, the slate placards with faded inscriptions. The afternoon flew by. They arrived back at the block where Eve was staying. She had been allocated a room in halls until she found a place to share.

"Well, thank you Adam for a lovely afternoon. It feels good to actually have a couple of friends now." She smiled warmly at him. He felt like he could fall into her eyes and drown. He shook his head to dislodge the errant thought. *Too soon, Adam. You'll scare the poor girl off!*

"Yeah, it has been lovely. It was really good to spend some time getting to know you." He took a deep breath to muster up a little courage. "I...I don't suppose you fancy going out with me sometime?"

That familiar pink glow made an appearance again, making Adam's heart do somersaults. "You mean like...a date?" She averted her gaze and he found her shyness very sweet.

He nodded. "Yeah...like a date." He felt the heat rise in his own cheeks, too.

She bit her lower lip and tucked a strand of hair behind her ear. "That...that would be... I would like that, yes... Thank you," she stuttered.

Adam wanted to thrust a triumphant fist into the air but reined himself in. "Great...great. That's great. How about Friday? We could go into town to this great place I know called *The Jekyll and Hyde* bar. It's really good... They sometimes have live music and the drinks aren't too expensive...not that it would matter... I'm not saying I'm broke... I just...well—"

She shrugged. "Adam, we're students. We're *all* broke."

"Yeah...I suppose that's true. So Friday? Half seven? I'll pick you up here?"

She smiled. "Lovely. I'll look forward to it."

"Me too, me too. But of course I'll see you before then."

"I'm sure you will. Bye for now, Adam." She leaned in and kissed his cheek. His hand came up to touch where she had kissed. A huge grin spread across his face.

"Bye, Eve," he almost whispered. As he backed away, he stumbled and nearly fell over the edging stones that surrounded the borders outside her building. She covered her mouth as she laughed and his cheeks burned with embarrassment. He waved, turned, and jogged away, trying his best to remain upright.

♥♥♥

Lily lay on her back in bed...wide awake. Checking her watch, she sighed when she realised it was seven o'clock, and she had been awake almost all night. Ditching Adam and Eve yesterday had been a pretty cowardly thing to do. She could admit that, as she lay there alone. Just seeing Adam gawping at Eve had made her chest hurt. She regretted introducing them the minute she saw the expression on his face. And of course Eve was everything she wasn't. She was pretty, blonde, and demure. Lily saw herself as gawky, plain, crass, and a bit clumsy, not to mention brash, opinionated, and well…the very antithesis of Eve. Okay, she had only just met Eve, so she couldn't really tell *exactly* what she was like, but…well, it was obvious.

Sighing, she clenched her fists and punched back onto the mattress, kicking her legs and growling at herself. Why couldn't she just effing get over him? He was out of bounds. He was her bestie. Her BFF. Her bro. Her buddy. Her pal. Except that wasn't *all* he was. He was tall and broad and muscular and strong and handsome and intelligent and funny and sweet and sexy and… *Shitty shitty shit! This is doing me no bloody good.*

She sat up and took in a deep breath. An inner conflict sprang to the forefront of her mind. *Maybe I should talk to him….and say what though? Adam…you know that you and I used to climb trees together and play cops and robbers in your back garden? And you remember that time you punched Stewart whatshisname because he pinched my snack? Oh and you remember when I drew flowers all over your cast when you broke your arm and you sulked because I couldn't draw dragons instead? Well the thing is, I've been in love with you for a while now, and I'd like you to forget about Eve and be my boyfriend, and maybe one day marry me so I can have your babies. Is that all alright with you?* She laughed out loud at the ridiculousness of her train of thought.

She trudged down to the shower and tried to scrub anything other than platonic thoughts of Adam away. Her first lecture wasn't until ten, and Adam hadn't called in last night to arrange breakfast, so she decided she would study. That would take her mind off him.

She had been back in her room for ten minutes when there was a knock on the door. Reluctantly, she opened it.

"Bloody hell, Adders, you're up early. Did you pee in your bed or something?"

He pursed his lips and frowned at her. "I fucking regret telling you that story, you know. I was twelve and I'd had a *nightmare,* for fuck's sake."

Lily shook her head. "Actually, I had totally forgot—"

"Anyway, you can't spoil my mood today."

"Oh damn, and I make it my life's work to do so." She smirked as he pushed past her and plopped down on her bed. "Come in, why don't you?" She snorted sarcastically.

"Get the kettle on, Lil. I'm parched." He flung himself back on the bed with his arms behind his head.

Sighing, she went over to the tiny table where her travel kettle, mugs, coffee, and little cartons of UHT milk— discretely pinched from every café they went to—sat in a pyramid. "So what's making you so chipper at this early hour?" she asked turning around to face him, her arms folded across her chest.

He sat bolt upright with a grin on his face. "I owe you a huge thank you."

Feeling a tad confused, she scrunched her nose. "For what?"

"For yesterday, silly. I know what you did." He grinned as he pointed a finger at her. "You could tell I was into Eve, and so you made excuses and left so that I could get to know her a little better."

Realisation dawned on her and a nervous giggle escaped. "Oh...yes, busted." *Wrong!*

"Yeah...well, we had a lovely afternoon just chatting and walking. She's a great girl, Lil... Anyway, I asked her out on Friday and she said yes." He beamed and punched the air with both fists.

Her heart sank. It was what she'd expected but maybe not this quickly. "Oh…that's…that's great, Adam…great… I'm happy for you."

"Bloody hell, you must be *really* shocked that a girl like her could fancy me! You called me *Adam!* That's only reserved for when I've pissed you off or…" He looked to the ceiling as he contemplated. "Well, mainly when I've pissed you off." He laughed.

She forced a laugh, too. "Yeah, shocked is about right." The kettle clicked off, making her jump. "Oh shit, Adders, I've just remembered I need to…erm…nip out. Can we do coffee later, maybe?"

He frowned. "You have to go out at *eight o'clock* on a Tuesday morning with wet hair?"

Thinking on her feet, she nodded emphatically. "Hmmm…yes, women's things." She cringed. She knew that would make him leave without asking.

His cheeks coloured and he stood quickly. "Oh right, right. I'll be off then. Catch you at lunch?" She nodded. "Okay, see you at the refectory then. Bye." He ducked out of the door.

Amazing how quickly the hint of the feminine monthly cycle could relieve a woman of an unwanted male presence. As soon as the door slammed shut, she walked over to her bed and slumped down.

With her head in her hands, she began to sob.

Chapter Four

Blue Eyes (Elton John)
October 2000 – Edinburgh University

Adam simply couldn't wait until Friday. It was all he had thought about since...well...Monday. It was the light at the end of the weeklong tunnel where he would get to spend the evening with the stunning Eve. And hopefully, if he had the guts, he would kiss her. He'd seen her on a couple of occasions during the week but only to wave to or say a quick hello in passing. She had smiled shyly and tucked her hair behind her ear in that cute way she had, but he hadn't even had a chance to check that their date was still on. *Shit, what if she doesn't show up?* Nah, he was picking her up so that was fine. *What if I call on her and she turns me down? Nah, she didn't seem the type to do that.*

He would just have to wait.

He was sure he'd driven Lily completely mad talking about Eve. He had asked her advice on all sorts of stuff...her being a girl and all. For the most part, she'd been really great. But she had been very moody. Mind you, she did mention *women's stuff,* so that would explain a lot.

Sitting at the table at lunch on Thursday, he was too nervous to eat. He had been waffling on at Lily for ages. So much so that she appeared to have glazed over and drifted off.

That is until she suddenly interrupted his latest round of *Oooh isn't Eve pretty* by blurting out, "I've met someone." The interjection pissed him off a little.

Adam huffed. "Have you? That's great. Who is he? Need me to vet him for you?" He smirked with enthusiasm. He enjoyed intimidating Lily's conquests.

She snorted. "Adam, we aren't at school now."

He felt a little stab of hurt at her tone and the fact that she seemed to be calling him *Adam* a lot lately. "Oookay…so who is he then?"

She sat up straight. "His name's Elliot Longthorne and he's studying music. He's in his final year. He looks a bit like Chris Cornell, and he likes Soundgarden and all the other music I love." She smiled enthusiastically.

"Oh…great. When do I get to meet him?" Adam was trying not to smirk, thinking that Elliott's name sounded like a cross between a *Harry Potter* character and something out of *Lord of the Rings.*

"Dunno. He's taking me out Friday. So you're not the only one with a date. We're off into Edinburgh. Think we're going to a party after at his mate's house."

Warning bells sounded in Adam's mind. "Well, just be careful, okay? You hardly know him and going to a house party might not be a great idea."

She rolled her eyes. "God, you sound like my dad." She huffed folding her arms in a teenager type strop.

Adam pointed a finger at her. "Yeah, well. *Your dad* trusts me to look after you whilst we're here, remember?"

She sighed as she leaned toward him narrowing her eyes. "Adam, how many times do I need to remind you that I'm an *adult* and I can watch out for myself?" She stood and stormed off. He followed her with his eyes. She made her way over to a group of longhaired *grunge* types. She locked mouths with the one he now presumed to be Chris Cornell or Pippy Longstocking or whatever the fuck he was called. What did he care anyway? He had Friday night to look forward to with Eve. *Aaaah…Eve…*

♥♥♥

After asking Lily's advice about what to wear, Adam had settled for dark jeans, a plain white T-shirt, and a pale blue shirt open over the top. He pulled on his brown suede jacket and his boots and set off. Lily told him there was no point taking her flowers because she wouldn't have brought a vase to uni. And a basket of flowers was something you bought for your Gran. Chocolates were a no-no simply because if Eve was like *most* women she would be weight-conscious, and it was far too early for jewellery. So he knocked on her door on time, but empty handed and feeling rather uncomfortable with the fact.

When Eve opened the door, he couldn't help but inhale sharply. She stood there in a long flowing multi-coloured skirt, a fitted white T-shirt, and a cropped denim jacket. Her golden locks fell just over her shoulders, and he had to fight the overpowering urge to take the shimmering strands into his fingers to feel their softness. She was utterly mesmerising. She smiled widely and blushed.

Realising he had stared open mouthed at her—*again*—he felt his cheeks heat. "Wow…you…you look…beautiful."

Eve bit her lip. "And hello to you too, Adam." Her warm smile melted his heart. He had to stifle a groan and cleared his throat.

"Are you ready to go?"

"Yes, I just need to grab my scarf and bag. She stepped over to her bed and did just that. "Ready now," she chimed, closing her door behind her. He held out his elbow and she linked arms with him.

After a walk filled with conversation, they arrived at the *Jekyll and Hyde* with its black paintwork and poster-laden windows. Dim lighting in the interior created an eerie, Halloween-esque atmosphere, which was enhanced by black chandeliers, dark gothic seating, and carved woodwork. The ambience was spooky but with an element of fun, too. There was a lively buzz of chatter, as it appeared that much of the student population had descended on the place at the same time. The bar staff weaved around each other with ease, and Adam and Eve chatted as best they could whilst they waited to be served. With drinks in hand, they went through to a quieter, separate little area off to the left and grabbed the last remaining table.

A shy silence descended on the couple. Then the typical situation where two people start talking at once occurred.

"So what music—"

"Have you made any—"

They laughed and then both gestured simultaneously. "*You first.*" It was enough to break the ice and they both relaxed.

Eve took a breath. "Okay…I was just going to ask what type of music you like." She tucked a strand of hair behind her ear. He loved how she did that. *So very cute.*

"Well, I have quite eclectic taste really… I love rock and Indie stuff. I've just bought Pearl Jam's latest CD."

She frowned. "*Binaural?* That's been out ages."

Adam cringed. "Yeah…never got around to buying it when it first came out."

A wistful look washed over her face. "*Yield* is my favourite. I just love *Given to Fly*. It sends shivers down my spine."

He smiled widely. "Hey, that's my favourite too." He took a sip of his beer. "It's funny, I never would have taken you for a grunge rocker."

She tilted her head to one side. "Ah well, they do say never judge a book by its cover."

He grinned. "They certainly do. So what else do you like?"

"I have a huge soft spot for Jeff Buckley. His music is just…well…transcendent."

"Yeah, he was a talented guy. I was shocked when I heard he'd died. Such a waste."

"I cried for days when I heard about it. *Grace* is one of my all-time favourite albums. Listening to *Hallelujah* still makes me cry now." She cleared her throat as if the emotions were bubbling to the surface.

He leaned forward, filled with enthusiasm that this beautiful girl seemed to be the whole package, stunning, intelligent, and a brilliant taste in music. He couldn't believe his luck. "The guy had an amazing voice, didn't he?"

"Oh yes, his vocal range was astounding." A glass collector came and removed some empties left by the table's previous occupants. Once he had gone, Eve turned to Adam. "What were you going to ask me? When we both started talking at the same time, I mean."

He gazed into her eyes. They were the most vivid blue he had ever seen. He was taken aback for a moment. She scrunched her eyebrows but smiled. Clearly, she was wondering why he was staring.

He cleared his throat and shook his head. "Sorry, sorry… Oh God, I keep staring, don't I? I was just going to ask if you had made any more friends since the other day. You'd said that you had arrived later than everyone else and had only met Lil and me."

"Oh right. Yes, yes I've made a few more friends now… Do you mind if I ask you something?"

Adam swallowed a mouthful of his beer and his eyes watered as some tried to descend down his wind-wipe. He coughed a little and with a croaky voice he said, "Not at all…fire away."

Eve tilted her head again and narrowed her eyes. "You and Lily…is there a…you know…a history there at all?"

Adam almost choked again. The question was unexpected. He cleared his throat and laughed. "Me and

Lily? Oh lots of history…nothing *but* bloody history. We go way back. We've been best friends forever. Inseparable since primary school." He leaned back in his chair to consider it further. "We've just never seen each other *that way*. Why do you ask?"

Eve shook her head. "Oh no reason really…it's just… Well, she's so pretty and highly intelligent… I suppose I'm just surprised that you and she never…"

"No. We were always needled about it by others at school, but it never bothered either of us. We just never had the attraction thing. We're just best friends."

She nodded, seeming to accept the explanation he had given. It was the truth after all. He'd told it how it was.

They had another couple of drinks whilst they talked about family, home-life, music, and cinema. They left the pub, stepping into the chilled autumnal evening air.

As they walked back to campus, they passed revellers whose night was just beginning. He tentatively reached out and took her hand in his. He knitted his fingers with hers and wondered if she would pull away. When she didn't, his smile widened. He looked over to her and discovered that she was smiling too. They continued their walk in silence until they reached her dorm room.

She was the first to break the silence as they arrived at her door. "I hope you didn't think I was being nosey."

He scrunched his face and looked upwards as if trying to decipher what she meant. "Nosey? About what?"

"You and Lily."

"Oh that? No it's totally fine. We're just friends. She's very important to me and she's usually the first one I tell about…well…you know…" He gestured between them. "This kind of stuff…but if that's weird—"

She shook her head. "Oh no, not at all… No, I think it's sweet that you have such a good relationship… It's just that I had to ask. I didn't want to be stepping on her toes."

Adam smirked. How did people *really* see his relationship with Lily? "Well yes, it must have looked a bit odd."

She stepped a little closer. "No, you don't understand… I had to check."

She was so close, he could smell the wonderful rose fragrance she wore, and he closed his eyes briefly as he breathed her scent deep into his lungs. "Check what?" he whispered.

"Check if you were an item…because if you were…I wouldn't have done this." Placing her hands on his chest, she reached up and kissed him gently on the lips. He inhaled sharply and stepped closer, his hands moving up her arms and into her hair. Her lips were soft and warm, and she made a little contented sound that just about melted his heart. Her hands gripped the lapels of his jacket.

When the kiss came to its natural end, Adam fluttered his eyelids open and looked down at the beautiful girl in front of him. She smiled up at him in return.

He blew out a puff of air and it clouded between them. "Wow."

Eve giggled at his reaction and then her face became serious. "Oh heck…look, I don't go throwing myself at men. That's the first time I've ever done anything like that. I don't want you to think I'm—"

He stopped her mouth with another heart melting kiss. When he opened his eyes this time he rested his forehead on hers. "I think nothing of the sort. I think that's the best first kiss I've ever experienced in my life." He brushed his thumbs gently over her cheeks. "Please say you'll let me see you again." His voice was a whisper.

"Adam, I would love to see you again. I was hoping you'd ask."

Chapter Five

Loud Love (Soundgarden)
October 2000 – Edinburgh University

Elliot kept a firm hold on Lily's hand as he pulled her through the writhing bodies in the dimly lit house. Her heart pounded in her chest as they stepped over and around people. As she glanced around the unfamiliar surroundings, she gulped. Couples were making out in full view of everyone else. Some were indiscreetly groping each other's privates, which shocked Lily to the core. The room smelled of alcohol and other things that she didn't wish to acknowledge.

Elliot had informed her that his friend, Jacko, was holding the party at the house he shared with several other young adults. None of them were students and she wondered how on earth Elliot knew them. Apparently the parties were notorious for their raucous music and free flowing alcohol. Lily felt rebellious. If Adam could go out and find someone, so could she. And Elliot was gorgeous, thin and sinewy, but muscular at the same time. His long curly mane and his resemblance to her biggest crush were helping her attraction in spades. When he kissed her, she felt a rush of heat to places as yet untouched by men. He made her feel good. But she didn't love him. She doubted she ever would. This was purely a physical attraction.

Eventually, they made their way through to a kitchen where a stocky, tattooed man greeted them.

"Elliot, my man!" Jacko slapped him on the back and then set his eyes on Lily. "Who's your gorgeous girl?"

"Jacko this is my girlfriend, Lily. Hot isn't she?" Elliot squeezed her into him and kissed the top of her head. She felt a little strange about his actions, and his words for that matter.

"She certainly is, my friend." Jacko reached out and shook Lily's hand. "It's a pleasure, Lily. Any friend of Elliot's is a friend of mine."

She shook his hand. "Likewise, Jacko. Busy place you've got here." She laughed as she was jostled forward by beer hungry folks, who were all clambering for the keg, which sat upon the kitchen countertop.

"Certainly is. My parties are always popular. Can't think why." He laughed as he handed out plastic cups filled with what smelled like cheap ale or home brew. Lily liked him immediately. His warm eyes made her feel at ease and his ink fascinated her. She would one day have a tattoo, she decided.

Elliot led her, beer in hand, through to a lit lounge with low wattage lamps covered in red scarves, which gave the room a strange glow. There were bodies all over the place just like the rest of the house. She sipped the beer and winced. *Eugh! Not going to be drinking much of that stuff.* Elliot turned to her and took her beer. He placed it with his own on the cheap-looking, nineteen seventies sideboard that was situated just inside the room. Soundgarden's *Loud Love* boomed out over the sound system. Not breaking eye contact, he leaned and kissed her. At first the kiss was gentle, but as need coursed through her veins, she grabbed for him to deepen the kiss. He eagerly reciprocated, fisting his hands in her hair. She felt a familiar throbbing between her legs as she did every time their lips locked.

Leaning into her ear he spoke huskily, "Want to come upstairs?" She did. She really did. But she thought perhaps her first time shouldn't be in a house packed full of other people doing the same thing. She scrunched her brow and thought on it. She looked up into Elliot's eyes. He leaned into her again. "Look, I'm not going to pressure you or anything... I just... God, I want you. That's all. You have an amazing body and…well, I really want to be inside you. I hope that doesn't sound too crude?" He cringed. "I know you're not that kind of girl. And I'm not actually that kind of guy. You'd only be my third. I…I just really want you." He stroked her cheek with the back of his hand, his eyes hooded with lust.

It wasn't the most romantic thing she had ever heard, and she didn't quite believe that she'd only be his third, but hearing his words did spike something inside her. She pulled him down for another deep kiss and felt her legs weaken. She was under no illusions that this was anything more than lust. Feeling that way made things a little easier. She knew her heart was safe. Well, actually her heart was in a millions pieces already thanks to the small matter of her unrequited love.

Elliot took her hand and led her toward the stairs. Again, they clambered over couples on the staircase deep in the throes of groping and openly kissing with tongues. At the top of the stairs, they were presented with several doors. He seemed to know where he was taking her as he opened the second door to the right along the corridor. He poked his head around the door and flicked on a light. The room was tidy and looked remarkably clean considering where they were. Posters of heavy metal bands adorned the walls and a black fake fur comforter lay stretched at the end of the double bed. Nervously, Lily stood glancing around as he closed the door and slid the bolt across.

He turned to face her and smiled warmly. "Hey…you look nervous."

"Elliot, we've only been seeing each other a short time and I've never done… Look, this may sound crazy, but I'm still a virgin."

He approached her and took her face in his hands. "There's no pressure. Let's just take things slow. If we don't go all the way, then that's fine. I just wanted to be alone with you for a while." He leaned and kissed her again. She knew exactly what he wanted and she thought she wanted it too. She was over twenty now after all, an adult capable of making her own decisions. Most of her friends had been having sex for ages. She'd been waiting, but all the waiting in the world wasn't going to get her the man she *actually* wanted.

She kissed him back deeply and felt the throbbing between her thighs again. He slid his hand up her top and fondled her breast, making her moan in pleasure. He pressed himself against her, and the firmness of his arousal pushed hard against her thigh. She breathed in sharply as he kissed her neck. Her eyes closed as she relished the sensations taking over her body.

He walked her backward over to the bed and pulled her down with him. When they were lying down, he slid his hand down and pulled up her skirt until his fingers were pressing her sensitive spot. She wantonly pushed herself against his hand as he circled her over her panties.

He gazed into her eyes. "Lily...please let me. I'll be gentle, I promise." His pupils were dilated and his eyelids were heavy. Without really thinking it through, she nodded her head. After fumbling around in his pocket for a condom, he pulled his jeans down slightly and rolled it on. He tugged her panties down her legs and off, and in a moment he was moving inside of her. She felt a searing pain and cried out. He swore under his breath and stopped moving. "Sorry, Lily, are you...are you okay? Should I pull out?"

"No, I'm fine...keep going...it's fine." She gasped, keeping her eyes closed. She bit down on her lip. It was awful. Not at all how she had wanted things to be. She had dreamed of sharing this moment, her virginity with Adam, but she knew that realistically it was never going to happen. Elliot kissed her and stroked her face. Lily opened her eyes and looked up into his lust-filled gaze. He came with a final thrust and repeated her name over and over, peppering her face with tender kisses.

She felt numb.

Once his breathing had calmed, he pulled himself away and rid himself of the condom. He rolled over to her again and kissed her. "Lily…I…I know it's really soon and I know I'm going to make a total idiot out of myself, but I think I should tell you something. I really, really like you…a lot… I think there's a good chance I'll fall for you if we keep doing that."

Lily gulped. A stray tear trailed down her cheek and into her hair. She wasn't sure she wanted to do that again with him. He had been sweet and as gentle as possible when taking someone's virginity, but she felt disappointed with herself for giving it so willingly.

She rolled to face him. "That's really sweet, Elliot. I'm just…I'm not there yet. I'm getting over someone—"

"Don't explain. It's fine. I get it. Do you think there's any chance your feelings might change though?"

She forced a smile. "Maybe," she lied.

A grin spread across his face. "That will do for now. I can wait." He kissed her again. "Come on, we'd better get back to the party. The bathroom is just next door if you want to…you know…clean up. I'll wait outside for you."

She made her way into the bathroom and found a pack of moist wipes. She cleaned herself up and looked at her flushed reflection and messed up hair in the mirror above the toilet. "You idiot." She chastised herself, feeling angry and even more disappointed now that she could look herself in the eyes. "You stupid, stupid idiot."

She had just handed her virginity over to someone she didn't love, just so that she could rid herself of it like she would discard an old item of clothing she no longer liked, as if it meant nothing. Elliot had been lovely but the earth didn't move. There had been no orgasm for her. And now the throbbing of desire between her legs had been replaced with something she didn't want to acknowledge. She dragged her fingers through her wild curls and took a few deep breaths hoping to fend off the tears that were stinging her eyes. *No point regretting it now. What's done is done.*

When she opened the bathroom door, Elliot pushed off the wall and circled her in his arms. "Thank you, Lily. It meant a lot to know I was your first." He kissed her and she let him. "I hope we can do it again and maybe that you'll enjoy it more. You didn't really enjoy it, did you?" He cringed.

"It was…nice." It was her turn to cringe now. Elliot shook his head at her words and looked upset. "Elliot, honestly, it was never going to be mind-blowing for me, was it? Not the first time." She took his cheek, trying her best to be reassuring.

"I guess…I just hate that your first time was…*just* nice. I'm sorry, Lily. It should have been better. You didn't even…you know." He looked awkward as he hugged her tight. *That's because you didn't even try.* She searched for the right words, but none came, so she just hugged him back. "It'll be better next time. I promise." *There won't be a next time.*

❤❤❤

Saturday morning arrived and presented Lily with the throbbing head usually associated with the over indulgence of alcohol. Elliot had dropped her off at her room at one o'clock in the morning after she had ended up consuming too much of the rancid tasting, brown liquid that Jacko was passing off as beer. She had drunk the vile concoction solely to rid herself of the memory of what she had done.

After giving up their bar work for the summer, she and Adam had vowed to go job hunting again, and Saturday was supposed to be the day. It had been arranged for a while, but they hadn't confirmed things, so she was surprised when there was a knock on the door while she lay there feeling like someone had carpeted her tongue with shag pile as she'd slept. She clambered out of bed dressed only in an old, faded, oversized Ramones T-shirt that had once belonged to Adam.

"Morning!" he trilled as she opened the door. His greeting was quickly followed by a sharp intake of breath. "Shit you look rough. What happened?" He pushed in and plonked himself down on her unmade bed.

"Beer and loud music." She yawned and stretched her arms over her head.

Adam suddenly averted his eyes. "Er, Lily, I know we're best friends and all, but all you have on under that T-shirt is a pair of flimsy knickers. I *am* a bloke you know."

She dropped her arms quickly and felt the heat rise in her cheeks. "Whoops, sorry." She cringed, grabbed a pair of yoga pants, and pulled them on as quickly as she could. "So, how did your first official date with Eve go?" *Not that I actually want to know.*

A grin spread across his handsome features. "Oh, Lil, it was fantastic. We kissed."

Her heart sank a little but she forced a smile. "Oh great. That's really...great."

He frowned, causing a familiar crease between his brows. "How was your night? Did you go to that house party?"

"I did...it was really...yeah...good. Elliot's really sweet."

He laughed coldly. "Sweet? That's not a word I would've associated with him. Just be careful okay? He's the kind of guy who you don't want to be handing yourself over to. I…I don't trust him."

She pulled her brow into a frown and gasped. "You don't even know him, Adam. You can't say things like that." She folded her arms across her braless chest defiantly.

"Look, like I just said, I'm a bloke. I know what he's after. And I just don't think you should go giving *it* to *him*."

She felt the heat rising in her cheeks again and her hands fisted on her hips. "Yeah…well…that's…you…it's…it's none of your business who I…" She shook her head as she stumbled over her words, the right ones evading her completely.

His mouth fell open and his cheeks coloured. "Please tell me you didn't?"

She turned her back on him and folded her arms once again. "Didn't what? I don't know what you're talking about."

He blew out a long breath as if he was trying to calm a rage. When he spoke again, his voice was quiet and controlled. "You know exactly what I'm talking about. Tell me you didn't sleep with him." They had always agreed it was better to wait until you were in love before you gave yourself to someone. Adam was very old fashioned that way and Lily had always thought it very sweet. She could almost feel his eyes boring into her back.

Her cheeks warmed as though they would burst into flames at any second. She had never been able to lie to Adam. Not successfully. She swung around to face him and narrowed her eyes. "Well, Adam, what I *can* confirm is that there wasn't any *sleeping* involved." *Shutupshutupshutup! Not helping yourself!*

He stood and walked over to her, his fists clenched at his sides, and a pained look had taken over his usually warm eyes. "You didn't?" She remained stoic. He dragged his hands through his hair and groaned as if she had kicked him. "Oh fuck, Lily, why? What did you do that for? Do you have feelings for *him*? Seriously? Fucking Pippy Longstocking?" The pain in his eyes turned to disappointment and he shook his head.

She gritted her teeth. "His name is Elliot Longthorne, Adam, and it is *none* of your business. So I had sex? So what? I enjoyed it." She lied. Her words were meant to hurt him as the anger both at herself *and* Adam bubbled to the surface. "It was great and I'll be doing a lot more of it with or without your blessing. I'm an adult. Remember? Now if you're going to stand there being all judgmental, then I suggest you fuck off out of my room!" she shouted pointing to the door.

He shook his head as he turned and walked out, slamming the door behind him. She let out an angry guttural scream and punched her mattress.

Chapter Six

Everybody's Gotta Learn Sometime (The Korgis)
November 2000 – Edinburgh University

Adam and Lily didn't speak for over a month after her admission she had slept with Elliot. Adam had no right to be angry or disappointed, and he knew this when he thought rationally about it. But it didn't stop the rage from bubbling inside him every time he thought of her giving herself to the lanky streak of piss so freely. What made things worse is that the relationship she had run headlong into fell apart soon after they'd had sex, just like Adam knew it would. He wanted to comfort her but his stubbornness wouldn't allow it, and so it fell to Eve to be Lily's shoulder to cry on. Not that there had actually *been* any crying apparently.

"So…what did she say at lunch?" Adam asked as he and Eve sat in his uncharacteristically tidy room after walking back together once lectures had finished for the day.

Eve sighed and furrowed her brow. "I wish you two would just *talk*, for goodness sake. You're both adults and I shouldn't have to be your go between. When I speak to her it's all *Is Adders still mad? Has he said anything?* And then I come to you and get the same." She hit him with a cushion.

Adam huffed. "I know, I know…seriously though…how is she?"

Eve rolled her eyes and placed a hand on his face. "She's angry as hell at *you* but loves you to bits and hates all this angst between you."

"Is she upset about Pippy?"

She pushed his arm. "You need to stop calling him that. No, she's not upset. They parted because…well…look just speak to her."

Adam sat upright. "Because of what? Please tell me Eve. You're worrying me."

"Look, she only slept with him to see what it was like. He turned her on and she wanted to try it. But when it came down to it, he wanted a relationship, and...well *she* didn't. Simple as that."

"Really? So *she* ended it?"

"Pretty much, Adam, yes." She kissed his nose.

"And you believe that?" Adam couldn't.

Eve rolled her eyes. "Of course, I believe her. I have no reason not to. Look, can I ask you something?"

He snuggled into her neck and kissed her. "Anything," he mumbled.

"Why are you *really* so wound up about her sleeping with him?"

He stopped his ministrations and pulled back to look into her eyes. He huffed again and ran a hand through his hair. "I told her dad I'd watch out for her. I feel like I've let him down. She should've waited until she was in love. She should've let it be special. She deserves that, Evie."

"But, Adam, she's not *your* responsibility. You need to let her breathe. You can't protect her forever."

"Look, can we please stop talking about her? You and I are what matters here. Not my stubborn arsed friend." He gently caressed her lower lip with his thumb. Leaning in to kiss her, he lowered her back on the bed and deepened the kiss. Her hands found his hair and she moaned into his mouth.

All this talk of sex had got Adam thinking. He had been seeing Eve for around six weeks. He hadn't tried to take things further. He respected her and wanted their first time to be special, not rushed at some stupid, alcohol fuelled house party. The most they had done is kiss and touch a little. She turned him on just by the way she returned his kisses and grasped his hair. Her moans of pleasure almost sent him over the edge on more than one occasion.

He moved his mouth to her neck, nibbling and sucking at her tender skin, getting the reaction he loved so much. Her fingers gripped his hair harder.

He wanted her.

Desperately.

His every waking thought now had Eve's smiling eyes and beautiful face slap bang in the middle of it. But he would only take the next step for love. His mouth stopped moving. His head snapped up and his eyes met hers. Their blue depths were filled with lust but there was more there. The realisation hit him like a ton of falling textbooks. He *loved* her. He really, *really* loved her. *Shit. I'm actually in love.* Suddenly he sat up and pulled away. The worry that he saw flash in her eyes momentarily melted his heart but he lowered his gaze. Fear coursed through his veins riding on the back of the adrenalin.

She touched her lips. "Adam...what is it? What's wrong?"

He turned to her and touched her cheek. "Nothing...I'm fine honestly."

Her cheeks coloured rose-red. "Did I do something wrong?" Her voice wavered as she spoke.

Shaking his head vehemently, he smiled. "No...not at all. I...I need to tell you something, but I'm scared you'll run a mile."

She backed away from him. "Oh God, Adam, what is it? You're really scaring me." Her eyes had become glassy and her lower lip trembled.

Clearly she feared the worst.

He pulled himself along the bed toward her. "Hey, stop." He took her hands in his. "It's nothing bad. I just don't know if it's the right time... I'm scared, Eve." He looked into her azure eyes trying to communicate his feelings so that she would understand.

"Just tell me...please."

He closed his eyes for a second, trying to conjure up some courage to say how he felt whilst terrified he was about to blow everything. Focusing on her once again, he took a deep breath. "Eve...I...I'm in love with you... I love you."

A tear escaped her eye and his heart sank. She didn't feel the same and he'd just ruined everything. He sat upright pulling his hands away and looked down at them where they twisted in his lap. He closed his eyes again as he felt the bed dip. She was leaving. He couldn't bear to watch her leave, and so he kept his eyes closed tight. He listened for the door but was greeted with nothing but a shuffling sound.

When he finally dared to open his eyes, he looked up and his breath caught. She stood before him completely naked. It was the most beautiful sight he had ever be held. Her golden blonde hair tumbled over her shoulders and caressed her round, pert breasts. The tight pink buds beckoned for his touch as he raked his eyes slowly over her flawless skin. His hungry eyes followed the curve of her waist to her hip, and the soft hair at the junction of her thighs brought a gasp. He swallowed past the lump lodged in his throat. Blinking up at her he opened his mouth to speak, but she reached and pulled his hand so that he was standing before her.

She lifted her hand to cup his cheek. "Adam...I love you too."

Relief washed over him and he thought his heart might burst with this new realisation. He leaned to kiss her, and stroking his fingertips down her bare back, he felt her shiver under his touch.

Anxious that he had somehow made her feel pressured, he said, "Evie, we don't have to do this now. I'm so happy that you feel the same, but we can wait. I'm not Elliot. I'm happy to wait." He kissed her again and his arousal betrayed the words he had uttered.

She pulled away and looked into his eyes. "Adam, I don't want to try to plan for this to be perfect. I don't want to put pressure on either of us by saying we'll do this on that day, in that place… I want to give you this gift now. I want to make love with you, Adam, please?"

He inhaled sharply as he looked down at her. "But I want it to be perfect and what if it's not?"

She smiled her usual breath-taking smile. "What makes it perfect is that it's me and you. We have all the time in the world to perfect things. We'll learn. But tonight we have all night. I've never done this before and although I don't know for sure about you I get the feeling that, whilst you have probably got some experience in other ways that maybe you've never done this either?"

"No…never. I've just never felt enough for anyone to go that far." He felt the heat rise in his cheeks at the admission. He wanted to be the experienced one. He wanted to rock her world and make her see stars but felt disappointed in himself. On the other hand it dawned on him that they were about to share this most intimate and special thing with each other.

She pulled at his T-shirt and discarded it on the floor. She was braver than he gave her credit for. Always assuming she would be the shy one, he realised he was wrong as he allowed her to unfasten the button on his faded jeans and slide them down his legs, taking the boxers with them. His arousal sprang forth and she bit her lip as she gazed upon it. He was glad she had no one to compare him to. At least he didn't have to fear he wasn't enough for her.

He pulled her into an embrace, his hands in her hair as he tilted her up for a long, deep kiss. Never in all his twenty years had he been more aroused or more in awe. Of course he had looked at magazines. He was a young man after all. But Eve truly was a sight to behold. And she was for his eyes only. He stepped back toward the bed, taking her with him. They lay down together and gazed into each other's eyes.

She giggled nervously. "Okay...now I'm scared."

He kissed her tenderly. "Me too...I want to please you so much. I want to make you feel amazing but—"

She placed her fingertips over his lips. "Shhh, no pressure, remember? Do you have protection?"

He nodded and leaned over to his nightstand. He shot a glance back over at her. "Oh God, Eve this doesn't mean I expected... I mean I hoped that someday... I mean—"

She stopped his mouth with a kiss and an encouraging, tender smile that told him he didn't need to explain. He took out a small foil packet and placed it beside them on the bed. He lay beside her and covered her mouth with his own. As theirs tongues danced, he smoothed his hand gently downward to her breast and caressed her nipple. She moaned into his mouth and gripped him tighter. Her skin was so soft, and he loved how she shivered under his gentle touch. With feather light movements, his fingertips travelled down her body until he reached the junction of her thighs. He slipped his fingers into her dampness and stroked her there for a while, taking note of the things that pleased her and the things that made her grab for him. Her breathing rate increased into breathy gasps and moans, which spurred him on. His movements became faster as Eve became more vocal. He touched and caressed until she tightened and cried out his name, clinging onto his shoulders, her eyes closed and her head back. He had made that happen. A sense of pride washed through his veins, the likes of which he'd never experienced before.

Nervously, as she watched, he sheathed himself and hovered between her thighs looking to her for consent. She stroked his cheek and pulled at his waist, urging him on.

He entered her on a long, low groan. "Oh, God, Eve...I love you so much... I never expected this... I never—"

She covered his mouth with hers once again and inhaled sharply. He watched her clamp her eyes shut tight. He knew she must be hurting but she continued to pull him in. Carefully at first, he moved inside the woman he loved, holding her close until he could hold back no longer and his movements became more urgent. He thrust into her one last time as pleasure rocketed right to his very core. Stars appeared and fireworks exploded throughout his entire body, the most wonderful sensations taking over him. He collapsed onto her and nuzzled her neck for a moment until his breathing returned to normal and his heart rate slowed. She held onto him and kissed his cheek and ear, sighing as she did so.

He pulled away from her and propped himself up on his elbows. Staring into her eyes he asked her, "Are you okay?"

She nodded. "I'm so much more than okay, Adam. I love you."

He kissed her again. "And I love you. Thank you. That was the most amazing feeling I've ever experienced. Thank you so much."

Suddenly feeling a little overcome with emotion, he bit the inside of his cheek and pulled away to unsheathe himself. Eve climbed under the covers and held her arms out to him. He climbed back in next to her and pulled her in to rest her head on his chest.

Wow. Just wow.

Chapter Seven

It's My Party (Lesley Gore)
June 2001 – Edinburgh University

"Adam! We're going to be late for Lily's party! Come on!" Eve shouted through the bathroom door of the shared house. He had been waiting ages to actually get in there thanks to the fact that all six housemates (including Lily) were invited to the party. Moving into a house with only two bathrooms and so many people was the most ridiculous decision Adam felt he had ever made.

"I'll be out in a minute, gorgeous!" he shouted back, nicking his chin with the razor. "Ah, shit!"

"You okay, honey?"

"Yeah, just bloody cut my chin."

"Oooh. I'll kiss it better when you come out," Eve replied.

He smiled at his reflection. "You can't talk about kissing me if you want to get to this damn party, Evie."

"Just hurry up, okay?"

"All done." Adam opened the door and scooped his girl up in his arms, kissing her neck.

Edinburgh was heaving with Saturday night revellers as Adam and Eve travelled to the party venue in the taxi. Many of the stone buildings on the Royal Mile had long since been converted into bars and restaurants giving the age-old road a modern twist with its bright signage and trendy exteriors. When they arrived at the club everyone was already there. Lily greeted them, glass in hand. "You made it finally! Thought you'd bloody decided not to come!" She hiccupped.

"How much have you had already, Lil?" Adam scrunched his brow at his best friend as he noticed the bruise on her cheek. "And what the hell have you done to your face?" He lifted a lock of her hair.

"Oh that…I walked into the door in my room, can you believe it?" She laughed. "Bloody clumsy cow, I am."

Adam shook his head. "Well, you need to stop drinking so bloody much."

Lily rolled her eyes in an exaggerated manner. "Okay, *Dad*." She turned and walked toward the bar. Adam followed her with his eyes.

Eve squeezed his arm. "You shouldn't be so hard on her, Adam. She's not your responsibility."

"So you keep telling me. But she doesn't take responsibility for herself, does she?" he snapped.

"It's her life, honey. Give her some breathing room."

He turned to her and slipped his arms around her waist. "What would I do without you to keep me level headed, eh?" he asked, leaning down to kiss her.

"Well…I think poor Lily would get even more stick than she does right now." Eve giggled.

They walked over to the bar which was brightly lit in contrast to the rest of the club. The optics hung with their multi-coloured liquid contents, almost like works of modern art. All Adam wanted was a beer, but it looked like he may end up with some fancy cocktail concoction instead. He scanned along the row of fridges and spied his favourite tipple hiding amongst some bright blue monstrosity that wouldn't be out of place in a laboratory. After ordering their drinks, he glanced over toward Lily, who was now tongue deep in her current boyfriend's mouth. *Carl. Dickhead.* Adam wasn't a fan. He pulled Eve onto the dance floor when a slow number came over the sound system. She nuzzled into his chest and he kissed the top of her head.

Later on, after the third or fourth song, he glanced around the club realising he hadn't seen Lily for quite a while. Scanning the dimly lit place as best he could, his search was in vain. She was nowhere to be seen. Worry set in.

"What's wrong Adam? You're so distracted tonight." Eve stared at him, lips pursed. He could see the frustration in her eyes.

"I'm sorry, Evie...it's just Lily. She seemed...odd. Don't you think? And now there's no sign of her. I feel uneasy about it."

Eve sighed. "To be honest, Adam, I'm getting rather fed up of this. You aren't *with* Lily. You're with *me*. Now I get that your friendship is strong but this is just getting—"

Adam gripped her arms. "Evie, I love you. And I'm sorry, okay? It's not like that between me and Lil. You've known that for two years now. But something's not right. Please believe me. I *know* her. I know something is off."

Eve gazed at him and then nodded. "Okay...I'll go check the ladies." She turned sharply and walked away.

❤❤❤

Lily sat in the end cubicle. Tears fogged her eyes and the bruise on her cheek throbbed. She wondered why things had started to go so horribly wrong. She blew her nose, which made her cheek hurt even more. The door into the restroom opened and closed.

"Lily? Lily are you in here, honey?" *Eve*. Lily remained silent. "Adam's worried about you. If you're in here can you just say, so that I can tell him you're fine?"

Lily sniffed as more tears came. "Lily? Is that you? Are you crying?" Footsteps moved closer to the end cubicle and the door rattled. "Okay, now I'm worried too. I was trying to defend you to Adam, saying that you were fine, but now I'm not so sure. Open up, okay?"

Lily stood and unlocked the door. Eve pushed it open. "What on earth is wrong, honey? What's happened to make you cry?"

Lily shook her head and crumpled her face as she began to sob uncontrollably. Eve enveloped her in her arms. "Oh honey, please tell me what's going on. Is it Carl? Have you split up?"

"Eve...please...please, don't tell Adam, please." She squeezed Eve's arms.

Eve narrowed her eyes. "Tell him what? What's going on?"

"He hit me," she whispered.

"What? Who hit you?"

"Carl...but it was only once." She widened her eyes pleadingly.

Eve's mouth fell open. "What? He *hit* you? Oh my God, Lily, why on earth would he do that?"

"It was only once and he said sorry. He got a bit drunk when I missed a period and thought I was pregnant. He...he said I was stupid and careless... He was right. It was my fault."

"No...hang on a minute. It takes two to bloody tango. That's just ridiculous."

"I know, but he said he was sorry. I...I think he meant it."

Eve gripped Lily's arms. "I don't give a flying *fuck* if you thought he meant anything. He shouldn't have laid a *finger* on you. And what happened was not your fault okay?"

"But it was my responsibility—"

Eve's eyes were wide and her face had lost its colour. "Bullshit, Lily. You know that's a load of rubbish. You're an intelligent woman, for goodness sake. Don't you dare defend him for doing that to you." Lily felt the inappropriate urge to snigger. She had never heard Eve swear before. The realisation that Eve must be very angry and worried enough to do so was quite a sobering thought.

"Please don't tell Adam, okay? Promise me?"

Eve shook her head slowly. "You know I can't make that promise. He's your *best friend* and he cares about you deeply. He needs to know."

Tears spilled over once again. "No! I trusted you, Eve. You can't tell him."

"Where's Carl now?"

"He went out for a smoke. He said… Never mind." Lily shook her head.

"He said what?"

Lily dropped her gaze to the floor. "He said my party was shit and my friends are pathetic. He thinks my friends are beneath him." She sobbed, feeling ashamed.

"Right. Come on. Get some water splashed on your face. We're going back out there to get Adam and we're going home."

"No…no, I'm fine… I'll just put more make-up on. I'll be fine," Lily insisted.

"No. We should get you out of here until we decide what to do."

♥♥♥

Adam paced near the bar. What the hell was taking Eve so long? He decided she must have found Lily in some kind of drunken stupor in the toilets. Worry got the better of him and he marched toward the ladies' room. Without stopping to think he pushed the door open. Eve and Lily swung around as he entered.

"What the fuck's going on with you two?" He clenched his jaw as he watched the two girls acting suspiciously.

Eve looked toward Lily. "Please tell him, Lily."

"No!" Lily's voice was strained.

Adam frowned. "Tell me what?"

Lily shook her head at Eve.

"Tell me what?" Adam raised his voice.

Eve cupped Lily's bruised cheek. "Lily, please."

Lily crumpled to the floor and Adam rushed to her side, crouching beside her. "Lily? What's going on?"

"He hit me."

"What?" His voice was calm, belying the storm that had begun to rage beneath his skin. "Who hit you?"

"It was my fault. But it's all fine now."

He took Lily's face in his hands and wiped the tears away with his thumbs. "Did Carl hit you?"

"Yes but it was my fault."

"Okay, on what planet is it ever okay for a man to hit his girlfriend?" he asked her gently. "Lily, answer me that. When is it ever okay?"

"I…I…but he thought I'd trapped him."

"What? What do you mean?"

"I missed a period. He thought I was pregnant. He said if I was that I'd done it on purpose."

"So he fucking *hit* you when he thought there was a chance you could be *pregnant*?" Adam spoke through clenched teeth. Lily just nodded. "Where is he now, Lily?"

"Adam, no…it's fine…he said sorry."

Adam let out a derisive laugh. "Oh well that's fine then…as long as he apologised." He turned to Eve. "Where is the lowlife piece of scum?"

Eve bit her lip. "He apparently went out for a smoke."

Adam stood slowly. "Keep Lily here." He flung the door open so hard it bashed into the wall and left a huge dent.

♥♥♥

Carl was leaning against the wall, puffing on a rather large cigarette that looked distinctly like a joint. Adam ran toward him, and before Carl had a chance to figure out what was happening, Adam's fist connected with his nose. "You bastard!" he shouted as he repeatedly punched Lily's boyfriend in the face. "You lay one finger on her again, and I swear I will fucking *kill* you!"

Carl flailed his arms before curling into a ball on the ground. "Whoa, mate, stop hitting me! What the fuck? You've broken my fucking nose!"

Adam stood over Carl, fists still clenched, chest heaving. "You stay away from her, do you hear me?"

Carl laughed through his blood stained teeth. "Whatever she's told you, mate, it's all lies."

"Don't you call me your fucking mate, you prick!" Adam's heart pounded in his chest and he had to will himself not to continue with the beating.

"She tried to trap me! She tried to get pregnant. You know what they can be like. They see a good thing and they don't want to let it go." Carl held his hands up.

Adam grabbed him by the collar of his shirt and dragged him to his feet. Moving to within an inch of Carl's face, Adam gritted his teeth. "You're not a fucking good thing! You're a fucking coward. If I *ever* hear that you've stepped within a foot of Lily again I swear to God I'll kick your fucking arse from here to Australia. Do you hear me?" Carl nodded. "Because next time, pal, I won't be as kind as to let you walk away with just a broken nose, you get me?" he shouted. People had begun to congregate outside the club where they were.

Adam shoved Carl again and he fell to the floor, hitting his head on the wall and yowling. Before he opened the door, Adam turned back to Carl. "Oh and while I remember, *Carl Denton*, if you decide that you're going to involve the police, don't worry, I'll be sure to tell them about the joint you've been smoking along with the fact that you hit your girlfriend when you thought she was pregnant and trying to trap you. As if anyone would want to trap *you*, you arrogant piece of shit!" Gasps travelled around the crowd that had gathered.

Lily and Eve were waiting by the bar when Adam returned shaking his sore hand. Lily's eyes widened. "Are you okay, Adam?"

He grinned. "I'm fine. Your *ex* is a little sore though."

♥♥♥

When they arrived back at the shared house, Adam walked Lily up to her room. He hugged her tight as they stood just inside the doorway. Her tears soaked his shirt.

He tilted her chin up. "Hey, why are you crying?"

"Because I'm so stupid...and because your knuckles are a mess...all because of me." She sniffed.

"Look, Lil, you deserve to be loved by someone *worthy* of you...you know all that stuff you were spouting about it being your fault he hit you was rubbish, don't you?" Lily nodded. "Because he's a wimp. He's not a real man and he's certainly not worthy of my best friend. Please keep away from him. And if he tries to come back into your life just remember how shitty you felt when he hit you. And tell me if he tries to make contact. I won't have it, Lil. I won't have anyone treating you like that. Not while I've got a breath in my body."

She gazed at him with watery eyes. "Thanks, Adders, I'm not sure what I would do without you.

He pulled her into him. "Well lucky for both of us we don't need to worry about that, eh?" He kissed her cheek and went back to his room.

Eve was reading in bed when Adam returned to his room. He undressed and climbed in next to her, snuggling up to her warm, naked body. "Thanks for staying here tonight, Evie. And thanks for your help with Lily."

She placed her book down. "It's okay...I think I owe you an apology."

"An apology? What for?"

"For doubting you about Lily. You clearly knew something was amiss and I just got jealous."

Adam pulled up to look into her eyes. "Jealous? Why jealous?"

She sighed. "Because of your relationship with her. It doesn't usually bother me, but sometimes I just see how you are with her and feel I can't compete with that level of love." Adam opened his mouth to speak but Eve placed her fingers on his lips. "And before you say anything, I'm aware of how ridiculous I'm being. Lily needed you. I just...sometimes struggle with how close you are." She dropped her gaze and her cheeks coloured.

He pulled her down so that their lips were almost touching, his eyes searching hers. "You do know how much I love you, don't you? And that you're the only girl for me? You're the one I want to wake up with, the one I want to share my body and my life with. You do know that, Evie, don't you?"

"When I'm not being paranoid and silly? Yes I know that. Now, what I really want is for you to make love to me. I want to forget about all the drama for a while."

"I can't think of anything that I'd rather do right now. I love you so much. Don't ever forget that. You and me are forever."

"Forever," she repeated. "And I love you too, Adam."

Chapter Eight

Skools Out For Summer (Alice Cooper)
June 2003 - Scotland

"How did it go, honey?" Eve's voice was music to Adam's ears.

"Well, it was gruelling to say the least!" Huffing the air out of his lungs, he collapsed back on the sofa. He shuffled his jacket down his arms whilst tucking his phone under his ear.

"Did you get any vibes at all? How did your presentation go? Did your lesson go okay? And did the kids seem to like you?" Eve's questions came out in a rush, making Adam smile.

He chuckled. "Erm…hang on…let me get this right…not really…quite well…great and yes."

"Adam!" She sounded frustrated.

"Sorry…the presentation went great thanks to you making me be *uber* prepared. The practise lesson was brilliant! We had a discussion about acrostic poems. I got them all to make an acrostic poem using their names. Some of them were amazing. I was so impressed. The kids were great fun. Awww, I really want this job, Evie."

She sighed. "You'll get it, honey. I just know you will."

"I wish I had your optimism. Anyway, when are you coming over? I miss you and I haven't made love to you in almost a week." His voice turned to a husky low whisper.

She moaned in his ear, sending shivers down his spine. "Hmmm, I was thinking the same thing. I would've come over tonight but I thought you might be too tired."

He sat upright. "Too tired for you? Never. Come over now if you like."

"I've just got some things to sort out for work and then I'll come over, okay?"

"Hmmm, can't wait. Hurry up, okay?"

♥♥♥

After leaving university Eve had moved with her friends into a house on the outskirts of Edinburgh, on the route to Jedburgh. Her post-grad internship with a small local newspaper didn't pay much, but considering she had three other housemates her rent was fairly low. She was stuck doing the births, deaths and marriages (AKA hatches, matches, and dispatches) at first but didn't really mind. Adam had attended several interviews but had been hitherto unsuccessful. High school English teacher vacancies were few and far between and the competition for each one fierce. More applicants than available posts; that was the issue.

This latest one had felt different. The high school was a fairly rural prospect but the kids had been great. Very respectful, unless they were lulling him into a false sense of security—a highly plausible prospect.

Adam shared a house with a guy named Max that he too had met at uni. He had been working, along with Max, in a large bookstore in the centre of Edinburgh to tide him over, and his work colleagues were rooting for him.

Lily? Well, Lily had inherited a tidy sum from a Spanish aunt and had gone travelling. She had spent less and less time around them lately and had a string of loser boyfriends who she joked she was just using for sex. Travelling had been something she had always dreamed of. And so when the opportunity arose, she grabbed it with both hands. Her gift of the gab meant she quickly made contacts and was soon busy working as a freelance journalist as she travelled, which kept her in the lifestyle to which she had quickly become accustomed.

Every so often either Adam or Eve would receive a postcard or a letter containing a photo of her in the arms of some Italian, Portuguese, or Spanish man. She looked as if she was having fun. Adam hoped she was. As if waiting in the wings, the phone rang as soon as he had hung up from his call to Eve. It was Lily.

"G'day, Adders! So are you soon going to be teaching the children of some poor unsuspecting Scottish parents or what?"

He held the phone away from his ear as Lily's voice boomed down the receiver into his ill-prepared cochlear. "Hey, Lil. No news yet. I think it went well though."

"Fantastic! So what are you up to? Is Eve there?"

"No, not yet. She's coming over soon, though. Where are you?"

She snorted down the line. "Durrr! Australia! Didn't you get that from my greeting?"

He nodded as if she could see him. "Ah, yes sorry. Fried brain. Having a good time down under?"

"It's awesome, Adders! And I have met the most goooorgeous guy! His name is Chris and he's really hot. He's a fucking *underwear* model!" She squealed.

"Hmmm, great. What happened to Alberto?" He remembered the last photo he had received.

"Oh…he went back home. Didn't follow the rest of us to Oz. We said we'd keep in touch but…"

Another notch marked on Lily's imaginary bedpost.

Hesitantly, he offered, "Lily…be careful, okay?"

She giggled. "What? Me? I'm always careful. I'm just having so much fun!" Her voice was bright, but Adam couldn't help the concern rising within him. "Hang on, Ad… What? Now? Okay, I'll just be a minute." She spoke to someone in the room with her. "Look Adders, I have to go. I'll call in a few days to see if you've heard anything. Bye!"

Before Adam could respond, the line went dead. A sense of unease niggled at his gut. He knew she was out there to experience life and to have fun, but she was taking it to the extreme. It seemed there was a different man at each stop off point on her travels. He just wanted to know she was okay, but he got the feeling that even if she wasn't she wouldn't tell him.

Half an hour later, there was a knock at the front door. Max was going out to his girlfriend's straight from work and so he knew that once Eve arrived they would have the place to themselves. He opened the front door and there she was. He inhaled sharply. She never failed to leave him breathless. She wore a long red coat and underneath a black and grey satin dress, which clung to her curves in the most delicious way. He felt the blood rush southwards just at the mere sight of her standing there. He scooped her up in his arms, kicking the door closed behind him.

"God, I've missed you," he whispered as he nuzzled her neck.

"Adam, I saw you yesterday."

"Yes but that was only a brief meeting. I haven't *seen you*-seen you in almost a week." He kissed her deeply, sneaking his tongue into her mouth.

She pulled away briefly and said, "You mean you haven't seen me *naked* in almost a week."

"Hmmm, that too." He nibbled on her bottom lip.

She groaned. "Now you come to mention it I have missed this," she breathed as his lips moved to her neck. She slid her hands up his arms and into his hair as his lips brushed hers once again. Pulling back she gazed into his eyes. "Hmmm, I'll take my coat off and then we can continue this."

He pulled away and helped her off with her coat. After hanging it in the hallway, he returned to find her reclining on the sofa, her shoes kicked off to the side. He immediately went to her and slid along her body, smoothing his hands over the curve of her hip and over her breast. Her breath hitched as he teased a nipple through the fabric of her satin dress. His lips found hers once again, and she opened to allow his tongue access. Their kisses became deeper and he could feel her heart rate increase against his chest as he slid his hand down...down. His palm caressed the silky skin of her thigh and slipped around to cup her bottom.

"Eve...I want to make love to you...right here on the sofa...right now." He gazed into her vivid blue eyes and could see his own need mirrored there. She grabbed his hair and pulled him down to take his mouth with her own. He couldn't get enough of her. Her taste, her smell, her body, and the noises she made when he pleasured her. She was simply intoxicating. He slipped one hand around to the front of her panties to cup her mound as he propped himself up on the sofa with the other. She closed her eyes and bit her lip. He loved that look too. He slid the panties down her legs and deftly unfastened the tie that held her wrap-around dress closed around her beautiful body. Moving the fabric aside so she was almost bared to him he devoured her first with his eyes and then he worshipped the junction of her thighs with his mouth, teasing her with his tongue.

Eve's chest heaved as she watched him. Her gaze was filled with a passion that matched his own.

She reached and stroked his face. "Adam...I need to feel you." He crawled up her body once again and lowered his head to pull her tightened nipple into his mouth through the delicate lace of her bra. She arched her back and cried out in ecstasy. He could wait no longer to connect to her in the most intimate way, and so fumbling with his belt and zipper, he freed himself and moved over her. With his eyes locked on hers, he found his most favourite place and inhaled sharply as he sunk inside. Her legs wrapped around him, pulling him deeper still as he caressed her breast with one hand, making her writhe beneath him. He could stay like this forever.

This woman was his life. She completed his soul and drove him wild with desire. As he moved inside her, his eyes bore into hers, and it wasn't long before they were clinging to each other as they ascended into the stars, calling out each other's name.

Adam rested his forehead on Eve's whilst his breathing and heart rate slowed. "I...love...you...so much...Evie."

"And I love you...more than anything." She kissed him tenderly as her hands stroked his back. They stayed there like that for a while, sharing kisses and staring lovingly at each other. Connected in soul, body, and mind.

Eve kissed Adam's nose. "I brought wine. I thought we could order a take-away and maybe have a nice long soak together."

He smiled. Her suggestion sounded like his idea of sheer bliss and he nodded. She knew just what he wanted, just what he liked, and he wanted to keep things like this. Forever.

Chapter Nine

Australia (Manic Street Preachers)
June 2003 – Australia

Lily awoke as the sun streamed in through a gap in the drapes, stinging her eyes. There was a rather long, naked man draped across her body. For a few moments she wondered where on earth she was. Then slowly it dawned on her. She was in Australia, which meant the naked man was Chris. *Mmmm...Chriiiiis...the underwear model...yum.* She rubbed her eyes and stretched, but when she did, she realised how achy she was. But then again there was no wonder, considering last night's lengthy *pash-sesh*—as Chris had called it in an accent as delicious as his body. He had stamina; that's for sure. She lost count of how many orgasms she'd experienced. She just...*lost count*. It was mind-blowing. She smirked at the memory.

She carefully slipped out of bed and hotfooted it to the en-suite to take a shower, thinking the hot water would go some way to relaxing her tired and aching muscles. It had been two days since she last spoke with Adam about his interview. She missed him. Chris was a welcome distraction, but she had no illusions about this fling going any further than the airport once it was time for her to move on. New Zealand was the next stop on the *Lily Macrae World Tour.*

Travelling in itself had been a welcome distraction from her predicament. She had seen some wonderful places and had met some fabulous people. The relationship between her best friend in the world and her good friend Eve had reached fever pitch. She just knew Adam would propose to Eve. And she was expecting it to happen almost as soon as he got a teaching job. So, if she thought about this realistically, it would occur sooner rather than later. As much as she loved Adam and wanted his happiness, hearing he was marrying another woman would crush her already broken heart, and no amount of distance would change that. It was sad that long before her current age of twenty-three she had lost her heart and fallen victim to the bitch that is unrequited love.

"Lily, come back to bed. I want to take up where we left off!" a husky voice called out. His Australian accent made her smile. She hadn't even climbed into the shower yet and toyed with the idea of going back in to him, but thinking about Adam had thrown cold water on any surge in her libido.

"Can't. I'm in the shower!" she shouted as she was climbing in. The water was hot and steam billowed around the room, enveloping her in a cloudy cocoon. Chris appeared peeking around the shower screen with a lascivious grin on his handsome face. His shaggy blonde hair was deliciously dishevelled, a look he carried with such grace.

Without invitation, Chris stepped in behind her, his state of arousal becoming evident as the steam cleared. "You're not going to leave me like this, are you?" He pouted as he prowled toward her, gesturing to his swollen manhood.

She tried to stifle the giggle that was determined to escape her body. "I would never do such a thing." She backed up to the wall as she looked down to find him already sheathed and ready to take her. Chris skimmed his hands down her body and effortlessly lifted her up so that she could wrap her legs around him. Her head rolled back and she tried her best to shake out the images of Adam that chose that precise moment to return and invade her mind.

Later on after their shower antics—which did nothing to alleviate her aching muscles—when Chris had left, Lily picked up her phone and dialled Adam's number. A croaky voice answered at the other end. *Whoops.* She would *have* to remember the time difference.

"Hello?"

"Adders? It's Lily!" She ignored the sleepiness in his voice.

"Oh...hey, Lil." She heard a fumbling noise. "It's okay, sweetheart, it's Lil." Hmmm, Eve was staying over.

Lily bit back the jealousy. "So did you hear about the job?"

"Yeah...yeah, I did."

Lily was becoming impatient. "And?"

"And...I got it!" he shouted into her ear.

Tears pricked at her eyes and she bit the inside of her cheek, knowing not only did that mean he had landed his dream job but that he would, without a doubt, soon be proposing to Eve. "Oh, Adders, that's brilliant!"

"Isn't it? I start after the summer break. Not long now. Anyway...how are you? How's Oz?"

"Oh still great and...still great!" she lied. She was homesick. Well actually, she was Adam-sick. But she wouldn't share that snippet of useless information. What good would it do?

"Great...I'm so glad to hear that, Lil. Look, I'll be honest...I'm worried about you."

Lily snorted. "Worried about *me?* Why would you be *worried* about me? I'm having the time of my life, Adders. I'm fine. Honestly. Anyway, gotta go. This call is costing me a bloody fortune! Speak soon. Bye!"

"Erm...okay, bye then. Call soon."

Lily hung up and threw her phone down as if it was on fire. She stared at it. He was *worried.* That wasn't what she wanted to hear. She wanted to hear that he missed her. That he wanted her to come home. That he was dumping

Eve and wanted to marry her instead. She laughed out loud at her ridiculous train of thought.

♥♥♥

Later on Lily made her way to meet with a group of friends she had met while travelling. She walked into the crowded bar and scanned the room. Suddenly a pair of big hands covered her eyes, making her jump almost out of her skin.

"Guess who?" the husky, deep, male voice tickled her ear. *Chris.*

"Hmmm…now let me think. There are so many people it could be…"

Chris dropped his hands from her eyes and huffed. "Charming."

She turned to look up at his handsome tanned face. "Oh Chris! It's you!" She feigned surprise.

Chris looked sullen. "Yeah. It's me." Lily immediately felt guilty. He actually looked genuinely hurt.

She tapped his nose with her fingertip. "Awww, Chris, don't sulk. I was only messing." She slipped her arms around his neck and kissed his chin. A smile made its way across his angular features. He really was rather delicious.

He leaned down and took her mouth with his. He really knew how to make her melt. A moan escaped her as her legs turned to jelly. He must have felt her wobble as his mouth curled into a smile against hers before he nibbled at her bottom lip. "Look, I wondered if we could get out of here instead of staying with the others. I want to take you to the beach." It sounded divine. After all she didn't really feel like drinking tonight.

"Do you think we can sneak out before they see us?" she whispered.

"No…they know we're here. But I told Marc earlier that I was taking you out, so they're cool."

"That was very presumptuous of you, Mr. Knight."

"Yeah, but I know you can't resist my Aussie charms." He was right. But it wasn't really his charms. It was his body and what he could *do* with it. Pure and simple. He was a player, not boyfriend material, and she knew this.

They made the short journey to the beach where the sun had begun its descent, casting a golden glow over the sand. They strolled together in silence for a while. Chris grasped her hand and pulled her to a stop in front of him. She turned to look at him. His brow was scrunched and he looked worried.

She pulled her brows inward to mirror his. "Chris? Are you okay?"

"No…I mean…there's something I want to say. You'll think I'm a complete idiot but just hear me out, okay?"

Pursing her lips, she cocked her head to the side.

"Ooookay. Look…I know I haven't known you for that long, and I know you think I have this bad rep like I'm a womaniser or whatever and that I have some kind of… I don't know…notching system or something on my bedpost but…well…sorry, I can't get my words out." He ran his hands through his hair and looked skyward as if to compose his thoughts. "It's just that…awww shit…look, I think I have feelings for you. And I know that it's ridiculous. We have amazing sex. And I can't get enough of your body, but I can't stop thinking about you either. I want to go to New Zealand with you next month. I want to spend some time with you…you know…see if this is going anywhere."

She stared at him open mouthed. Her heart was hammering its way out of her chest. To say she was shocked would have been the understatement of the year.

He stroked his thumb over her cheek. "Lily…please say something, eh? You look like you're catching flies."

She bit her lip and then released it with a sigh. "Chris...I...I wasn't expecting this...I was...I thought..."

He huffed out through puffed cheeks and rolled his head back placing his hands on his hips. "Fuck. I'm a *fucking* idiot."

She snapped out of her trance-like stupor. "Chris...hey, no...you're not an idiot. Not at all." She grabbed his hands and pulled them down, wrapping them around her. Deep down she knew this relationship could never go anywhere. He was gorgeous. He had the body of an Adonis and boy did he know what to do with it. He could melt her underwear simply by kissing her...but *love*? Love wasn't something she could foresee in their future. She couldn't imagine *ever* falling in love with anyone else. Adam was the only man she could ever imagine truly giving her heart to. But Adam wasn't hers. And he wasn't here. Chris was. Where would be the harm in seeing where it went? Maybe she was wrong? She pulled his face down toward her. "I was just shocked...that's all."

Chris's face lit up with the most beautiful smile. "So is that a yes? I mean...will you give us a chance?"

She took a deep breath and closed her eyes for a moment, wishing on every star in the sky that she could fall for him. "It's a yes." Chris scooped her up in his arms and swung her around.

Chapter Ten

You And Me Song (The Wannadies)
July 2003

Lily arrived home from New Zealand toward the end of July. The country had been amazing and definitely somewhere she would love to spend more time. The lush green of the forests and the majestic mountains painted a backdrop in her mind that would stay with her forever.

Chris had stayed there, reluctantly, even though he had begged Lily to let him accompany her home for a while.

"It'd be good for me to meet your friends and family, Lily. I think there's a real future here, don't you?" He caressed her cheek as they lay naked in bed.

"Yes…yes of course there is a future here, Chris. I just think maybe I need to go home alone this one time. I'm coming back to New Zealand in a month. I'm only going home to help my best friend celebrate a new job."

"Yeah, well I hope she appreciates you going all that way, Lil. She's a very lucky girl to have such an amazing friend." He spoke in his sexy Australian drawl as he nuzzled her neck. "I'll miss you like crazy when you're gone. I hate to be without you…you know that, Lily."

"I know, Chris."

She kissed him deeply trying her best to reassure him of something she hadn't even really decided. His assumption that her best friend was a girl showed just how much she had allowed him to get to know her. Would she return to New Zealand? Possibly not. Did she see a future with Chris? She really, *really* wished she did.

❤❤❤

Adam had booked a few tables at Glitterati, a posh new restaurant on George Street close to the city centre of Edinburgh. He was so excited he could hardly contain himself. To top it all off, Lily had flown across the world just to be there. The night was going to be fantastic. The job was such a huge deal to him, and he couldn't wait to share the celebrations with close friends and family.

Eve's parents had come down from Skye for a wee break and so this had been the perfect time to get together and celebrate. Tables were booked for eight that evening, and Eve was making her way there with her parents. He glanced at his watch. Six thirty. He had showered already and chosen what to wear—black trousers and a blue shirt—but he had paced up and down with excitement so much that he was on the verge of needing to shower again. The doorbell chimed the arrival of someone, and he dashed down the stairs to the front door.

Flinging the door open he was greeted by a curly haired, tanned Lily, standing there in a pretty lilac dress with a huge grin on her face. "Adders!" She jumped into his arms and he swung her around.

"Cheesy! I've missed you." He planted a kiss on the side of her face as she buried her head in his neck.

"How are you doing pee-pants?"

"Oy…I'm great actually. Not even your name calling can squash my mood."

"Erm, may I remind you that you started it?"

"No you may not. Now are you coming in to wait for the cab or am I shutting the door in your face?" Lily looked skyward as if pretending to decide. He grabbed her arm and pulled her in. "God, you never grow up do you?"

She scrunched her face in mock disgust. "Not if I can help it."

He went through to the tiny kitchen and pulled two bottles of cold beer from the fridge. "So, where's this man you've been swooning over?"

"Chris? Oh he…erm…had to stay in New Zealand. Couldn't get the time off work, you know how it is."

"What is it he does again?"

She blushed. "He's an underwear model at the moment. But he wants to be a chef," she informed him. "He's a bloody good cook."

"Aye but enough about his bedroom skills, what's his food like?"

She smacked his arm playfully. "I said *cook* and you know I did." She took a long gulp of her beer. "He's a great guy." She looked wistful.

"I sense a *but* and I'm not talking about the sexy one he keeps in his boxers."

She rolled her eyes. "God, you are in a good mood today. Your jokes are worse than normal."

He pulled a face at her. "So…the *but*?"

She sighed and placed her beer bottle on the kitchen counter top. "I get the impression he's really into me. The *L* word hasn't been mentioned yet…"

"So he doesn't know you're a lesbian then."

She smacked him again and he laughed heartily. "Will you bloody stop with the shitty jokes, Adders. You asked me a serious question and I am *trying* to give you a serious answer."

He held his hands up in surrender. "Sorry…sorry…continue."

"I don't think it will be long until he tells me he *loves* me." She cringed.

He scrunched his brow. "And you don't feel the same?"

She shook her head slowly, gazing down at the label on her beer bottle.

"But you enjoy his company, you have amazing sex, and he is as fit as they come. I don't get it, Lil? What's the problem?"

"It's hard to explain, Adders. But I just...I don't feel that way about him. I've tried really hard...believe me I have."

Adam slipped an arm around her shoulder. "That's the thing though, if you have to try *really hard* then it's not meant to be." He squeezed her into his side. "You shouldn't have to *try* to love someone. You either do or you don't. What are you going to do?"

"That's just it. I really don't know. I'm supposed to go back there in a month. But I'm thinking about not going back at all."

"Ah...I wish it was different. But having said that, if it did turn out you'd fallen for him, you'd probably move to the other side of the bloody world and I'd never see you. Can't say I'm a fan of that scenario." He squeezed her again.

She blushed and turned to try and hide it. "Well, it's a moot point. It's not happening." She turned back to him and smiled sadly. "Anyway, enough of my love life. How's Eve? What time is she getting here?"

"We're meeting her there at Glitterati. Her folks are down from Skye and they're staying at a hotel in Edinburgh, so she's gone up there after work. Max and Tia will be meeting us there too."

"Ah, yes, Max and his new lady love. Is it serious?" She took another draw of her beer.

"I would say so. They're talking about her moving in here."

She almost choked. "In here? What about you? He can't do that."

Adam laughed. "Well, he is. I'm thinking of moving on anyway. The job at school will give me more money, so I can maybe afford a bigger place. Might even *buy* somewhere."

She gaped, open mouthed. "Good grief, Adders, what's happened to you whilst I've been away? You appear to have grown up."

"Bloody cheeky sod." A car horn beeped outside. "Right, that's us. Come on. Let's go party!"

❤❤❤

Getting a table at Glitterati was no mean feat. Securing several was a pure miracle. Adam was eternally grateful to the people who had made the cancellation, considering this was the space his party was now filling up. He was over the moon to be celebrating in such style. He and Lily walked through the glass doors into the open expanse of white walls, white chairs, and white booths. And to top off the white…a little more white. All this was married with a gazillion sparkles donning the expensive looking chandeliers. As they moved in the breeze from the opening door, tiny rainbows were being cast on every spare area of wall and floor. It really was stunning.

"Bloody hell, Adders, you've gone all out." Lily gasped as she took in the luxurious surroundings.

Adam breathed in a contented relaxing breath, a wide smile fixed on his face. This was perfect. Just perfect.

A group of people were waving at them from a seating area over by the bar where white leather sofas surrounded a large faux-sheepskin rug. A long glittering chandelier hung just above the low glass table.

Adam's parents, as well as Max and Tia and a few colleagues from Adam's current workplace, all shook his hand and greeted Lily. But his eyes soon settled on his most desired guest.

Eve.

His breath caught and most of his blood made a rapid journey south when he saw her. She wore a fitted silver dress that showed off the curves he adored to perfection.

On her dainty feet were silver stilettos, and she carried a jewel purple clutch. Long silver strand earrings fell to her shoulders and her golden blonde hair had been straightened, hanging just below her shoulders. A heart-melting smile spread across her face as his eyes trailed up her body to meet her shimmering blue depths. Quickly he made his way over to her and slipped his arm around her waist.

"My goodness you have to be the most beautiful thing I've ever seen," he breathed into her ear and felt her shiver at his words.

"You look rather gorgeous yourself. I can't wait to get you home." She playfully squeezed his bottom. It didn't help the rush of blood below his belt-line. He kissed her neck and waited for his insides to settle before turning to greet her parents.

♥♥♥

The meal was as wonderful as they had all hoped. Everything cooked to perfection. Portion sizes meant everyone was satisfied but not overly stuffed. Everyone was happily chatting and drinking while Massive Attack's *Teardrop* played in the background. Adam smiled as he lazily stroked a finger up and down Eve's wrist.

After the whole party was finished with desserts, Adam nervously stood and clinked his glass with a spoon. The tables closest to him quieted. "Sorry to interrupt your wee chats everyone, but I just wanted to say a few words if that's okay." He smiled as he looked around the area of the restaurant where his nearest and dearest sat. "I can't tell you how wonderful it is to have you all here with me to celebrate tonight. Getting this role as English teacher in such a fantastic high school is a massive thing for me and I'm absolutely thrilled about it." Rumbles of appreciation travelled amongst his friends and family.

Adam took a deep breath. "But I'm afraid I lulled you all here under false pretences." Confused looks were exchanged but he continued. "Getting this job means the world to me...obviously...but there is one thing that means even more to me than that...well I say one thing...I mean one *person*." The Wannadies began playing in the background and Par Wiksten's quirky vocals filled the air with the sweet lyrics of *You and Me Song* as it floated out above the low mumblings of the restaurant clientele.

Adam turned toward Eve and took her hand. "Eve, you mean more to me than any job...than any other woman...than anything in this whole world, in fact. I wasn't unhappy before I met you but I was incomplete. Meeting you wasn't just an accident. We were meant to be. We go together like...like haggis and tatties...like bees and flowers...like fish and chips... Okay, enough with the food comparisons when we've just eaten." Giggles and chuckles traversed the group. He fumbled about in his pocket and retrieved a small box.

He dropped to one knee in front of Eve and gasps filled the air as he spoke with trembling lips and fingers. "Eve, if I'm honest, I think I've loved you since the moment I first met you that day Lily brought you into the refectory, and if it's possible, I love you more each passing day. You're the sun in my sky...my light in the darkness. Okay, the clichés are coming out now but... Well I don't care. You're the most stunning woman in any room you walk into. You make me laugh. You even laugh at my jokes and that's a sure fire way to show you're a keeper. You rein me in when I'm impulsive...but I really hope you don't rein me in this time. You've filled my heart with a love I could never have imagined feeling. And if you'll have me, I'll try my very best to make you as happy as you make me feel with just one of your beautiful smiles. Eve...will you marry me?"

Eve's eyes were glassy; her fingertips were resting on her lips. Her bottom lip quivered. "Yes, oh yes." She lurched forward and wrapped herself around Adam as the whole restaurant burst into spontaneous applause. Adam and Eve kissed passionately to seal their engagement.

♥♥♥

Tears streamed down her face, as Lily watched the scene unfold before her. She didn't try to stop them. People hugged her, presuming she was overcome with happiness for her best friend and his romantic proposal. After all, she'd been the one to introduce them. But deep inside, unbeknownst to anyone else, her heart broke all over again. The ache in her chest was almost unbearable, but she put on a brave face and applauded along with the rest of the witnesses to this magical event. Her smile was forced and felt like a mask. But it was a mask she would have to wear for the rest of her life. And wear it she would. Just for Adam. Just because all she wanted, apart from Adam, was his happiness.

Chapter Eleven

Move On Up (Curtis Mayfield)
August 2003

"How many more boxes are there, Adders?" Lily called from the top of the staircase. Her arms felt like jelly and her legs weren't much better. Eve was in the kitchen unpacking all the necessary bits and pieces to make cups of coffee for everyone.

"Oh, only another fifty or so. Don't worry…it'll keep you fit," Adam mumbled over the top of the large box marked *CDs* that he was manoeuvring through the front door of the new house.

Lily sighed and growled. "Why did I stay for this? I could be sunning myself on a beach in bloody New Zealand next to a half-naked male underwear model right now." She had extended her stay long enough to help Adam and Eve move into their new place. They were renting with the option to buy, which meant things were easy and would speed along nicely once their finances were all in place.

Eve came through with two mugs of coffee and the end of a packet of chocolate cookies grasped between her teeth. "Awww, Willy, we weally appweciate dis you know." Lily came sliding down the stairs on her bottom and took the packet of biscuits from Eve's mouth. "Thanks, I'm not sure if you caught any of that but I was just saying—"

"You appreciate it. Yes, I got it. And I know you do. And I honestly don't mind. I'm just knackered." Lily ripped open the packet and shoved a cookie into her mouth. Whole.

Adam returned from the lounge and took a mug from Eve, kissing her on the cheek. "Thanks, gorgeous. Have I told you today how much I love you?"

Eve rolled her eyes. "Yes about a million times."

Lily's stomach lurched as the happy couple kissed. "Oh good grief, get a bloody room. In fact, there are three of them upstairs, go take your pick." She slapped Adam around the head.

"Ouch! Watch it or you'll get all the heavy boxes next."

She huffed. "Yeah? Like I haven't been getting them already?"

"You two have a wee break, and I'll go out to the van and bring some stuff in," Eve suggested.

"No, you have a break too. We've all been working bloody hard this morning." Adam glanced around the hallway. "Awww, Evie it's going to be fantastic, this house. I can just see it now."

The terraced cottage was fairly plain which—Eve had insisted to Adam—was a very good thing as they could easily put their stamp on it. They had both been saving for a while and had managed to purchase some extra pieces of furniture to make the house feel like a home. *Their* home.

Downstairs had a small entrance hallway and to the right was a good-sized lounge. Through the lounge was a newly fitted kitchen. It was fairly modern but had a country feel to it. Cream shaker style units sat under solid wood block work surfaces. Silver coloured appliances finished off the smart room nicely. The previous owners had bought the cottage as a shell and had gutted the insides, modernising it with a view to sell it for profit. The cottage garden at the back had an area to sit and a small lawn. Right at the back was a veggie plot that Adam couldn't wait to get stuck into. It was an exciting prospect, growing his own spuds.

From the small hallway led a wooden staircase and on the top floor was a small but perfectly formed bathroom complete with roll-top bath. There was a small room that would be great as an office and then two further bedrooms, one of which Lily had named as her room and the other which was earmarked, obviously, for Adam and his gorgeous future wife.

♥♥♥

After unloading the last of the boxes, Lily had declined the offer of a take-away, a bottle of wine, and crashing at the new house. She had informed Adam that he should spend the first night in his new home with his fiancée. He hadn't taken much convincing.

He stretched and looked at the clock. It was only ten thirty, but he was keen to get to bed. He yawned dramatically and slipped his arm around Eve's shoulders, leaned in, and whispered into her ear, "I think I'm going to turn in. Can I tempt you?"

She visibly shivered, turned to him, and breathed, "I don't think I'll take much tempting."

Leaning forward he covered her mouth with his own and slipped a hand through her hair. "I want to take you upstairs, undress you, slide inside you, and stay there all night." His voice was a low growl.

She gasped as she ran her hands up his chest. "Well, what are you waiting for?"

He scooped her up in his arms and made his way to the hall. Careful not to drop his precious cargo, he climbed the stairs and pushed open the bedroom door with his foot. Placing her on the floor he gazed down, deep into her vivid blue eyes, which had darkened slightly now that lust had taken over. Her hands slipped around his waist and tugged at the old T-shirt he wore. She pulled it upward and he stooped to help her remove it.

He inhaled deeply as she smoothed her hands over his bare chest and around his neck. She laced her fingers, tugged at the dark strands of his hair, and pulled him down so that his mouth was over hers again. He went willingly, darting his tongue into her mouth, desperate to taste her. Everywhere. Slowly he pulled her tank top over her head until her lace-covered breasts were revealed to him. He dragged his fingertips down from her collarbone to the rise of her soft curved mounds. "You have the most beautiful breasts I've ever seen, Evie," he said as his thumbs circled her hardening nipples through the lace. She moaned. He hardened.

Slipping the straps of her bra down, he freed each breast, caressing each nipple in turn with his tongue. Her head rolled back and she sighed her pleasure. Sliding down her sides and enjoying the curve of her hips, his hands dipped into the waistband of her yoga pants and down to her perfectly rounded bottom. He squeezed and slowly descended to a kneeling position in front of her. "I want to taste you." He gazed up at her through hooded eyes. She leaned on his shoulders whilst she stepped from her pants. The lace panties followed very soon after. Adam kissed her smooth skin just below her naval making her groan again.

She grasped his hair as he peppered kisses across her lower abdomen until he slid his tongue into her sensitive flesh. She gasped and he felt her legs almost buckle. Lightly he pushed her back so that she tumbled onto the bed directly behind her. He moved forward to blow through the soft curls at the apex of her thighs and she grasped at the soft, silky comforter.

"Adam…please…I need you…now." Her breathing was ragged and her voice huskily caressed his senses. Kissing all the way around the tops of her thighs and prolonging his own delicious agony, he eventually slipped his tongue into her heat again and groaned as he took his prize. He could stay there all night, just tasting, kissing, and caressing her with his tongue, but he had promised her other gifts. Once she had cried out his name, he stood and removed his jeans and fitted boxers. Never taking his eyes from hers, he climbed onto the bed between her thighs and lay on top of her. He rolled onto his back taking her with him until she straddled his waist. And then he guided her down onto his arousal, gripping her hips so that he could move her. Her head rolled back, and it was evident she was beginning to climb once again. He could feel her tightening around him and it pushed him over the edge. His hands reached for her and pulled her into his chest as he thrust into her one last time, calling her name and then kissing her deeply.

He stroked her back as they both fought to calm their breathing. "Evie." She pulled herself back to look into his eyes. "Evie...don't ever leave me. I don't know what I'd do."

She smiled as she stroked the hair back from his damp face. "I'm going nowhere, Adam."

"I...I just...I could never love someone as much as I love you...you're it for me. This is it. I don't want to be without you. You're my life. You have...all of me."

"And you have all of me. I'm yours."

Chapter Twelve

Don't Say You Love Me (Free)
September 2003

Lily nervously walked through arrivals towards the meeting point at Christchurch airport. The spring day was bright and sunny, quite a contrast to the autumnal temperatures beginning to occur back home. She scanned the crowd looking for Chris and eventually her eyes fell on a tall, blonde, handsome man holding a single red rose, a wide, gorgeous grin fixed in place on his flawless features. Her heart skipped ever so slightly, filling her with a tiny shred of hope. Could she begin to love him?

He began to walk toward her, his steps faster the closer he got. She stepped out from behind her trolley and was immediately scooped up by strong muscular arms.

"God, Lily, I've missed you so much. I got scared," he whispered into her hair.

Pulling away from him, she peered into his bright green eyes, which were now filled with emotions that she didn't want to read. "Scared? Why?"

He tucked her hair behind her ear. "You stayed away so long I thought you weren't going to come back to me." His jaw clenched. "But I would have had to come and find you, Lily. I...I—"

Dreading the next words to fall from his mouth, Lily interrupted, "Well, I'm here now," she trilled, "and I'm shattered. Can we go home so I can sleep?"

He pouted. "Sleep? I haven't seen you or held you in weeks and you want to sleep?"

She bit her lip. "Well...sleep first and then..." She kissed him deeply, igniting a passion in him that she knew she would definitely benefit from later. He groaned into her mouth as he held his hand knotted in her tangled curls.

They arrived back at his rented apartment and she dumped her bag in the bedroom. He followed her in and slipped his arms around her waist again, nuzzling her neck.

Turning in his arms, Lily looked up at him. "What do you see in me, Chris?" she asked.

His brow furrowed. "Are you kidding me?"

She shook her head. "I don't get it. You're a bloody model, and I'm…well—"

"And you're a sexy, talented, intelligent, and fun woman with an incredible body who drives me insane in bed and who I love spending time with." He kissed just below her ear and she shivered. "Does that answer your question?"

She scrunched her face. "I have an incredible body?" She found that very hard to believe. She had always thought herself rather ordinary in the looks department and felt her hips were too big and her breasts matched her hips. *Hourglass* was what people called it when they were trying to be nice. *Fat* was what Lily called it on her off days.

"Take it from me, Lily, you have the most sexy curves…and your breasts…" He slipped his hand inside her shirt and caressed one as if to prove his point. "Are just my favourite part of you…apart from your mind of course." He chuckled. "And your smile." Shivers travelled down her spine as he continued to caress her. "And your hair…and—"

"Okay, okay I think I get it now." She smiled, feeling boosted by his words.

"Good…well that's why I'm attracted to you, but I love you for all of that and more." Lily gasped. *Shit…what do I say?*

He must have noticed the look of horror on her face as he cupped her cheek with his free hand. "Hey…it's okay. I know you're not…you know…in that place yet and that's fine. I'll wait. No matter how long it takes, I'll wait. Because you're worth waiting for."

She felt the familiar sting of threatening tears as she gazed up at the handsome, caring, sweet man before her. More than anything, she wanted to feel the same. Maybe in time. But why the hell did this keep happening to her? Why couldn't she give her heart? It was so unfair.

Once again, he noticed the change in her emotions. "Hey, shhh, don't cry, babe. You can't help wanting to take things slow and I accept that. Come on, let's have a nap, eh? I probably shouldn't have dropped that on you when you're suffering from jet lag, eh?"

She smiled. He was probably right for the most part. Jet lag always made her emotional. That and leaving Adam. But she really wasn't good company when she was tired. After slipping out of her clothes, she climbed into bed. Chris followed suit and climbed in behind her. He snuggled up to her, and with his arm around her waist, he pulled her back into his front. It didn't take long before she drifted off.

Sometime later—she had no clue how long—she was awoken by the most amazing feelings of pleasure radiating from her core and stretching all the way to her fingertips. She let out a long croaky, sleep-filled groan as she felt pressure building deep within her. She gripped the sheets as Chris continued with his amazing ministrations from somewhere under the bedclothes. She exploded in an intense orgasm, which sent her soaring above the rooftops and up into space. He knew how to play her body like an instrument. He climbed back up toward her face as she gasped, eyes closed. She opened them and looked up into vivid green eyes smiling down at her.

He kissed her nose. "Thought that might be a nice way to wake you up."

She stretched, allowing every muscle in her body to lengthen. It felt good. *She* felt good. His arousal pressed into her stomach, and with a grin she wiggled her body, causing Chris to close his eyes and emit a low growl. Opening and keeping his eyes locked on hers, he reached down and fumbled around in the nightstand drawer. Once he was sheathed in latex, he slid himself into her and began to move.

♥♥♥

Chris really was amazing. He seemed to understand Lily's need to take things slow better than she could have expected or hoped. She pondered explaining to him *why* she was so filled with trepidation about their relationship but worried that perhaps her admission would do more harm than good. Perhaps he would run a mile. That wouldn't be good. The fact that she was worried about losing Chris made her smile. Perhaps she was beginning to have feelings for him?

Several days after returning to New Zealand she logged onto her email and was reminded about why she could never love Chris.

Dear Lil

Eve and I just wanted to check that you arrived okay. Having seen no news about plane crashes we presume that all is well and that you are too busy bonking Chris's brains out to contact us. Okay, Eve says I have to tell you that she had no part in the construction of this email. But you know different, eh? (I'm winking at the screen…with my eyes I hasten to add!) Okay…now I am in deep shit and Eve is demanding I get off the computer so she can spank me. Oh sorry, not spank me…kick my arse…and apparently there is a difference! Whoops! Better go.

Write soon, Cheesy.

Hugs
Adders

Lily smiled to herself as she read. Typical bloody Adam. She hit reply.

Hi Pee Pants and lovely Eve

I arrived safe and well if a little knackered. Chris has been pampering me for the past few days, and so my body clock is slowly returning to normal. Whatever normal is! We're going out with some friends tonight, so I'd better be awake by then or I'll be falling asleep in my beer. Lol! I know that Adders is saying 'nothing new there then.' Cheeky!

Anyway, enjoy your lovely new home and I will see you at Christmas.

Hugs
Lily
Xxx

Chris came over as she clicked send. She had no clue how long he had been watching her. He had walked by as she started reading, but had he read her message over her shoulder? Well, it didn't really matter if he had. He sat beside her on the sofa looking quite serious. "What's up, hun?" she asked rubbing his arm.

He leaned forward, resting his elbows on his knees and dropping his gaze to the floor so that locks of his scruffy blonde hair fell forward. "Erm…how long are you hoping to stay in New Zealand, babe?"

She bit her lip. "I hadn't really thought about it much. Why?"

"It's just that…I've been offered a place on that cookery course that I wanted to take. Remember me mentioning it?"

She was puzzled. "Yes. Yes I do, but you weren't supposed to be doing that until next year."

He glanced up at her, sadness and frustration seemed to be fighting for pole position on his features. "I know, but my dad knows someone who knows the head chef at Alonzo's in Sydney. It's the best restaurant there. It's where almost every top chef has been trained. They've offered *me* an apprenticeship if I start the course next month. *Me*, Lil. This is huge. I really want to take it but I'm afraid…" He dropped his gaze to the floor again and picked at his nails.

She grasped his hand to stop him from fidgeting. "Chris, you seem to be spending a lot of the time *afraid* at the moment." *Is this down to me?*

He turned to face her. "Lily, I *have* to go back home. Soon. But I'm afraid you won't want to come with me. Coming with me means making some kind of commitment. I know you're not really ready and I need to understand *why* that is. Is it because you know about my past? Because I'd hoped that you knew I'd changed because of you."

She knew exactly what he'd been like before they met. He'd been completely honest with her. Too honest if the truth be known. He'd played the field and had his fair share of conquests behind him. With his looks and that Adonis-like body, he could have had any woman he wanted. But for some reason he wanted *her*. She still didn't understand why.

She shook her head. "No, your past is your past. I don't really care about that."

"Then can you be honest with me as to why you don't want to make things work with me?"

She stood. "It's not that I don't *want* to make things work with you, but you said that you would wait. You've said it more than once. I don't understand why starting this course will change things."

"It won't. Not really. But I've been thinking... I thought a lot whilst you were away in the UK, and I've been thinking since you've been back, too. I know what I said about waiting and I...I did mean it at the time... It's just that I get the feeling I'm wasting my time here and all the waiting in the world won't change things." His eyes looked pained. He had seen right through her at last.

She sighed. "Chris...it's...it's complicated. I really do like you. I do *care* about you. And I find you incredibly attractive. The sex is mind blowing—"

He stood and grasped her by the arms, staring deep into her eyes. "Then marry me, Lily." He stared intently at her, pleading with his eyes.

She gasped. "What? Chris...what? I...I don't know what to say. We've been together for what feels like two minutes... I can't think..."

"But you've said you care about me and the attraction is clearly there. The rest will come, surely? We can work toward love. And when it's right you know it's right, and I just know, Lily."

Heat rose in her cheeks and her heart hammered at her ribs as if making a determined effort to burst out of her chest. "But...why the urgency? Why all of a sudden do we have to rush into this?"

Chris exhaled a noisy, shuddering breath. "Can you honestly tell me that we're going somewhere, Lily? Can you honestly tell me that one day...however far off in the future it may be...that one day you'll marry me?"

Her heart continued to pound as her mind raced through a million different scenarios, a million different answers she could give. "I...I...Chris...marriage...it's..." She tried hard to clamber through the fog of her mind at this preposterous and unexpected turn of events. *Why is he doing this now?* Should she lie and say that yes, one day she could marry him? No, that would be cruel, and lying wasn't something she could do to this wonderful man. He deserved so much more.

He dropped his arms to his sides, sadness in his beautiful green eyes. Sadness *she* had put there. Guilt stabbed her heart.

He shook his head. "If the immediate answer isn't obviously *yes*, Lily, then I think maybe it's time I let you go."

Anger spiked within her and the tears came. "But you said you'd wait! Why are you doing this?"

He stroked her cheek. "It's called self-preservation. I've never felt this way about anyone. There's something about you and I can't get past it. I'm pretty sure I can't be the first one you've affected like this. I want a future with you but I want *all* of you. Not the scraps of your heart that you're willing to offer. I know it's sudden but it's sudden for me too. But all you've done since you arrived back is look at your phone and check your emails. I haven't seen you type a single thing until this morning…like you were waiting for something." His brow creased as regret washed over his beautiful face. "Lily, you lit up as you read whatever it was and then you were the same as you typed. You lit up for someone else. Not for me. And the look on your face was the look someone has when they're in love. I should know…I have it when I look at you—"

"Chris—"

"Let me just finish okay? I'm not angry. I love you, Lily. I'm *in love* with you and as much as that won't change for a long time, neither will your feelings for me whilst you're clearly in love with someone else." He cupped her face in his hands. "If I don't let you go now it *will* get harder and harder for me to do that as time goes on. And I will have to let you go eventually. And if I'm honest with myself, I think

I know the truth, babe. It doesn't matter how long I wait, I'm never going to mean as much to you as he clearly does. Am I right?"

Tears trailed down her face as she nodded and sobs burst from within. He encased her in his arms. "Thank you for being honest. I know this isn't easy for you either. Can I ask you something?" Unable to speak through her tears she nodded again. "Why don't you just tell him you love him, whoever he is? You may be surprised and find that he feels the same."

She closed her eyes and swallowed hard. "He doesn't." *And never will.*

He wiped her tears away. "But how do you know if you don't speak to him?"

She took a deep breath. "Because he's my best friend in the whole world...always has been...and he just got engaged and moved in with the love of his life." Her legs almost gave way as she finally made the difficult admission that she had contemplated making to Chris only a few days before.

He held her and stroked her hair. "Oh, Lily...sweetheart..."

After letting her cry for a few minutes, he pushed her away and smiled sadly into her eyes. "Unrequited love is a complete, fucking shit-head of a bastard, isn't it?"

She choked out a heartfelt laugh through her tears. "You certainly got that right."

Chapter Thirteen

No One Knows (Queens of the Stoneage)
November 2003

"This is the best flat we've seen all day, Lily. What do you think?" Eve asked when the estate agent ducked outside to answer a call on his mobile phone. The flat was in a beautiful, converted Victorian terrace on the outskirts of Edinburgh. The ceilings were high and the large, original sash windows let in lots of light, making the small but perfectly formed space feel bright and airy.

Lily sighed. "Yeah, it's small but I don't suppose I need anything bigger."

Putting an end to her travels, she had decided to return to Scotland and begin the arduous task of finding work. She had several interviews lined up and a string of excellent references under her belt thanks to the work she had gotten in Australia, New Zealand, and other countries she had visited. She was determined to do well at... Well, whatever she ended up doing. It would become her life and her main distraction.

Being back in Scotland caused a mixture of emotions to bubble to the surface for Lily. Eve and Adam were loving being in their new home and had initially insisted on Lily moving in with them until she found a place to live. Finding somewhere had now become a matter of urgency. Being under the same roof as the loved-up couple was difficult to bear. As much as she loved that Adam was happy, hearing him make love to Eve through the not-so-thick walls was the worst kind of torture. She knew they were holding back and trying to be quiet but why should they? It was their house after all. She felt so very uncomfortable.

The estate agent returned to the lounge of the one bedroom flat. "So Miss Macrae, what do you think?"

Lily looked at Eve who nodded encouragingly. "Where do I sign?"

♥♥♥

The two friends sat opposite each other in their favourite city centre coffee house. Eve opened her mouth to speak but seemed hesitant.

Lily took a sip of her vanilla latte. "What's wrong, Eve?" she asked, tilting her head to one side.

"Look, Lily... I hope you don't think we're trying to get rid of you. You're welcome to stay at our house as long as you need, you know."

"It's fine honestly. I want to get out of your hair. You two need your space. You're planning a wedding, and as much as I love Adam and you, I think I need my own space."

"As long as you didn't sign up for the flat because you feel pressured to leave. It's not necessary. There's no pressure. You haven't been back long, and I'm just worried that being alone will give you too much time to think about Chris."

Lily paused with her cup halfway to her lips. She hadn't discussed what had happened between her and Chris with Adam and Eve for reasons obvious only to herself, but of course they were concerned that she had suffered a broken heart. She had of course, but not at the hands of Chris and not really through anyone's fault.

She closed her eyes for a second and tried to compose herself. "Chris and I parted as friends. It really is fine. We just... Well, we wanted different things. He wanted a commitment and I wasn't ready for that with him. That's all. We parted so that he could move on and do his cookery apprenticeship. It was what he wanted and he needed to concentrate without worrying about me and whether we had a future." This was the most she had opened up since her return. She had tried to avoid talking about the situation and had been quickly changing the subject any time the matter arose.

"I see…" Eve nodded. "And you're sure you're okay? I mean *really* okay?"

Lily smiled and for a moment forgot whom she was out with. *Big* mistake. "I'm *really* okay. Chris is a great guy. He has a lot to offer a woman and I don't want him waiting around for me forever when I'm still in l—" She stopped mid-sentence, a feeling of panic washing over her at her almost slip of the tongue. She could feel her cheeks burning, a dead giveaway. "Wh-when I'm in no position to offer what he needs." Lily's eyes darted to Eve whose eyes were wide for a split second, but then Eve re-arranged her pretty features into a smile and nodded looking down at the table. Had she realised? *Oh shit, that's not good. Not good.*

Eve lifted her gaze and unreadable emotions clouded her vivid blue eyes. A sad smile tugged at the corner of her mouth as she leaned across the small table to squeeze Lily's arm. "As long as you're okay, Lily. A broken heart can be tough to get through alone."

♥♥♥

Back at the house, Adam was in the kitchen making dinner when the girls arrived home. After hanging their coats on hooks, Lily excused herself and went up to her room. Eve made her way through to the kitchen and slipped her arms around Adam's waist.

He turned to face her and enveloped her in his embrace. "Well hello there, sexy. How are you?" He leaned down and kissed her passionately.

She smiled when the kiss ended. "I'm better now."

Adam looked down at her and furrowed his brow. "Better *now*? What do you mean? Is everything okay?"

She nodded. "Yes, yes, everything's fine. Just ignore me."

He was filled with concern. "Come on, Evie, I know when something's bothering you. Tell me."

She shook her head. "It's fine honestly. I love you Adam…more than anything. You know that, don't you?"

He slipped his hands into her hair, stroking his thumbs over her cheeks. "Of course I do. Is there something you want to tell me?"

"No, everything is fine. It's nothing… Oh, Lily found a flat though." She changed the subject and Adam knew that's what she was doing, but he let it go.

"Oh great. When does she move in?"

"Adam! You can't ask things like that," she whispered loudly.

"What? Why? I'm just interested."

"Yes, well, I don't want her feeling like she has to leave if she's not ready."

He chewed his lip before speaking. "Why? What makes you think she's not ready? What has she said?"

She sighed. "She hasn't *said* anything, Adam. I just… Well, I don't know, but I just think things are harder for her than she's letting on, that's all."

Adam wondered what had been said while they were out. Clearly something had. "Should I talk to her?"

Eve gasped and shook her head. "No! That's the last thing she needs right now. Just let her be and if she wants to talk she'll talk. Just don't pressure her about moving out, okay?"

"I wasn't going to, sweetheart, but you're worrying me now."

She placed her hands on his chest. "No need for worry. Just…I don't know…don't be your usual brash self around her, okay?"

Adam chuckled. "Awww, you're spoiling all my fun. But okay…I won't." He kissed her again still feeling puzzled.

♥♥♥

Lily lay on the bed in the room she was *borrowing* at Adam and Eve's house. The way Eve had looked at her when they were at the coffee house preyed on her mind. She knew. Something told Lily that Eve had seen through her, and now Lily felt, more than ever, that she had to leave as soon as possible. She *had* to get out of here. How could she possibly stay now? Okay, so nothing had been confirmed, but the knowing look in Eve's eyes… *What if she says something to Adam? Shit! No…no surely she wouldn't. And what if she starts to act differently around me? Oh nooo. This is not good, Lily. Not good.*

She wanted things to remain as they were and was terrified of awkwardness. The thought of Eve being upset with her made her heart sink and her stomach tie up into knots. There was a gentle knock on the door.

"Come in." Her voice croaked.

"Hey, are you okay?" Eve asked as she pushed the door open.

Lily sat upright. "Yeah, yeah, everything's fine. Just a bit bushed still, I suppose." She forced a smile.

"Look…Lily…you don't have to move out right away you know. Really, you don't. You and Adam have been best friends for so long it's like having part of the family staying with us. I don't want you to feel—"

"Honestly, Eve it's fine. You guys need your space and I really need mine, too. It'll do me good to get sorted somewhere, and then I can really start looking for work in earnest. I'm fine, so please stop worrying. I hate that I'm causing you to worry."

Eve bit her lip and nodded and seemed to hesitate before speaking again. "Lily…erm…"

Lily's heart pounded in her chest and she gulped. "What is it?"

Eve smiled and shook her head. "It's…it's nothing. Dinner's ready."

"Okay, I'll be right down."

Eve turned to leave but paused and looked back toward Lily. "I consider you my best friend, too, Lily." Her voice was just above a whisper. Lily swallowed hard and opened her mouth to speak but no words came.

Eve left the room and closed the door.

Chapter Fourteen

Last Tattoo (Rehab)

January 2004

Lily nervously sat on the black leather sofa in the waiting area of the tattoo parlour. She was surrounded by blue walls and cabinets packed with all manner of paraphernalia from mugs to messenger bags. There was a smell of disinfectant permeating the air and the sound of buzzing filled the large space. The thud of her pounding heartbeat throbbed in her ears.

Across the room a young man was stretched out on a black leatherette chair where a pretty, blonde haired, female artist was concentrating on an intricate design on the man's thigh. He looked quite relaxed for the most part, except for the odd wince every so often. *What am I doing? I must be bloody mad!*

The good-looking guy behind the counter smiled at her. "You look terrified," he commented, snapping Lily from her own thoughts.

"Yeah...yeah...I am a bit to be honest." She smiled as she fiddled with her nails.

"Is this your first time?" he asked, leaning on the counter.

She cringed. "Oh God, is it that obvious I'm a tattoo virgin?"

The man chuckled. "I can tell 'em a mile off. Don't worry though. You'll be fine." She recognised his voice from the telephone.

"I'm guessing you're Joe?"

"Yep, guilty as charged," he said as he glanced down at his diary. "And I'm guessing by my amazing powers of deduction that you're Lily?"

"Yup, that's me, lily-livered Lily." She pointed to herself and rolled her eyes. Heat warmed her cheeks, which was a wonder considering most of the blood had drained from there.

Joe laughed at her and shook his head. "Honestly, you'll be fine."

She narrowed her eyes. "How can you be so sure, though?"

"Call it experience. It's never as bad as you build it up to be."

"But what happens if I pass out or throw up?"

"Well, if you pass out it takes longer coz they have to stop. If you throw up, we give you a mop and bucket." He winked. "It happens so rarely though. Like I said, you'll be fine. I have faith in you."

"Well, I'm glad one of us has." She wished she had his confidence. "I bet you don't get many women like me in here, do you?" She had moved on to fiddling with the hem of her top.

He scrunched his face. "Women like you?"

"Yeah…you know…normal, boring, ink and piercing-free women."

"Hey, you'd be surprised how many people you know have tattoos. They don't all look like Stubbs." He nodded over his shoulder at the other artist wielding a tattoo needle.

"Really? I thought maybe I was…I don't know…out of the ordinary."

Joe huffed. "Nah, not by a long way. We had an author in here not so long ago. She was a woman of about forty. She was having her first tattoo done to commemorate the publishing of her first book." He smiled. "To look at her, you'd have thought she was the last person to have one, but like I say, you can never tell. Her husband came in awhile after her to get his first done, too. He's had a few more since then."

"Oh? It can't be that bad, then?"

"Well, put it this way, there's more return visitors than not. It's kind of...how do I put it..." He looked up to the ceiling. "Addictive, in a way."

She sniggered at his last comment. "Erm, I'm pretty sure I'll just be having the one."

He wiggled his eyebrows. "Hmmm, never say never, eh?"

She appreciated his attempts to reassure her as she glanced around and took in the photographs of previous tattoos that adorned the walls. *These guys are some bloody talented artists.*

A muscle-bound, giant of a man with hardly a tattoo-clear inch on his exposed arms walked over. "Lily?" he asked as he smiled. She nodded. "Come on lass, you're up." She walked over to his workstation, which had been prepared and covered ready for her.

Once she was sitting in the chair, he laughed. "Joe was right, you look absolutely terrified. Don't be. It'll be done before you know it. I'm Stubbs by the way." He held out his gloved hand and she took it. He had a firm grip and such a friendly face she momentarily forgot her fear. "So, you're having some Gaelic script on your lower back, is that right?"

"Yep, that's right."

Stubbs held out a sheet of paper with a phrase printed on it. "This is what you emailed in, are you happy with it?"

She looked over the words that had been written in beautiful script designed especially for her and a lump of emotion lodged in her throat.

"Yes...yes that's beautiful."

"Right, lass, I need you to sit sideways in the chair with your feet through the arm, and you need to lean slightly forward, okay?"

She followed his instructions. Joe from the desk pulled up a chair and sat in front of her. "Want me to keep you company until you get used to the sensation?" His head cocked to one side.

She breathed a sigh of relief. "Oh yes, would you? Thanks." He pulled his chair nearer as Stubbs prepared the positioning of the script.

Joe leaned forward resting his elbows on his knees. "So, what's the occasion?"

She sighed. "It's a long, complicated story."

He shrugged and held out his hands. "I'm not going anywhere."

She took a deep breath and was about to speak when Stubbs interrupted. "Erm, sorry there, Lily, but I'm about to start now. Are you ready?"

She glanced over her shoulder. "Yes, ready as I'll ever be." The buzzing began again and she gritted her teeth.

"So…you were going to tell me, Lily?" Joe pulled her focus away from the sting that had begun near her bottom.

"Oh…erm…yes… Well, I fell in love with this guy years ago." She flinched at a particularly sore patch.

"Is he your boyfriend, then? I don't see a wedding ring."

"Sadly no… He's…he's my best friend."

The look on her face must have spoken volumes as Joe simply nodded and said, "Ah."

"Anyway he doesn't feel the same way about me."

"How do you know? Have you told him how you feel?"

"No, but it doesn't matter. He's getting married."

Joe mouthed the word *Oh*, and then sitting back in his chair he rubbed a hand over his close cut hair. "That'd just about ruin things for you, I guess."

She nodded. "Little bit."

A look of confusion spread over Joe's face. "So can I ask why you're getting that *particular* tattoo done? I've seen the translation."

She rolled her eyes again. "I know…I know… It makes me look pathetic, but I felt I needed to express how I felt even if he never knows. You know? It's out there. If ever he does see it he'll never know it's for him. He'll never know what it means, but somehow I feel I need to do this."

He folded his arms across his chest. "Lily, people come in here having all sorts of tattoos done for all sorts of reasons. We don't judge. We just aim to do exactly what the customer wants. And as long as you leave here happy with our work, then we're happy."

The phone began to ring and Joe cringed. She waved him away. "Go on. I'm actually pretty fine." She smiled. The pain wasn't quite what she had expected. It wasn't excruciating. It was okay. Suddenly a sense of pride washed over her and she drifted off listening to the music of *Soundgarden* as it ironically played in the background.

♥♥♥

Once Lily's newly inked back was covered in special lotion and covered in film, she left the tattoo parlour, saying good bye to the artists who had made her feel so welcome and at ease. The whole experience had been fantastic. All of her preconceived notions had been blown out of the water. And in a strange way, she could understand why people went through this more than once. Although she was sure she might think differently at bedtime when she had to figure out how to lay down.

Adam texted and invited her around for a take-away with him and Eve and a guy from Eve's work. She knew this was a lame-assed way of trying to fix her up with Dominic. She had mistakenly commented on the fact that he was cute when she had met Eve for lunch at the newspaper one day. She wished she had kept her opinions to herself. Dominic was cute, yes. But that was it. She wasn't about to embark upon any kind of relationship with him or anyone else for that matter. Not for a while. She had plans, plans that didn't involve her staying put. Plans that involved more travelling, but this time the travel would be work related.

Another text arrived.

A: Come on, Lil. Don't be a mardy cow. Dom fancies you and he's a really great bloke. Adam was persistent, that was for sure.

L: Sod off, Adders! I said no! Stop trying 2 fix me up. Am happy being a singleton. Lily insisted.

A: Well when u decide 2 get a house full of fucking cats for your spinster lifestyle don't forget I'm allergic!!

L: How can I? U were a wheezing blotchy mess at my Auntie's that time! Was hilarious! Lily sniggered as she typed.

A: One word Lil… BOLLOCKS! Came the reply.

L: Language Adders! Remember you're a teacher. Now eff off n leave me alone. Have a hot date with John Cusack.

A: You wish, you bloody nutcase. See u 2morro Cheesy. Adam had given up finally. *Phew!*

Back at her tiny flat, she slipped into her most comfy jim-jams, poured herself a glass of red wine, and opened a packet of popcorn. She stuck in the DVD of her favourite film, *Serendipity*, and gingerly curled up on the sofa to have an evening of ogling John Cusack. Lily had thought long and hard about this. Of all the men in the world John Cusack and Chris Cornell were the only two men who Lily could *ever* imagine replacing Adam in her affections. So that was it. She would worship John Cusack from afar tonight and tomorrow her Soundgarden CDs would be played for the first time in ages.

Chapter Fifteen

Goodbye My Lover (James Blunt)
August 2005

Lily stood before the mirror. She was impressed with the way she looked in her grey pin striped trouser suit. *Best woman, a little ironic really. Clearly not the best woman for Adam.* She sighed and fiddled with her hair, which was already perfect. There was a knock on the bedroom door.

"Come in," she called.

The door opened and Adam walked in. She gasped at the sight before her. There he stood. The man of her dreams in a grey suit that matched hers. The stunning crimson red tie and vest to match her silk blouse. He looked so nervous.

He looked *so* beautiful.

He stepped forward and threw his arms around her. "Oh God, Lil, you look amazing… I mean really beautiful." His voice wavered as he spoke.

"Oy, you'll crumple me, you soppy git." She forced a laugh but had to bite the inside of her cheek to halt the threatening tears.

He released her and held her at arms-length. "Sorry, Lil. I'm just a wee bit overwhelmed today, you know? Terrified actually."

She nodded as she pursed her lips, struggling to keep her emotions in check. "I know…I know."

He smiled with glassy eyes. "You look how I feel." He wiped at his tears.

If only you knew. "Yeah, well, it's not every day you get to marry off your best friend in the world, eh?"

He shook his head. "True…very true."

She pondered for a second. "Do you know I was expecting you to go all out tartan, Adders? Yet here you stand with not one scrap of it to be seen."

A grin spread across his face. "Erm… Well, I've not completely let you down there, Lil." He pulled up his trousers to show the bright Stewart tartan socks he sported.

She laughed "Ahhh, that's more like it."

"But that's not all." He dipped into the front of his trousers, and she wondered what on earth he was doing. Fumbling a little, he retrieved the waistband of his boxers.

She gaped at her friend. "Tartan knickers, Adders? Really?"

He continued grinning and bobbed his head rather like a nodding dog. The doorbell chimed and she looked out of the window before heading for the door. "Come on, Adders, the car's here."

He eagerly followed. "Oh great! I've been waiting to see what you organised. I hope it's not a tractor!"

She stopped in her tracks and turned. Adam almost barrelled into her. "Oh, Adders, you've spoiled it now!" she said, her face deadpan.

Adam opened and closed his mouth like a goldfish. "You didn't? No, tell me you didn't get me a tractor to transport me to my wedding."

She burst out laughing. "Ha ha! You tit! As if I'd hire a bloody tractor to take you to the church. Honestly, do you know me at all?"

He breathed a sigh of relief and followed her to the front door as she flung it open. He gasped. "Fucking hell, Lil! You hired me a Bentley?" His eyes were wide like a kid on Christmas morning. "I can't believe you did this!" He grabbed her and hugged her so tight she had to fight for air.

She gasped into his chest and patted his back. "Dead best-man-woman can't breathe…dead best-man-woman…"

Evidently he realised he was almost suffocating her and released her with a laugh. "Shit, sorry, Lil. I'm just…I can't believe…thank you so much!" He grabbed her once again.

After an exhilarating drive to the pretty little church in the village where Adam's parents lived, she stood beside him at the front by the altar. Best friends. Suddenly the wedding march began and everyone stood. *This is it. This is goodbye. This is forever.* Lily's heart pounded in her chest and she felt like her legs would buckle. Tears stung her eyes. Adam linked his hand with hers, making the pain in her chest so much worse. He glanced at her with a beaming smile on his face and mouthed the words, "Thank you". She wasn't sure what he was thanking her for. But she held on tight to his hand trying her best not to cry.

Suddenly she heard Adam gasp and her eyes followed his. Eve was walking down the aisle. She really was a vision. Her long blonde locks had been pinned up and curls cascaded down around her beautiful face. The dress was off shoulder and fitted to the waist where it fanned out. Not huge…but just enough to be Princess-like. Her bouquet of crimson red and cream hung before her and her arm was linked with her father's. The look of pride on that man's face was enough to make the hardest heart melt. It was clear why Adam loved her so very much. Not only was she stunning but she was the warmest, kindest person you could ever wish to meet. Once again, Lily was reminded that Eve was everything she wasn't.

Seeing Adam look so adoringly into Eve's eyes as they exchanged their vows was the most excruciating thing Lily had ever witnessed. The ache in her chest was so real and so painful she had to take deep breaths and clutch the pew behind her for support. What was to come would be harder still. *The speech.*

♥♥♥

The meal was lovely but Lily could hardly stomach anything. The champagne was flowing and just about took the edge off her nerves. The time was looming when she would have to stand and tell the world how happy she was to be losing the only man she had ever loved. The one man she could envisage marrying. The only man she could ever imagine having children with. He was lost. He was in-love. She was happy for him. But in being happy for him, she'd had to say goodbye. How could she ever let go? A love so deep wasn't something you could just forget.

After a nod from the master of ceremonies, she stood and clanked her glass with a fork. The room fell silent. All eyes turned to her.

She cleared her throat. "Erm…as many of you know, Adam and I go way back. Way back to little school in fact. He used to defend me against the bullies who tried to take my crayons and pinch my carton of milk. In that first few years I knew…" She glanced at her mother who had tears in her eyes. Lily swallowed hard. "Erm…sorry…in those first years I knew that Adam and I would be friends for life. We've been through some entertaining experiences together…like the time we got locked in an old house down his street that everyone said was haunted. We sat there for ages hoping someone would realise we were missing, but really I think they were relieved to have a break from our constant chatter. Anyway, Adam was a big baby and cried the whole time, but I let him wipe his nose on my T-shirt so he was fine in the end."

Laughter travelled around the room. "Oh…and there was the time he spilled juice on his crotch at my house, when we were about eight..." Lily sniggered at the memory. "My mum had to dry off his shorts, but he had to borrow a pair of my knickers to go home in!" The laughter grew louder and Lily glanced over at Adam who was beet-red and peeking through his fingers as Eve laughed heartily beside him, squeezing his leg. "Yep, he's never lived that one down." Lily took a deep breath. "Anyway, I'm not going to embarrass him anymore. In fact, I've written a little poem that I'd like to read out... So okay, I might embarrass him for a few seconds longer." The room fell silent again

Taking a deep breath and glancing over at Adam and then down at the paper she held in her trembling hands, her emotions began to get the better of her again. She began to read aloud.

As little kids we'd graze our knees
We'd laugh and climb and know no fear
The path we took toward this day
Who would have thought we'd end up here?
You've been my rock and my big brother
You've fought my enemies 'til the end
My best friend, protector, and confidante
The someone on whom I could always depend
I've watched you grow and been so proud
The secrets kept are ours forever
I won't tell if you don't tell
The trouble we've caused will be known never
We always stuck together fast
Nothing could put our friendship asunder
But we knew it couldn't last
I got fed up of you...there's really no wonder
You've met your love and your heart is whole
You share a love so deep and true
I'm so glad for you my dearest friend

And know how much she truly loves you
So when it all is said and done
And all the joking's put aside
I'm sure you know but I'll tell you now
You really do have the most beautiful bride
And so you go off to married life
Here I stand and say goodbye
I wish you both happiness, love, and joy
And now I'll stop before I cry.

The tears she had been holding back and had joked about escaped down her cheeks, and she felt the urge to run, but the room exploded in applause and glancing up she could see there was hardly a dry eye in the room. Adam and Eve enveloped her in a bear hug as she congratulated them. Every emotion she had ever felt erupted from within under the guise of happiness. Only she knew the real truth. Only Lily knew the heartache.

Chapter Sixteen

She's Out of my Life (Michael Jackson)
August 2009

"Adders? Adders where are you?" Lily called when she arrived to find Adam's door unlocked. There was no reply. She made her way through the dishevelled lounge into the kitchen at the back of the house. Dirty dishes covered every surface. An unpleasant odour assaulted her nostrils. "Fucking hell, it stinks in here, Adders. Where are you?"

She still got no response. Walking back through the lounge she made her way up the stairs. The unpleasant smell seemed to follow her wherever she dared to tread. *I'll need to have my effing clothes fumigated at this rate.* She dodged discarded shoes, socks, and other items on the stairs and made her way to Adam's bedroom. On opening the door, her nose encountered the pungent smell of unwashed male. *Delightful.* Adam was lying face down on his bed, curtains drawn.

She plonked down beside him, switched on the bedside lamp, and poked him in the back. "Adders, for fuck's sake, come on man, get up."

He sniffed and rolled over. His eyes were puffy and his face unshaven. "Thanks for your sympathy. Now fuck off." He covered his eyes with his arm where a fresh batch of tears sprang forth.

"Because you're my best friend and because your wife is dead, I'm going to let you off for that. Now get up and get a shower. You stink. We're going to go for a walk and then we're coming back here to clean up this shit hole."

Adam groaned. "Why do you have to be so harsh, Lil? Why do you say *because your wife is dead* so matter-of-factly?"

"Because, Adam, I'm sorry but it *is* a matter of fact. And you sitting here aiming for the most unwashed and hairy man of the year prize isn't going to change that. People are too nervous to be straight with you. Your mum sent me round to knock some sense into you. She feels too scared to kick you up the arse in case you jump off a cliff." She rocked his body back and forth. "I, on the other hand, know that you are too much of a chicken to do such a thing, seeing as you're scared of heights, and so I'm here to tell you to get the fuck out of bed, get washed, and get on with your life!" She raised her voice at him but immediately felt guilty. She pulled his arm away from his face. "It has been almost six weeks since the funeral. School has been back in session for two weeks now. I know you're grieving, believe me I do. I still keep crying about it all. But there comes a point when you have just got to start to try and get on with life again."

He sniffed and pointed at her. "You said there was no time limit on grief. When did that change, Lil?"

He was right. She remembered saying those very words. He sniffed again and rolled away from her. She manoeuvred around the piles of dirty clothes and sat at the other side so that he was facing her again, her voice softened. "I'm sorry for being so harsh. I don't want to upset you more, Adders. I love you, and it's hurting me seeing you hurting."

"Well fuck off and don't watch then. I didn't ask you to come here with your shit attempts at helping."

She sighed. "No...but look around you. Is this how Eve would want you to be?"

"Don't you fucking do that." He almost barked the words.

"Don't do what?"

"Don't do the whole *oooh-Eve-would-want-this-and-Eve-would-want-that* shit. It's a low blow."

She pulled in her lips to stop a harsh retort from firing out. Instead she rubbed his arm. "Come on...think about it...*would* she want to see you like this?"

He sat bolt upright and glared at her, his bloodshot eyes boring into her so intensely she recoiled. In his unshaven and unkempt state he looked quite menacing. "It's a moot fucking point isn't it? Because as you so clearly and so lovingly put it SHE IS DEAD!" He punched the mattress as his voice boomed around the bedroom, rattling off the walls along with the raw emotion emanating seemingly from his very being. He placed his head in his hands as growling, angry sobs wracked his body. She encircled him in her arms and bit her lip to stave off her own threatening tears. She rubbed his back as his almost palpable pain poured out.

Once his sobs had subsided he pulled away. "I'm so sorry...I'm so *very* sorry. I shouldn't take it out on you." His desolate expression made her heart ache. She wanted to take his pain away. Seeing the man she loved like this was ripping her heart to pieces.

She brushed his greasy hair off his forehead and smiled. "I'll let you off. You are a grieving widower after all. I think you've got a good excuse." Her voice was soft and just above a whisper.

His lips curled slightly and he shook his head. "You're right, Lil. This place stinks." He glanced around the room as if realising this for the first time. "And God, it's such a mess."

"Right. Go get a shower. I'll make a wee start on downstairs. When you're done we're going for a walk down to the park. We'll pick up sandwiches from Berengers, and we'll have ourselves a wee picnic. Deal?"

Adam nodded and sniffed. "Deal."

Lily made her way back downstairs and began to collect the empty beer cans and pizza boxes scattered around the lounge and kitchen. She found some refuse sacks under the sink and disposed of the abundance of rubbish. Buying her own house two years before Eve's death, as an investment, had enabled her to move out of her tiny flat, and she was fairly house-proud. Adam had always been the same when Eve was alive. Clearly now, however, cleanliness was not on his list of priorities. Eve would have been furious.

Once the floor was visible again, she got out the vacuum cleaner and swept the carpet. The place was beginning to resemble a home again as opposed to the council dump. She opened the windows and locked them on the latch to let some fresh air circulate. Already the bad smell was beginning to vacate the premises, leaving something akin to freshness in its wake.

Adam walked into the lounge where Lily sat waiting. "Bloody hell, Lil. You've worked wonders."

She gazed up at the Adam she knew well. Clean shaven, fresh clothes, and washed hair. He looked wonderful, apart from the red circles around his eyes. "That's better." She stood up to hug him. "You look like *you* again."

He hugged her back. "Thanks, Lil… I think you were right about me needing a kick up the arse."

She cringed. "Well, maybe I could have been a little more compassionate, eh?"

"Nah. You know me better than anyone. I think people have been pussy footing around me and I've been letting them. Look where it led. I was becoming Jedburgh's very first home-owning tramp." He twitched the corner of his mouth at one side.

She giggled. "Well, I did think I'd found a dead rat under your sofa but it turned out to be some former foodstuff with a thick layer of furry fungus."

His eyes widened. "Oh God, no?"

"Oh yes. I would have screamed but then you'd have laughed at me for being a big girl."

He shook his head. "Are you kidding? I think I'd have screamed like a big girl if I'd have found it." It was so good to see him smile again.

The pair grabbed their coats and set out of the house for some much needed fresh air. Luckily the weather was decent and the sky was blue. The walk to the park took them straight past Berenger's bakery. It had been a favourite of theirs for many years. Passed down from father to son, the bakery had a traditional appearance with its dark wood windows and the little bell that jingled on entry. The aroma inside made her stomach growl loudly and the few customers in the shop all turned to her. Her cheeks heated and Adam burst out laughing. It was the most wonderful sound she had heard in a long time. She felt good that it was her that had brought it out of him...well, her grumbling belly anyway.

They headed for a bench by the duck pond in the small park. He took several deep breaths as if to cleanse the stale air that had been filling his lungs for the past six weeks. A family of mum, dad, and two toddlers were there feeding the ducks with bread from a supermarket wrapper. Lily watched as the little girl kept letting go of the bread whilst it was behind her instead of throwing it forward. Her parents were giggling and trying to teach her how to throw properly. Lily smiled at the scene and wondered if she would ever find herself doing something similar.

Realising she had drifted off a little, she looked back to Adam. He was watching the same scene with tears in his eyes. Poor Adam. He and Eve had been talking about starting a family only a short while before the accident. Lily nudged him with her shoulder. "So, when are you going back to work then? The kids must be missing you like mad. I know it's only two weeks into the term, but...well..."

He picked at the bread at the end of his baguette and nodded. "Yeah, I really should go back soon, eh? They've been so great at work. But I suppose...life goes on. I just... I'm just scared of going back and seeing sympathy in the kids' eyes. It'd tear me apart. I don't know if I could cope with that."

"Yes you can. And it only means that they care. Those kids worship the bloody ground you walk on. They must be worried about you. And no one would be angry if you got choked up in front of them. It shows you're human. You're a teacher, Adders, not a robot."

"Yes...you're right. I miss them. I miss work. I miss...normality."

"Well, why don't you speak to the principal? Tell her that you want to come back next week, eh? It's Monday now. You have a week to prepare."

He looked confused. "That's a point...it *is* Monday. So what the hell are you doing here? Why aren't you at work?"

She rolled her eyes. "Well, I just happen to have this friend who's lost his wife and needs to get back on his feet again, and he won't do it unless I'm behind him giving his arse a push."

He smiled warmly and nudged her shoulder. "Lil...you're the best."

Her heart did a somersault. "Aye and don't you forget it."

Chapter Seventeen

Against All Odds (Phil Collins)
September 2009
Adam walked out of the staffroom and took a long, deep breath. The staff had been lovely, very supportive and kind. He had found himself fighting to swallow the lump lodged in his throat on numerous occasions. But just being here, in the school building with its familiar smells and sounds seemed to ease his pain ever so slightly. His first lesson of the day was going to be the hardest. The class of fifteen-year-olds had been with him since they started at the school. They were his favourite class of all. Not that a teacher should have favourites. They were by no means the brightest kids. But they were passionate. Before he had left, they had been running through *Romeo and Juliet* as a play. The kids had struggled with the language at first but acting the scenes out had helped immensely.

He walked into his classroom and wiped the board of all the notes made by previous supply teachers. He rolled down the next panel and stopped dead. Scrawled in bubble writing across the board was the message *Welcome back Mr. Langton, weve reely mist you.*

He chuckled and shook his head. "It's good that I'm back if that's how they're spelling these days," he said aloud. Feeling unable to wipe that section of board clean of the touching sentiment, he stepped away, leaving it in full view.

The bell sounded to notify the pupils of the beginning of the school day. He waited for the kids to appear. The first to enter the classroom was probably the graffiti artist herself. Jenny Milton. Her bleached blonde hair and heavily made up face hadn't changed.

"Mr. Langton!" She ran over and stopped short of flinging her arms around him. He inhaled sharply, panic washing over him at the thought that she might follow through. She stood in front of his desk with a big grin on her orange face. "You got our message then." She pointed to her handiwork.

Adam breathed a sigh of relief when he realised she wasn't going to hug him. "I did, Jenny. Thank you." He thought about mentioning the atrocious spelling but decided against it.

More pupils filtered into the room and crowded around his desk placing envelopes down which Adam presumed were condolence cards. It was very sweet. "Are you alright, sir? We...you know...heard about Mrs. Langton. It must have been awful."

"Yeah, we're really sorry, sir. If we can do anything just tell us."

"Shall I hand the books out, sir?"

"It's good to have you back, sir. That supply teacher we had was shit!" With a loud gasp the whole class fell silent, and everyone's focus was turned to the owner of the foul mouth.

Adam cleared his throat and stifled a laugh. "Okay, Tom. I think that's enough now."

The spotty teenager bit his lip and cringed. "Sorry, sir...sorry for swearing I mean... I'm not sorry for what I said though...cause it's true!"

Jenny Milton punched him hard on the arm and glared at him. "You'll get us all detention you spotty weasel," she hissed. Tom chuntered under his breath that the whole class had thought it and he'd just said it.

Once everyone was seated and the books had been handed out, Adam took a deep breath. He had prepared a speech to deliver to the class, but it felt a little contrived now.

He blinked a few times to rid the tears stinging at his eyes and began. "Okay, kids, we have a lot of catching up to do. But first of all, I just want to say how great it is to be back with you all. It's been a rotten few weeks. Losing someone you love is never easy. I loved my wife more than anything in this world, and so you'll have to please excuse me if I get emotional at any point. I'm trying very hard not to bring what happened into the classroom, but as my best friend has informed me...I'm a teacher not a robot. But I want to get on with life now. I want you all to do well in your exams, and you were making great progress before...well...you know. So let's get cracking, eh? Onward and upward." Silence fell on the usually rowdy group.

Suddenly, Jenny Milton stood and began clapping. She was immediately joined by Tom. One by one all of the pupils stood and joined in the applause. Then came whistles and cheers. Adam was taken aback as the class of loud-mouthed and leery teens showed their appreciation for his words. He soaked up the positive energy coursing around the room. He was back. And it felt good.

♥♥♥

Lunchtime came around quickly and Adam heaved a long breath of exhaustion as he flopped into one of the squashy armchairs in the staff room. Resting his elbows on his knees and his head in his hands, he closed his eyes. Someone patted his back and sat in the chair beside him. He glanced up into the eyes of Diane Silverman, head of Performing Arts. She was a good friend and had been at the funeral.

"How are you holding up, Adam?" she asked with a kind smile.

He rubbed his face. "I'm shattered. I honestly don't remember ever being this tired after a morning of teaching."

She nodded. "I can imagine. You've been through a lot. I hear you got a standing ovation during first period." She grinned.

His eyes widened. He'd forgotten how fast news travelled around school. "Erm, yes. That was a bit of a shock."

"They adore you, that lot, you know. I've lost count of how many times Jenny Milton has asked for your address so she could bring you some soup."

He pulled his brows into a frown. "Soup?"

Diane giggled. "Yes. Apparently she's heard that you're supposed to bring chicken soup to someone in your situation as it will, and I quote, *help to heal your soul.* Bless her heart."

The lump appeared in Adam's throat again and he swallowed hard. "Oh...that's...that's so...sweet." His voice cracked as he spoke. He couldn't quite get over the fact this group of kids, whom most people had given up on, had shown such kindness toward him. He pushed his thumb and finger into the corners of his eyes and bit his lip as his emotions pushed toward the surface once again. He could feel his chin quivering.

Diane squeezed his shoulder. "Oh Adam, I'm sorry, love. I didn't mean to upset you. Are you okay to be here? I can have a word with the principal."

He held up his hand and shook his head. "No, no, Diane. Thanks but I'm fine. I *will* be fine. It's all just a little overwhelming."

Her hand was still on his shoulder. "Look...if you need anything..."

He covered her hand with his own. "I know."

♥♥♥

Adam walked through his front door at four thirty. There was a strange silence to the place now. Somehow coming home from work for the first time since Eve was killed was like losing her all over again. He closed the door behind him, slid down it until he hit the floor, and leaned his head back to rest. The emptiness inside him mirrored the emptiness of the pretty little cottage he had shared with Eve. He closed his eyes as his shoulders began to shudder and the tears began to flow.

Suddenly, there was a knock at the door. He cleared his throat. "Who is it?" he called up toward the letterbox, his voice breaking.

"Adders, you big cry baby, it's me," Lily said as she reached through the slot usually reserved for bills and junk mail and ruffled his hair.

He whacked her hand, making her yelp. "Subtle as ever, eh, Lil?" He pulled himself up and opened the door. She stood with her arms wide open.

"I knew today would be shitty. Come here." She stepped inside, kicked the door closed behind her, and enveloped him in her arms. He crouched to meet her height and pulled her into him, letting his emotions run free. Once he had calmed down, he pulled away, wiping his eyes on the back of his hands and sniffing.

He rubbed his hands over his face and huffed out through puffed cheeks. "Sorry, Lil. I just can't seem to stop fucking crying."

She smiled. "That's coz you're a big cry baby, like I said." She prodded him.

He rolled his eyes at her callous but jovial manner and couldn't help but smile. "Thanks for that."

"You are *so* welcome. Who can mock you in your time of need if not your best friend in the world, eh?" Grabbing his arm, she pulled him through to the lounge. "Right, Adders, you have a choice. We either stay in and watch a movie while we eat crappy food all night, or we go out and get pissed. Now seeing as it's a school night I'm thinking option one. Whaddya say?" She held her arms out, palms flat.

He thought about it for a few minutes. "Ah…to be honest, Lil, I was just going to do a bit of marking and get an early night."

"Tough titties. I'm here with the choices. Pick one."

"Honestly, Lil—"

She stomped her foot and raised her voice. "Pick one!"

He huffed at her like a petulant child. "Oh for fuck's sake, Lil. Option one then."

She beamed like a little kid who had just been granted extra pocket money. "Great! Hang on there. I've got supplies." She skipped out to the car and returned soon after with two carrier bags full of junk food.

"I got pizza, popcorn, kettle chips, a huge bar of chocolate, and a couple of bottles of beer," she announced looking rather proud of herself.

He couldn't help but smirk at his loopy friend. He wasn't entirely sure what he would do without her at the moment. Although, it would probably involve tears, sad songs, and old photographs.

She rummaged around in the bottom of her bag. "Okay, I took the liberty of completely jumping the gun and renting two films. So you have another choice… Monty Python's *Life of Brian*…or…*Wayne's World?*"

Adam burst out laughing. "Good grief, Lil, did you happen to travel to the rental store in a Delorean?"

She looked puzzled. "Huh?"

He rolled his eyes. "Delorean…Michael J Fox…Marty McFly?"

Her face was scrunched. "What the heck are you on about, Adders?"

He threw his hands up in exasperation. "*Back to the Future*, you dufus!" He shook his head. "The films you've picked are blasts from way back in the past."

A look of realisation spread across her face, and she blushed at her own silliness. She slapped her forehead. "Oh, that's the car from the film! The Delorean!"

He ruffled the top of her dark curls. "Bloody hell. That took some sinking in. I reckon senility is setting in early."

"Oy! Cheeky pig. It's a good job you're grieving or I'd punch you."

♥♥♥

They sat huddled on the sofa eating pizza as Adam recounted the tales from his first day back at school. "Who would have thought it, Lil? Those kids really do care."

"I had no doubt in my mind. That Jenny Milton though. That thing about the soup made me fill up. Bless her." Lily sniffed

"Oh God, don't you start. It made me do the same this morning in front of all my colleagues. She's a character, that's for sure. Every time I saw her today she gave this sad smile. I had no idea she had a heart underneath that crusty orange façade."

Lily sniggered. "I don't get this need to trowel make-up on. Girls that age don't need to do that."

"I agree but they all do it. Anyway, get the film on and pass me the choccy."

"Bossy sod. *Life of Brian* is it then?"

"Absolutely."

Chapter Eighteen

Given to Fly (Pearl Jam)
October 2009

"So when are you going to be back, Lil?" Panic was thick in his voice and Lily's heart lurched. Adam had been back at work for four weeks now, and she'd been assigned a story in the United States. It was a great opportunity and she couldn't pass it up. She'd been asked to go out and report a piece on the differences between the education system there and the one in place in the UK. Okay, so she wasn't going to be signed up as an anchor on some flashy US news show, but at least she would get to meet people. It would be good for her. She knew it. Adam didn't seem to get it though.

"I should be back in a month so don't worry. Anyway, you're doing fine. Have a little faith, Adders." She squeezed his arm. She had left it until the day before she flew before calling around to his house and telling him the news. He'd had enough on his plate, reacquainting himself with the normalities and routines of school life.

He slumped down onto his old sofa and huffed out a held breath. "A month... Lil...what will I do?"

She sat down beside him. "Adders, sweetie, I'm not your only friend. You have family, too. And Max is down the road. It's a month. That's all. And I have to go for my career."

He rubbed his hands over his face and loosened his tie. "Yeah...I know you do... It's just...well no one really gets me like you do. You know how to deal with all this grief shit."

"Grief is shit, Adders, it really is, but I'm not a crutch. You can't expect me to just be here at your beck and call. I know that sounds harsh but it's true."

A pained look washed over his face and he winced at her words. "Is that what you think I'm doing? Using you as a crutch?"

She nodded. "I know you don't mean to, but I've been here almost every day for the past month, and when I haven't been here, I've been talking to you on the phone. I have to get back to my own life at some point." She spoke as gently as she could, but knew her words stung.

He pursed his lips and glanced sideways at her. "You're right. I'm a big boy. So I've lost the love of my life...so what...so I'm all alone...so what...so—"

"Adam, shut up," she snapped. "Stop with the woe is me crap, will you please? I have been there for you throughout this. You know that. I've helped in every conceivable way. But at some point you have to start helping yourself. Stand up on your own two, huge bloody feet. Please?" She stroked his cheek. He flinched and pulled away.

She stood. "Right, well I'd better go. I have to be at the airport early and I need some sleep."

Adam stood to face her. "Stay here." He held her arms. She had longed for those words to fall from his lips for so long. But the meaning behind them now was not the one she'd hoped for. He was being selfish trying to cling onto her for as long as possible. Not because he loved her any differently than before. But because in some crazy part of his head he thought he needed her. He thought he couldn't function without her. Yup, she was definitely a crutch. And she wouldn't have it anymore.

"Adam, I'm not going to do that. My stuff is all packed and ready at home. My bed is at home. I'm going home."

Adam slumped down again. "Fine." He folded his arms like a sulky teenager once again.

She couldn't help but snigger at his demeanour. "You've been taking too many lessons from those kids at school. I could balance my mug on that bottom lip."

He looked at her again as a grin struggled to break out on his face. He bit his lip, clearly wanting to stay angry. "Fuck off." He chuckled.

"You fuck off." A grin spread across her face.

He stood up again. "No you. Give me a hug and then fuck off to America." He grabbed her arm and pulled her in.

She wrapped her arms around his middle and hugged him hard. "I'll be back before you know it."

"Don't care."

"Liar," she said into his chest.

"Cheesy head."

She sniggered again. "Pee pants."

"Right, you can really fuck off now."

She burst out laughing and made her way to the front door. "You'll be fine, you know."

The flight was a long one. Lily arrived in a chilly New York City airport and climbed into a yellow cab. She gave the driver the address of her hotel and slumped into the seat.

"Business or pleasure?" the rotund driver asked over his shoulder.

She snapped out of her semi-conscious state. "Sorry?"

"Are you here on business or pleasure?"

"Oh right, sorry. It's been a long day. Business."

"What line are you in?"

"I'm a journalist. I report for a pretty major news station in the UK."

"Well, lar-dee-dar. Ain't I the lucky guy today, huh? What brings you to New York?"

"I'm doing a piece on the education system in the States."

"Ha…well, alls I can tell you is my boy, Deano, he's a bright kid, but they don't do squat to encourage him at school."

She rubbed her eyes. She really didn't want to converse. She just wanted to relax and doze. The cab journey was going to take an hour, and she would rather have silence than make small talk with some guy she'd never met before and who she was never likely to meet again. "Is that so?"

"Yeah…he could be a doctor or a…what do you call it…news reporter. He could even sell real estate if he put his mind to it."

She stifled a giggle. "Well he sounds very bright indeed."

"Yeah, the brightest. Anyways, you tell 'em over in the UK that my boy needs more help."

"It's not really my place—"

"Yeah, I mean so he took a knife to school one time. One time! It's like they hold it against the kid. I mean, whaddya gonna do?"

"I really don't—"

"Yeah well, me and the missus, we told 'em, you gotta give the kid a chance here. He ain't gonna use the damn thing. It's just…you know…protection."

She gave up trying to interrupt the monologue that ensued in the front seat. She switched off and added a nod every so often. The man could really talk! They pulled outside a beautiful old building.

"Anyways lady, you need anything, you call Pauly, okay? I can pick you up and take you wherever you need to go. It was real nice talking to you."

She climbed out and handed him a wad of notes. He fumbled through them and tried to hand her change back. "No you keep it, Pauly."

"Awww, lady you're too kind, too kind. Thank you. You have a good stay in the Big Apple now."

"I will certainly try, Pauly. Thanks again. Good luck with Deano."

The yellow cab pulled away and as it did so the driver waved at her. The concierge opened the door and doffed his rather spiffy top hat as Lily nodded and smiled. Immediately a bellhop came over and took her bags, loading them onto a trolley. She checked in at the reception desk and made her way to her suite.

Once her bags had been deposited, she removed her coat and shoes and flopped onto the bed. She fumbled in her handbag and pulled out her cell phone. When she turned the phone on, just as she expected, there were several messages from Adam.

A: I miss you already, Lil. Can you come home please? ☹

A: Hi Lil, it's me again, sorry about my last message, I know you can't come home yet but I'm bored and sad. ☹

A: Me again, what time do you land? You're not answering me and I'm worried.

A: Hi again, please can you reply when you get this message? My mum is trying to get me to go stay over the half term break and I don't want to. I need help with a good excuse.

A: Too late she has convinced me to go stay. My mum that is. She wants to feed me coz she says I'm getting too thin!

A: Lil, where the fuck are you? You should be there by now! TEXT ME!!

She threw her phone across the bed where it landed and bounced onto the floor. *Oh shit.* She scrambled to the end of the bed, expecting the phone to be in pieces. Thankfully it wasn't. She glanced at the clock on the nightstand. It was eleven at night. Guilt washed over her, and with a groan she picked up the phone and dialled Adam's number.

He answered after one ring. "Lily? Are you okay? I've been worried sick."

"Adam, I'm fine. You have to stop worrying. The flight was delayed that's all. Then I got in a cab with a sweet old guy who wouldn't stop talking, and I have just collapsed onto my bed and found half a dozen messages from you."

"Ah...yeah...sorry about that. I don't like it when you don't answer." Silence took over the line for several moments. "I worry, Lily. I don't know what I would do if anything happened—"

"I'm fine. Please stop okay? I'm shattered and need to sleep. I have an early start in the morning."

"Okay...sorry...I just worry."

"I know. It's fine. I'll talk to you later in the week okay?"

"Okay...night, Lil."

"Night, Adam."

"Lil?"

She sighed. "What now?"

"You keep calling me *Adam*. You only do that when you're pissed off."

"Sorry. I'm not pissed off. Just tired."

"Okay, night."

"Night." She hung up before the ridiculous conversation could carry on.

Chapter Nineteen

Alone in This Bed (Framing Hanley)
March 2010

Adam had been dreading his thirtieth birthday. If Eve had been here there would have been big plans afoot. The simple fact that this was his first birthday without her made his chest ache. Other than the anniversary of her death and Christmas…and her birthday…and their wedding anniversary…this was the date he was dreading most. Who was he kidding? Every day was difficult. But for this day to be so significant made the ache grow deeper. He pulled the pillow back over his head. Thank goodness it had landed on a Saturday. People at work had been very kind. There had been lots of knowing looks during the week, which had just made him feel more and more lost.

He thought back to the birthdays he had celebrated when Eve was with him. She always made a fuss. He would usually awake to the smell of bacon cooking. She would bring a tray up to him and sit beside him whilst he tucked in to his favourite food. She would shower him with thoughtful gifts and little tokens of love. His favourites had been the small things. A heart shaped key ring, a mini Statue of Liberty ornament, even a white pebble she had found on the beach and had written *Forever Yours* in twirly writing on. Memories of those times made him so happy…so angry…so very, very sad. His eyes began to sting.

He was torn from his reverie by banging on the front door. He groaned loudly. Glancing at the clock, he realised it was after eleven. He had no real reason to get up, however, so what did it really matter? Sinking back under the duvet, he ignored the hammering.

"Oy! Adders, you lazy pig! Get up and open the effing door before I resort to breaking in!"

Lily.

He clambered out of bed and made his way downstairs in just his boxers. He yawned widely as he opened the door.

She gaped. "Good grief! Put your flesh away, Adders! It's your thirtieth! No one wants to look at a naked old man!" She shoved past him and dragged him by the arm toward the stairs. "Get your arse upstairs and get a shower whilst I make you a fry up. Then get your *clean* and *clothed* arse down here because I have something to tell you."

Reluctantly, he followed her instructions and once showered in jeans and his favourite old grey T-shirt, he made his way back down to the kitchen, following the teasing smell of bacon and sausage. He sat down at the small table as she placed a full plate of heart attack inducing food in front of him.

Sitting opposite him without any food, but with a smile on her face, she slid an envelope across the table. "Happy Birthday, you old git."

Chewing on a mouth full of crispy bacon, cooked just the way he liked it, he glanced at her. "Oy! Less of the git." He grinned and opened the card. He shook his head at the joke inside. *Typical Lily.*

She giggled for a few moments, but then her laughter subsided and her face became serious. "When you've finished that, I need to speak to you about something…something very important." She chewed her lip.

His interest piqued, Adam placed his fork down and took a gulp of the fresh orange juice in his glass. "That sounds ominous. Is everything okay?"

She nodded. "Just finish your food, okay?"

He munched away until his plate was empty and his belly was *very* full. He followed her through to the lounge with his cup of coffee, and she gestured for him to sit next to her on the sofa. He sat down. His brow pulled in at the middle.

Placing his cup on the floor, he turned to her. "Lil, you're worrying me. Please, can you tell me what's going on with you now?"

She took a deep breath. "Okay…you have to promise that you won't get angry, okay?"

He pulled his lips between his teeth. His palms were sweating, "Awww, now I'm really worried. And usually when people say *don't get angry* it means that you will do just that. What have you done?"

"This is going to be difficult…for me too…but just hear me out."

He was getting annoyed. "Lil, just spit it out, will you?"

"Right…okay…here goes… Last year…before Eve died, she and I were talking about your…about your thirtieth. She wanted to plan something big for you, and she wanted my help. So together we planned something pretty huge. It was all done using my credit cards so that you wouldn't find out…but…" Her lip began to tremble. "But then she was killed by that fucking idiot drunk driver…and…I wasn't sure what to do."

He slid across the sofa, his own emotions needling at him just beneath the surface. "Hey, hey…don't cry. It doesn't matter, Lil. Don't worry. I'm not bothered—"

"No, Adam…you don't understand…let me finish…" She took another deep breath. "Anyway, Eve knew how much New York meant to you. How much you had always wanted to go. She wanted to be the one to visit Times Square with you…to visit places like the Empire State Building and the Statue of Liberty…"

Adam caught his trembling lip between his teeth as the salt water welled in his eyes. "You didn't?" he whispered.

"No...*I* didn't, Adam...*Eve* did." She handed him an envelope. With shaking hands, he took the white envelope from her and opened it. Two first class flights to New York.

He gasped as the tears overflowed from his eyes and covered his mouth with his hand as he read the note that accompanied the tickets.

June 20th 2009

My Darling Adam

It's a bit weird writing this letter when you are sitting at home wondering why I'm spending so much time at Lily's. But all I can say is it was important for me to write this now whilst I'm so very excited about what I've done! I hope that, seeing as when you get this almost a year has passed and the money has been spent, that you will simply smile across and hug me. No doubt I'm sitting biting my nails as you read this! Go on, look at me and check. See told you!

New York has always been our dream destination and so I know that when you calm down you will forgive me for booking the Waldorf Astoria for four nights...whoops! I forgot to mention that before (hee hee hee). But ever since we watched Serendipity, *it's been a dream of mine to stay there, and so I know you will enjoy it too as all you have ever wanted to do is make me happy. Well, now it's my turn, my gorgeous, wonderful, handsome husband. Have I told you today how much I love you? I'm guessing I have but just in case I have been too pre-occupied making your favourite breakfast I will write it now... I LOVE YOU! More than anything in this world. Never forget that.*

Now get over here and kiss me!

Eve

Xxx

A painful sob broke free from his body as he slumped forward, head in his hands. His body shuddered as he clung to the note. The note that Eve had written. The note that was his last connection to his beautiful wife. The note that told him she was thinking about him but was expecting to be sitting opposite him as he read it. Why wouldn't she have been expecting that? It was too much to bear. His sobs were loud and unabashed, and all the raw emotion connected to the day poured out of him. He felt arms encircle him and squeeze him tight. A damp face pressed into his neck.

Eventually his sobs subsided and he lifted his face. Lily's red-rimmed eyes stared back. A look of worry plagued her features. "I'm so sorry, Adam... I didn't mean..."

He frowned and shook his head, touched her cheek. "No, don't be sorry, Lil." He sniffed and wiped his hands over his tear stained face. "It was just a little overwhelming...the letter...the tickets...the fucking *Waldorf Astoria?*" He smiled. "But after everything that's happened...with her not being here...the note alone is the best I could have hoped for."

She returned his smile. "The thing is the flights are tomorrow. I spoke to the head teacher at school and you're booked off for the week. Special dispensation."

His eyes widened at the realisation. "That explains the looks I've been getting this week."

She squeezed his arm. "You can go and just enjoy it. Think of her and know how much you meant to her."

He looked at the envelope containing the tickets, which had fallen to the floor. "But there are two tickets, Lil. I...I don't really want to go alone."

She rubbed his arm. "Then ask your mum. She would *love* to go. She really would, Adam."

He chuckled. "Erm, I don't think it's the kind of place I want to go with my mum. Can you imagine her face if I get drunk? No, you helped plan it. *You* should come."

Her heart pounded. She felt a little lightheaded. "Erm…erm…I…erm."

He placed his hand over hers on his arm. "Look, you helped to organise this and you're my best friend. If anyone should go with me it should be my best friend. Don't you think?"

Chapter Twenty

New York, New York (Frank Sinatra)
March 2010

"Oh...my...God!" Lily gasped as they stood in the entrance of the suite at the Waldorf Astoria. "This is the most luxurious place I've ever been in, and I've stayed in many hotels. Some of them quite nice. But this..."

Adam swallowed the lump in his throat. "Yep, my girl had taste alright." He glanced around and his damp eyes settled on the huge king-size bed. "You take the bed, Lil. I'll sleep on the floor or...or the sofa."

She swung around. "You'll do no such thing you, Muppet. We're both adults. We'll share the bed."

He felt the heat rise in his cheeks. "Oh...okay."

She cringed. "Oh heck, Adders...I didn't mean...I mean I know that Eve and you were meant to... I'll take the sofa." She stumbled over the right words to say.

He shook his head. "No...no it's not that at all. I just didn't think you'd want to share the bed, you know?"

"Yeah, well we used to share a bed when we were kids. It's no different. We're best friends, Adders. It's fine...as long as you don't mind, that is."

"Nah. I've put up with your snoring before. I'll just poke you or slap you if you get too loud."

"Me? Snore? I don't think so, matey. I think you'll find it's you that turns porcine in your sleep!"

"Yeah? We'll see, eh?" Adam chuckled.

The friends unpacked their belongings, rested a short while, and then made their way out onto the busy and bustling Park Avenue. They were greeted with a cacophony of car engines, sirens, aeroplanes, and loud chatter. Lily went into David Bailey mode, snapping pictures of anything and everything that stood still long enough. She had visited New York before for work but had told Adam she had never had the time to do the sightseeing, touristy part. It was almost like she was seeing the place for the first time.

Adam puffed out his cheeks as she made him pose for the hundredth time. They walked across town to the famous Bloomingdales store where Lily was like a woman possessed. Adam ended up loaded down with bags and bags of clothing, gifts, toiletries, and goodness knows what else. He just smiled. It was good to see her enjoying herself.

Eventually, both exhausted, they stumbled across a nice looking coffee shop and collapsed into a booth. "I think you bought the whole of New York, Lil. You do know there's a limited baggage allowance on the way back, don't you? The bloody plane won't get off the ground at this rate!"

She giggled as she looked at the mountain of purchases. "Whoops! I think you may be right. I may have to charter my own private jet to get home."

He took a drink of the nectar-like coffee in his mug. "Jeez Louise, that's a damn good cup o' joe."

His fake American accent made Lily laugh out loud. "Yeah…I hueard it was gooyed caawfee hea." She mocked in her best attempt at a Brooklyn accent but it came out a little nasal and whiny.

He threw his head back and his shoulders shuddered as he guffawed. Coffee was not quite as good when it went up your nose. He spluttered and wiped his nose and chin. "Eeeuw!"

She was laughing so hard she had to stagger up from the table and make a dash for the restroom. Tears rolling down her face.

That evening they sat across from one another in the beautiful restaurant at the Waldorf Astoria sharing a bottle of wine. A pianist played *As Time Goes By*.

Lily glanced over at Adam who was clearly taken, watching a young couple. They were evidently in love. "Hey, Adders, are you okay?" She reached across the table and covered his hand with hers.

Turning his attention to her, he smiled. "Yeah…I'm fine…just thinking, that's all."

"About Eve?" *Stupid question.*

He nodded and took a drink of his wine. She could see that his eyes were a little glassy. He set his glass down and cleared his throat. "Thanks for coming, Lil. I know I'm not being the best company."

She shook her head. "Nonsense. We're having a great time. And I know I'm not who you'd like to be here with, but I hope I'm not spoiling it too much."

"Don't say that…that makes it sound like you're second choice, Lil."

She leaned and squeezed his hand again. "Come on, Adders, I know you'd rather be here with Eve. That's understandable. You don't need to feel bad."

He sighed and closed his eyes for a few moments. "I just… I still can't get my head around the fact that I'm alone…you know?"

"You're not alone. You have me…and your family."

"Yes, and I'm grateful. I just wish I still had Eve, too. I keep reading that note. The part where she said I should go kiss her… That ripped my heart to shreds." His voice cracked as he spoke.

"I know… But how wonderful that you have it, eh? I'd forgotten she'd written that and put it with the tickets or I would've given it to you sooner."

"No...no, I think it was good to get it when I did." He twirled the wine in his glass. "It was like...it was like she was still here."

The waiter brought their food and placed their plates down in front of them. "There you go Mr. and Mrs. Langton...enjoy."

She gaped open mouthed and lifted her hand as if she was going to correct him but Adam stopped her. "Don't, Lil, it's fine. Goodness knows what people would think if we told them the truth. And the room is in that name. It's fine."

Later that night, Adam climbed into bed in his T-shirt and boxers, and Lily made her way over to the bed in her shorts and tank top. They'd both got a little tipsy at dinner, and she suddenly felt very nervous about sharing a bed with the man she adored. He was on his back, eyes closed, with one hand on his stomach and one behind his head. He looked so incredibly sexy. She wanted to snuggle up to him, kiss him...make love to him. But instead she gingerly climbed into the empty side of the bed and lay as far away from him as possible.

After a while, she heard him sniff. She rolled over toward him and realised his hands were covering his face as he shuddered. Sliding across the bed to him, she pulled him into her arms and let him cry until he fell asleep.

♥♥♥

Adam awoke to find himself wrapped around Lily's body. *Shit!* His arm was laid across her bare stomach where her tank top had ridden up in the night, his nose nuzzled into her neck, and his legs were entwined with hers. He remembered her holding him as he let his anguish pour out all over her. *Again.* She would be so pissed off if she woke up and found they were laid together, rather like lovers, in the middle of the large, luxurious bed. Carefully he untangled his limbs from hers and re-arranged his boxers. He stood and watched her sleep for a moment.

She really was beautiful. With her darks unruly curls spread across the pillow and her olive skinned abdomen exposed to his gaze. His eyes followed the deep curve of her waist to her hip. He swallowed. How strange things had worked out this way for them. How strange she thought of him as a brother. He fondly remembered the poem she had written for him as part of her *best man-woman* speech. *My best friend, my protector, my confidante*. How different things could have been if either one of them had crossed that arbitrary line in the sand. *Too late to think like this now, idiot, and how completely inappropriate.*

She shifted in her sleep, pulling him out of his reverie. Her tank top shifted to expose the bottom curve of her breast. He realised he had been staring at her. Quickly turning, he made his way to the bathroom and switched on the shower.

He turned the dial to cold.

♥♥♥

Lily awoke to the sound of running water coming from the en-suite bathroom. She stretched and glanced down when she felt a cool breeze across her middle. Realising her breasts were almost out there for the world to see…well for Adam to see anyway…she pulled her top down. Hopefully that happened *after* he'd gone to get a shower. Her inner voices reigned once again. *Otherwise he's had a really good view of my goods… Hmmm, I wonder what he thought if he saw them… Stop it, Lily, for goodness sake.*

Adam returned from the shower, towel drying his hair, in a pair of joggers slung low around his narrow hips. Ever since she teased him about the weights he bought when they were teens, he had always denied the fact he worked out, but looking at him, half naked before her, she knew he did. He had defined abs and that delicious V that disappeared into his joggers. She drew her eyes back up his body, feeling her skin heat. *Good grief, Lily, seriously get a bloody grip. He's a half-naked man. You've seen them before. Lots! But this one is Adam and we love him. Oh God I sound like bloody Gollum now!*

♥♥♥

Adam cleared his throat. "Erm, morning, Lil… Listen, I wanted to apologise."

Lily scrunched her brow. "Apologise? For what?"

"Erm…for crying on you like a big girl."

"Oh that. Don't worry. I'm used to it now."

He huffed. "Thanks." He slung the towel over his shoulder. "And for waking up after pretty much sleeping *on* you all night." He cringed at the memory and at the fact that he had been quite turned on at the time. He noticed her cheeks flush at his words, and he pulled his lips in to stifle the smile trying to make its way across his face. It took a lot to embarrass Lily, but it looked like he had succeeded without intending to.

She fiddled with the sheet she had pulled over her legs. "Oh, don't worry. I suppose you're used to having the whole bed to yourself nowadays, eh?" His half smile disappeared. Her eyes widened. "Sorry…was that really insensitive?"

"No…it's true… I just don't like to think about it, I suppose."

"No wonder, Adders. I'm so sorry," she whispered.

He took a deep breath. "Look, we can't go on feeling this awkward all the time we're here. This is clearly a lot different to sharing a bed as kids, eh? I'll sleep on the sofa tonight. I think it'll be easier."

"No! That's not fair, Adders. This is your holiday. I should sleep on the sofa."

"Absolutely not. I won't argue about this. That sofa is comfy and twice as big as mine at home. It's practically a double bed anyway. I'll be fine. It's decided. Let's get ready and go sightseeing."

Her demeanour changed as if she had acquiesced about the sofa. She climbed out of bed and made her way toward the en-suite.

She glanced over her shoulder. "Where do you fancy going today?"

"The Empire State Building," he said with glee in his voice.

"Oooh, you can be Tom Hanks, and I'll be Meg Ryan." She smiled.

"Nah…I think, after my behaviour last night, it should be the other way around."

She stopped and turned so that she was fully facing him with her hands on her hips and her lips pursed. She narrowed her eyes. "Are you saying I look like a man?"

He bit his lip. "It's the dark curls…very Tom Hanks." He smirked and ducked as she pulled a cushion from the sofa and threw it at his head.

Chapter Twenty-One

I Will Remember You (Sarah McLachlan)

The following day Adam awoke on the sofa. He'd had a fitful night's sleep filled with dreams of Eve. He pulled himself to a sitting position and rubbed his hands over his face. Today would be hard. Today he would tell Lily he needed to be alone for a while. Today he would say goodbye properly. He had no clue why he felt it had to be today, but it just had to be. There were places he wanted to walk. He wanted to be alone here with his memories of Eve.

"Morning, Adders. Coffee?" Lily yawned as she slumped onto the sofa beside him.

He turned toward her. "Lil…I need…I need some time alone today. Is that okay?"

She scrunched her brow. "Sure…of course. Is everything okay?"

"Yeah…I just feel like…I don't know…like I need to be with my memories today. Does that sound mad?"

She smiled warmly. "No, it sounds like you." She stood and walked to the bureau to make coffee. Adam walked into the en-suite and turned on the shower.

♥♥♥

Whilst Adam was in the shower Lily ordered room service. Adam needed a good meal before he went out. She knew how difficult today would be. He had a list of the places he wanted to visit. He had decided to do a harbour tour first to take in the views of the spectacular Statue of Liberty and then make his way back to take a walk in Central Park. These two places were the ones he and Eve had been most excited about. Later in the evening, he was going to visit Times Square when the billboards were lit brightly, dazzling pedestrians and drivers alike with their vibrant coloured images and advertisements.

He came out of the en-suite with a towel wrapped around his waist. He dried his hair. His eyes had the red-rimmed, telltale signs of tears cried once again. *Poor Adders.*

"I ordered pancakes and maple syrup. They came with bacon. How dodgy is that?" She giggled as she lifted the silver bell shaped lids from the warm plates.

"Dodgy? I think it sounds amazing. Oooh, and the bacon's all crispy too."

"Yeah...crozzled more like." Lily scrunched her nose up at the crispy pinkish coloured strips.

"Nah, this is perfect. Nice and crunchy. You've got no bloody taste."

The two friends ate their breakfast in silence. He still sat in his damp towel while she tried not to imagine him naked.

Eventually, she pushed her chair back from the table. "Well, I'm stuffed. I don't think I'll need lunch now!"

"Awww, you're a lightweight! You used to be able to eat a tattie more than a pig, Lil. What's happened to you?" he asked with a mouth full of bacon and pancake.

She pretended to gag. "Adders, I can see everything smushing around in your mouth! That's disgusting!"

A wide grin spread over his face as he opened his mouth and stuck his tongue out. "Blaaaaargh!" He shook his head from side to side.

"You really are a pig!" She threw her scrunched up napkin at him, and he laughed as she made her way to the en-suite. "Get some clothes on, too. I can see your arse!"

"You know you love me, really!" he shouted after her.

♥♥♥

An hour later Adam walked onto the busy sidewalk of Park Avenue. He hailed a cab and one pulled up beside him immediately. After giving the driver his destination, he pulled out a photo from his wallet. It showed him and Eve cuddled together beside a model of the Statue of Liberty they had seen on a weekend trip to Amsterdam. It was built from tiny building blocks, the type that children play with. Done this way, however, it looked more like a sculpture. He smiled and stroked his thumb over the image of his wife and got lost in his thoughts.

I'll see the real thing today, Evie. You'll be there with me in spirit…I know you will. I wish you were beside me now…for me to tell you how much I love that you did this for me. This amazing trip. Being here just…makes me miss you more. But I think I need to let you go now. Although I really don't know how to start that process. I know how much you loved me and I hope you always knew how much I loved you…still love you. I dreamed about you last night. It was so real. You were snuggled up on the sofa next to me. The curves of your body molded to mine just like they always did. I held onto you so damn tight, but…when I awoke you were still gone.

The cab pulled up to the curb where Adam could wait for the water taxi and he climbed out handing bills to the driver. He made his way over to the booth and bought his ticket. Standing in line with the other eager tourists his thoughts drifted back to Eve.

Well, here I am, Evie. I'm waiting in line to do one of the things you and I were supposed to do together. I'm glad it's a nice bright day. It feels like you're smiling down on me. I can see the statue off in the distance. I don't know what I expected, but…well…it's huge, Evie. It's beautiful. I wish you could see it. I hope that you can. The sun is shining down on it, and it looks like it's lit up with a gigantic spotlight just for me…for us.

People began to move and eventually he boarded the boat that would take him closer to the statue. There were people of all nationalities surrounding him. Funnily enough, he ended up sitting right next to a Scottish couple. From what little conversation he overheard between them, he could tell they were on their honeymoon. He secretly envied them.

It's typical, Evie. Everywhere I turn there are couples. Everyone here is with someone. Except for me. I'm here with my memories. Memories of you and how beautiful you were. How happy you made me. How amazing it felt to be with you. We could be anywhere and it didn't matter.

He felt the familiar sting of tears as the boat travelled nearer to the imposing lady, looming forty-six metres tall over New York Harbour. He gulped back the tears and bit the inside of his cheek. He pulled his jacket around his body to guard against the sea breeze that bit at him through his clothing.

Wow…there she is, Evie. She's even more beautiful close up. I can't quite believe I'm here. And…I can't quite believe you're not.

People frantically snapped photographs as the tour guide reeled off fact after fact about the icon which was a gift from the French and symbolised freedom and the dedication to liberty as an ongoing concept for the American people. Adam couldn't help the overwhelming emotion that surged from deep within. A stray tear spilled over and he quickly wiped it away.

Once the boat was safely docked once again, Adam looked back over his shoulder one last time.

Goodbye Liberty. It was nice to finally see you in real life…not that the building block version wasn't impressive…but…well you're the real deal. Oh, Evie…I remember that day like it was yesterday. We vowed then and there that we'd see the real thing…one day. I think Central Park is next. You'd been desperate to go there ever since we watched Serendipity. *That film has a lot to answer for.*

He smiled as he began to make his way in the direction of Central Park. After walking for thirty minutes, his restless night began to catch up on him, and his legs grew more and more tired with each step. He hailed a cab and made the rest of the journey in air-conditioned comfort.

Central Park was like an oasis of calm in a sea of chaos. The skyscrapers skirted the edge of the vast green space as if waiting to step inside. Budding trees framed the pretty lawned areas where families were picnicking on plaid blankets despite the March temperatures, making the most of the glimpse of sunshine. Adam bought a hot dog and a bottle of water from a vendor who stood reading the *New York Times*. Adam inhaled deeply as he glanced around himself.

Oh, Evie, you would just love this…the place is amazing. It's so colourful even at this time of year. It's busy, yet somehow peaceful at the same time. What I wouldn't give to be able to lay out a blanket and sit with your head in my lap whilst I stroke your hair. You'd read a book and I'd be people watching. I love that this place exists amongst all the hustle and bustle of the Big Apple. Oh…a horse and carriage…and yet another couple who look deeply in love.

He watched the horse and carriage pass by as he licked the relish that had begun to drip down his arm. An elderly couple walking hand in hand toward him stopped.

"Here you go, doll. Looks like you need this." The lady, clearly a New Yorker from her accent, was wearing lilac trousers and a yellow fleece jacket embellished with diamantes. She held out a folded paper handkerchief to him. "It's clean." She smiled.

He cringed, realising ketchup was now dribbling down his chin. "Oh heck, thank you…thank you very much. That's very kind." He took the hanky and wiped the sticky mess away.

"You're welcome, honey. Can't have a handsome young fella like you getting all icky on the way to meet his lady." She winked and she and her husband carried on walking. Adam smiled to himself and shook his head.

Now if you had been here, Evie, we'd be going for coffee with that old couple right about now, and you'd be inviting them to visit us back home in Scotland.

He came across a pretty little arched bridge and walked up to the mid-point. He stood and watched a couple of teenagers as they rowed a little boat along and argued jokingly about who was doing the most work to propel them forward. He inhaled deeply once again.

It'll be time to go home soon, Evie. Back to Scotland. Back to life in the real world. The world that no longer has you in it. But you'll always be in my heart, Evie. No matter what. Even if...and it's a big if...but even if I meet someone...I'll still love you. I hope you know that. I'll never forget you. How could I? I have so many happy memories, Evie. But I need to get on with moving forward. Looking back can only sustain me for so long. I hope you understand. It doesn't mean I've forgotten. It doesn't mean you've been replaced. Because you were one of a kind, Evie. My beautiful girl. My love...the missing piece of my soul. My Evie.

Chapter Twenty-Two

I Miss You (Stevie Nicks)
March 2010 (35,000 feet above the Atlantic)
"Are you okay, Adders?" Lily whispered when she glanced over at Adam, who sat staring into space in the dim light of the plane. Lily always hated flying but at least flying at night usually afforded a little sleep. Not tonight though.

"Sorry?" Adam turned to her.

"I just asked if you were okay. You've been quiet since we left the hotel, that's all."

He smiled but it was fleeting. "Yeah. I think this was always going to be difficult for me. I took the time to say goodbye whilst I was out yesterday. But coming home feels like I'm leaving her there...you know?"

Lily reached and squeezed his hand. "I know."

"I just... I suppose I know that eight months isn't such a long time and I'm wondering if maybe it's too soon."

"Too soon for what?"

"Too soon to let her go, Lil."

"Adam, please don't take this the wrong way...you know how much I loved Eve... But well...you're young. You can't live in the past. I can't imagine how hard losing her was. I know how hard it was for me but... She was your wife, so I know it was a hundred times harder. But you have to look forward now. I'm not saying jump into a relationship with the first woman that comes your way. But at least give yourself the chance to be *open* to meeting someone. You know?"

He huffed and leaned his head back. He didn't speak for a few moments as if processing her words.

Turning to her again, he had a sad look in his eyes. "But she was one of a kind, Lil. And I have no clue *how* to meet someone else. I've been with Eve forever. I'm not sure what to do. And I'm not sure I actually *want* to do anything."

"You don't *have* to do anything. Maybe... I don't know, maybe you'll just meet someone naturally...you know? Maybe you'll meet someone at school."

His brow creased. "At school? Are you having a laugh, Lil? I *work* with those women. The last thing I want to do is *date* one of them."

"It was just an idea. What about one of the student's mums?"

He laughed, trying his best to do so quietly. "Er...no way, Lil. Don't you think that would be a tad inappropriate? I can just imagine parents evening. 'Oh yes Mrs. Johnson, little Simon is doing really great in English, but anyway, are we shagging at your house or mine tonight?' Absolutely no way." He shivered as if the idea made him feel dirty.

"Okay, yes, I get your point." She sat back and pondered for a while. Suddenly, she sat up and blurted out. "I've got it!"

His eyes darted around. "Shhh!" he whispered, spraying her with saliva in his eagerness to quiet her. "People are sleeping and *I've got it* isn't something you want to be announcing in the small confines of an aeroplane."

"Eeeuw, Adders! Ever heard the phrase *say it, don't spray it*? I had a shower before we left, okay? I don't need another one."

"Okay, sorry. What have you *got* then?"

"Eh?"

"You said *I've got it* remember?"

"Oh, yes right. Okay...what about...and keep an open mind, okay? What about online dating?" She held out her hands as if it was the most obvious thing in the world.

He did not agree. His face contorted into something akin to disgust. "Not a fucking chance."

"Come on, Adders! It makes sense. I can help you set up a profile if you like."

"Nope." He folded his arms, leaned his head back, and closed his eyes.

"Why not?"

"Because…and I don't mean this to be offensive in any way…but I always imagine those websites to be filled with desperate people who can't find someone anywhere else and have resorted to the last chance saloon, that's why not."

Lily huffed. "That is *very* offensive. And actually that's where you're wrong. I know several colleagues who have met their partners that way."

"Don't believe you." Adam was not prepared to budge.

"Okay… Hannah, one of the editors at the channel. She spends so much time at work that she has no time to go out. She signed up two years ago and met Graham. He's a really nice guy and they hit it off. They're getting married next year."

"Ha…then he will murder her and chop her up into little pieces and eat her remains or something."

She shook her head at him and pulled her face into a look of incredulity. "Don't be so bloody melodramatic."

He peeped out from his half-closed eyelids. "Well…anyway. I'm not doing it."

She persisted. "Jeff in the weather room… He met Sonya through online dating and they're expecting their first child."

"Then he will announce he's gay and it's all been a cover up."

Ever determined to convince him she continued. "Stefano in the finances department—"

Adam snorted. "Green card."

"Clara and Phil…married three years."

Adam opened his eyes and turned to face her. "Look, Lil, I am not and I repeat…I. Am. Not. Signing. Up. For. Online. Dating." He repeated the words slowly and clearly.

She was the one to get huffy now and turned in her seat so that she faced the window. "Whatever…I was just trying to help."

"Yeah…I know…but just…I don't know…*don't*, okay?"

♥♥♥

Lily couldn't get to sleep. Plans were whirring around in her head. She had to show him online dating could work for him. It would be a start anyway. If he was too scared to get out there…and if he didn't want her—which he clearly didn't—then she had to figure out a way to get his confidence up. *No he definitely doesn't see me that way. We shared a bed in New York, and I was half naked for God's sake. He had a perfect opportunity then and didn't bloody take it. More's the pity.* She just had to come up with a plan. But she would have to be devious. Very devious. Make him think it was his idea. Yes that would work…wouldn't it? Or she could just… *Oh yes, that's it.* Operation *Get Adam Laid* was going to come into full force. Soon.

Very soon.

Arriving home in the early morning hours whilst it was still dark, Lily's mind was still whirring. Adam had offered for her to stay at his house but she declined, preferring her own bed and surroundings in which to cogitate on her mischievous plan. She stripped and dressed in her comfy pyjamas and collapsed onto her bed.

Sleep eluded her for hours, and after dozing, she made her way downstairs. She fired up her laptop and did an Internet search for the website that Hannah had tried to get *her* to sign up for. Made For Each Other was quoted as being the *matchmaking experience of a lifetime for individuals whose lives are just so hectic that love takes second place.* She quickly scanned through a couple of profiles and decided that this was the one.

She clicked on *Build Profile* and began to do her best to make Adam sound as appealing as possible. *Who am I kidding? He is bloody gorgeous. And he's funny, kind, caring... Hell, I wish he didn't think of me as his bloody relative or something.* She sighed and went to make coffee. Once she had shaken her self-destructive train of thought, she returned to her computer to continue with her mission. After completing the personal details of her best friend, she began to trawl through the photos she had of Adam in order to find a suitable one for his profile. There were so many, and if he ever saw them he would wonder why on earth she had them all. To say she was slightly obsessed would be an understatement.

Once the profile was complete, she flicked through it to make sure it was the best it could be. The photo she had chosen showed him with a beautiful smile on his face and his hair flopping onto his forehead. A line of stubble enhanced the strong square line of his jaw, and his eyes had a come hither glint to them. The photo alone would attract any female with a pulse.

Feeling herself getting tired, she decided to nap on the sofa. She awoke abruptly when someone sat at the end near her feet. Looking up, she realised it was Adam.

She sat up. "Hey. I didn't hear you come in." She yawned.

"No...I was very quiet." He smiled that smile that made her core clench and she stifled a moan.

"What's up? What're you doing here? I thought you'd be shattered after the flight."

"I was, but I needed to see you."

"Oh? Why? What's up?"

He stood and gazed down at her. The look in his eyes was one she had never seen before. It looked like...like *lust*. She gazed into his hooded eyes feeling more than a little confused. He dropped to his knees and without speaking he ran his hand down her cheek and to her breast. He molded it in his hand and she gasped.

"Adam?" He stopped her mouth with a deep, wet, luscious kiss. This was really strange behaviour. She had no clue what was going on, but couldn't bring herself to stop him. Especially when he reached up and removed his shirt. She lifted her hands to touch his sculpted abs and they trembled under her touch. He closed his eyes briefly, and when they opened, he bent again to kiss her. His hand began to slip lower...lower...lower until she arched her back and closed her eyes as he slipped his fingers inside her pyjamas and caressed her. The feeling was like nothing she had ever experienced, and she couldn't help the whimper that escaped.

Somewhere she could hear music playing. She felt as though she were at the end of a tunnel as the sensations of Adam's skilled touch washed over her body. On the verge of exploding, the music got louder...louder...louder.

Suddenly, she sat bolt upright. *Shit*. That had been one very vivid, very erotic dream. She reached for her phone.

"Hello?" She answered breathlessly.

"Good grief, Lil, what've you been doing?"

Adam.

Heat rose in her cheeks. "Erm...nothing, I was just...erm...sleeping and you woke me."

He chuckled down the line. "Oh yeah? Did I wake you from a dirty dream or something?"

How the hell? "Don't be ridiculous, Adders, I just had to hunt for my phone. I thought maybe it was an emergency or something and I panicked. That's all. Good grief."

His laugh got louder. "I think the lady doth protest too much."

She huffed. "Okay…you got me…you and I were shagging, Adam. Is that better?"

He stopped laughing. "Alright, stroppy cow. So you weren't having a dirty dream. I was only jesting." He sounded sulky. He was even oblivious to the bloody truth!

She sighed in exasperation. "What do you want, Adders?"

"I was just sitting here feeling bored and wondered if you fancied getting a take-away or something?"

"Yeah…okay. What time is it?"

"It's…erm…six thirty." Shit she had been asleep hours. And clearly looking through her Adam photos had *not* helped her current state of mind.

"Okay. Give me an hour to get a shower and change. Pick something up on the way over. I'll have my usual. I've got wine." And with that she hung up, threw herself back into the sofa, and blew out a long breath. Her thoughts flitted back to her dream and shivers traversed her spine. She smiled to herself. *If only it had been real.*

Chapter Twenty-Three

Back in The Saddle (Aerosmith)
May 2010

"I seriously cannot fucking believe I let you talk me into this, Lil." Adam stood in front of his mirror reluctantly combing his thick, dark hair. "It's only been ten months and you're trying to marry me off again already. Do I cramp your style that fucking much?"

She giggled at his sulky face. "Oh shut up, you misery. And stop swearing. She sounded really nice. And no I'm not trying to marry you off. I'm trying to get you laid."

He snorted in derision. "I don't fucking want to get laid. And if I did I could find someone by myself. I cannot fucking believe you set me up on a fucking dating site! What were you thinking?"

"It's the way things are done these days. It was a very reputable website. And this woman sounded just your type. And *stop* swearing." She really hoped the photo that had been sent was a true representation and not one that was taken twenty years ago.

"She could be an axe murderer or...or a man!"

Lily burst into hysterical laughter. He folded his arms across his chest, clearly not amused. "A....a man!" She held her stomach and made a squeaking noise as she laughed. "Oh shit...I need a pee." She scurried out and headed for the bathroom.

He was overreacting, but then again, she couldn't really blame him. It was a little unfair of her to do this to him without his knowledge, never mind expecting him to go through with it. All that said, he *had* agreed, albeit reluctantly. Perhaps he *was* ready to get back in the saddle, so to speak. She was only in the country every few months, and so she had to do something. She knew she could never have him herself, but she wanted to see him happy. Maybe if she had some control over *whom* he was happy with…

She returned to the bedroom where Adam sat on the bed. He was leaning forward and resting his elbows on his knees. He was wearing black trousers and a black shirt, open at the neck. His grey jacket gave a smart image but the lack of tie added a casual edge.

"Right you. Get on. She'll be outside the Dragon at eight. I'll call you at half past and if it's a no go… Well, you know the drill." She had even booked the Chinese restaurant for them to dine at. In her own opinion she was a bloody good friend. It was a shame that Adam didn't agree at that present moment.

♥♥♥

Adam reluctantly walked toward the Chinese restaurant cursing Lily under his breath. There was a woman waiting outside. As he approached her, he saw her face scrunch. *Oh great. That's a bloody good start.*

"Are you Adam?" she asked as he got closer.

"Yes…I am. Molly?"

She smiled and held out her hand. "That's me." She snorted. "I couldn't see what you looked like until you were in front of me. I usually wear specs but I didn't put them on tonight…you know…I wanted to make a good impression." She snorted again.

He was a little befuddled. "Why? Is that because bespectacled people are all bad?" he said dryly.

Molly snorted again and smacked his arm. "Oh…hilarious! I can see you're going to keep me entertained."

He forced a smile. She was quite pretty really. But there was no spark. And that snort… Well, that was akin to nails down a chalkboard. He held the door open for her. *God, if you are listening, please let Lil ring on time.*

They were shown to the waiting area. The restaurant was busy and their table wasn't ready yet. "So what do you do, Adam?" Lily had told her exactly what he did for a living on the profile that she had created. Had Molly even bothered to read the damn thing?

He cleared his throat. "I teach English in high school."

Another snort. "Oh yes! Of course you do! Silly me." Good grief she could give Peppa Pig a run for her money. "I hate kids, personally. Horrible little swines, they are."

He felt like he was in hell. He pulled his phone out of his pocket and checked the time. *Great.* Another twenty minutes to endure until Lily was due to ring.

"Well, I'll just go to the little girl's room," Molly informed him. "I need to make room for the nice bottle of wine I'm sure you'll be buying us." And yes, there it was…the snort…*again.*

He nodded frantically. "Well, I'm driving actually, but…yes…yes, that's fine…take your time." He smiled. Once she was gone, he grabbed his phone out and dialled Lily. She answered breezily after one ring.

He growled at her down the phone. "I'm going to fucking kill you."

"Well, I hope this is Adam because if not I'll be reporting whoever you are to the police." She sniggered.

"She's gone to the toilet, so get me the fuck out of here…now. I can't spend another second in the company of this kid-hating-porcine-impersonating woman!"

"Yikes…that good, eh?"

"She snorts, Lil. She snorts *a lot.*" He could hear Lily laughing at the other end of the phone. It only served to make him more cross.

"Oh dear, that doesn't sound good, Adders."

He glanced up and saw Molly making her way back to the table, he had to think on his feet. "Oh no, what a shame. Of course I'll be right there." He feigned disappointment.

"Is she back?" Lily sniggered.

"Yes, yes that's right. Isn't it terrible?"

"Has she snorted at you again yet?"

He bit his lip to stifle the laugh trying to erupt. "No, no not yet. We've only just arrived. Don't worry about it."

"So back to mine for a take-away then, eh?" Lily was clearly enjoying his discomfort. She would pay later.

"Oh yes, that would be a good idea. Yes, you'd better give them a call about that." Molly's expression showed concern.

"Right, I'm on it like a car bonnet, Adders. Indian or Chinese?" Lily asked

"Oh, I think maybe the first option would be the more acceptable."

"Okay, see you in ten."

"Yes, yes, ten is good. See you soon. Take care."

"Oh and Adders?"

"Yes? Yes?" After a brief pause Lily snorted long and loud down the line into his ear. He burst out laughing and covered his mouth, disguising his hysteria as a cough, and hung up.

Molly sidled over and patted his back. "Oh, Adam, are you okay? Should I get you a drink?"

He held his hand up and shook his head. Once he had composed himself, he sat up straight. "I'm so very sorry, but that was my…erm…sister. She's…erm…broken down and I have to go help. She's…erm…going to ring her insurance company, but I need to go and…well you know…help out." He was a terrible liar. He knew that his story was full of holes, but thankfully Molly was clearly quite dense as she patted his knee.

"Oh no, that's terrible. You should go. Family is clearly very important to you. We can do this another time."

He suddenly felt very guilty.

They said their goodbyes and he took her number, feeling yet another twinge of guilt as he knew there was no way on earth he was likely to call her.

Ever.

He got into his car and drove over to Lily's. He leaned on the doorframe suddenly feeling drained. He pressed the doorbell. She opened the door and burst out laughing at him.

He scowled. "Shut up, you cow." He shoved past her in a major strop.

"Oh come on, Adders. It can't have been that bad."

"Oh yes, it fucking can. Honestly, Lil. She snorted after every sentence. I swear at one point I expected her to tell me she lived in a house made of sticks!"

Lily held her stomach as she laughed. "That's so funny!"

He slumped onto the sofa. "Funny for you." He sniggered, suddenly allowing himself to see the funny side. "Oh, Lil, don't do that to me again, eh?"

She plopped down beside him and smacked his leg. "It won't be like that every time though. Whether it's from the website or anywhere else, eventually you'll have to give someone a chance, you know."

His expression became serious again as he turned toward her. "Lil, why are you so hell bent on matchmaking for me?" He caught her eyes in his gaze. She opened her mouth to speak but closed it again.

After what felt like an eternity she jumped up. "Ooh, I bought wine! You can sleep in the spare room if you like." She skipped off to the kitchen.

♥♥♥

After their take-away had been delivered and they had eaten their fill, they sat in silence drinking red wine. They had already sunk two bottles and Lily had bought a third. Adam knew he would feel shocking in the morning. But he was a big boy…he would cope.

Feeling emboldened by the imbibed alcohol, Adam decided to ask the million-dollar question. "So, Lil, have you ever actually been *in love*?"

A look of horror spread over her face and she seemed to be struggling for the words to reply. Her mouth opening and closing rather like a goldfish. Her brow scrunched and she fiddled with the hem of her lace top.

He sniggered. "What's up? It's not a trick question you know." His words slurred slightly.

Finally she laughed out loud. It sounded forced. "Me? I don't have time to be in love. I'm either travelling around the world reporting on shit going on abroad, or I'm looking after you. When do *I* get the time for love?"

He pouted at her insinuation that he needed looking after. "Nah, come on, there must have been someone. In *all these years*, there must have been someone? Chris! That guy from Oz! You reeeeally liked him." He nudged her with his shoulder.

"He was fit…and he was good in bed. But that's kind of where it stopped. He wanted more but…"

"But what?"

"Oh for fuck's sake, Adders, is it interrogate Lily day?" She looked angry now. "Just drop it, okay?"

He formed an *O* with his mouth. "There *was* someone! I can tell by how cagey you're being. Come on, Lil, I'm your best friend. Come on, you can tell me."

Her chest was falling and rising at a rapid rate and her lips were pursed. "I. Said. Drop. It." Her words were sharp and measured.

He grinned widely. "Oooh, I've hit a nerve...wait a minute." He suddenly sat bolt upright. "Oh fuck...I...I think I've figured it out." He felt the colour drain from his face.

A look of panic washed over her features. "You have?" She scraped the hair back from her face, clearly alarmed.

He leaned in close again and rested his forehead on hers. "I'm so sorry I never realised, Lil. And it's okay...it really is okay. It explains such a lot."

She closed her eyes and bit on her bottom lip. "Oh shit."

"I always wondered why you couldn't be around us, and why no relationship you ever had was very long. It's okay, Lil." He stroked her cheek as she held her breath.

"Is it?" she breathed.

"Of course it is. How could it not be?"

"I was just...scared to say..."

"I know, I understand, but you're my best friend in the whole world. I couldn't care less if you like girls, and I totally understand why you were in love with Eve."

Chapter Twenty-Four

Sketches of Spain {*For Miles*} (Buckethead)
June 2010

Two weeks after Adam's apparent light bulb moment, a cab was dropping Lily off at Edinburgh Airport. Soon she would be bound for the Spanish sunshine on a research trip for an upcoming piece for a Scottish television news channel about package holidays, the increased prices, and the effect it was having on tourism. She was happy to be escaping once again.

She had informed Adam that he was, in fact, totally incorrect about his conclusion that she was gay…or bi. He had blushed and apologised profusely, and thankfully his embarrassment at his presumption had rendered him incapable of pushing her further, even though she was sure he must have questions. After all, she had allowed him to know that there was *someone* she'd been in love with. Fortunately, he appeared too dense to put two and two together and come up with anything remotely close to four.

It would be good to be back in Spain. She felt quite at home there. Lenora Abalos, Lily's mother, had met her soul mate Alexander Macrae, Lily's father, when he was on a holiday with his friends. It had been love at first sight. Lenora had come to Scotland to live, and since then, the two had had a wonderful marriage. Lily craved what her parents had, the togetherness and closeness. Lily's looks had definitely come from her mother, and her dad had always called her his little Spanish jewel.

The distance from Adam was needed again especially after the drunken conversation following his disastrous date. She thought he'd figured it all out and was rather gutted when she realised he was way off the mark. Her secret would remain in place indefinitely now. She would be home again in a couple of weeks and would have to face him again. She couldn't avoid him. Anyway, she needed her Adam fix. He was, after all, her drug of choice.

Descending the plane after the short flight was a welcome relief, although the wall of heat that hit her when she exited the airport had her gasping for air. Her hair had done that crazy wild thing it did whenever she was around humidity. She jumped in a cab and headed for her hotel. After checking in and locating her room, the first thing she did was jump in the shower. The cooling water lowered her temperature sufficiently to ease her discomfort.

She tumbled onto her bed and reached for her phone. She had missed a call from Adam, and he had texted. Against her better judgment, she clicked to open the message.

A: Wish u had let me take u 2 airport u daft bat. Hv had another request for a date from pig-woman n another from someone called Sapphire...wot do I do?

Lily huffed her frustration and hit reply.

L: Stop being so mean abt pig-woman. She can't help it. N how the F shd I know what u shd do abt Sapphire?! What do u want 2 do?

Moments later a response came.

A: Spose I cd meet her? U neva know eh? Although I think it's all 2 soon to try and meet 'the 1'

Lily had secretly hoped he would give up on dating. It had been a bad idea on her part, but she appeared to have created a monster. And what the hell? He was talking about meeting *the one*? Dammit. This had well and truly backfired on her, hadn't it?

She hit reply.

L: Go 4 it. Can you manage to dress yourself without me there? She sniggered as she hit send. And as expected the reply was lightning quick.

A: F off! Cheeky sod! Will let u know how it goes. Bye Cheesy. Okay, so the childish nicknames were back, were they?

L: Later pee pants. She chuckled to herself as she hit send. He didn't reply.

Lily decided to go for a wander in the touristy part of town and check out what was on offer in this commonly sought after holiday destination. It wasn't yet time for the major school holidays, but she would have the opportunity to earmark some locations prior to her next trip, which is when the camera crew would join her.

She walked along a promenade lined with huge hotels, all white washed against the blazing Spanish summer heat. There were a wide variety of stalls selling handmade jewellery and locally made artefacts. She honed in on an artist's stall. He sat there, bare chested and tanned, grinning at her. His dark hair was thick and wavy. He had the beginnings of a beard, but was probably around twenty-four-years old.

Handsome guy nodded at her as she perused his artwork. "Hola, bonita." He grinned.

"Hola." She smiled back and felt her cheeks heat.

"Ves algo que te gusta?" he asked her, raising his eyebrows and curling his mouth up sexily. *Do I see something I like? How about you?* She bit her lip trying not to giggle at his obvious double entendre.

"Sí, ¿Cuánto es este dibujo?" she asked how much for the sketch she was pointing at.

"Is you English?" the handsome Spaniard asked.

"Sí, pero yo hablo español." She informed him that she was happy to converse in his language.

"Yes…and you speak it very well," he complimented her. "I give you the sketch, but in return you give me…erm…dinner?"

She gasped at the forward nature of the shirtless Spanish hunk. "You want me to buy you dinner?"

The man shook his head, clearly exasperated with himself. "No…mierda…my English is not as best as your Spanish, bonita. I think I ask you to go for dinner conmigo…*with* me. I take you, si?"

Lily stood for a few minutes gawping at the man whilst a beautiful smile played on his lips. He was quite a few years younger than her, but she couldn't find any reason why that should matter.

After discovering the gorgeous, muscular Spaniard was called Rafael Gaspar and was in actual fact twenty-five, she agreed to go to dinner with him. It became apparent that his uncle owned a restaurant on the seafront, and she agreed to meet him there at seven thirty. He had wrapped the beautiful sketch of the promenade and given it to her as a gift.

After showering, she dressed in a white linen dress that came just below her knees. The fitted bodice negated the need for a bra, but she draped a cerise pashmina around her shoulders and cerise jewelled sandals on her feet. Her pretty woven wicker bag finished off the look perfectly. Thankfully, her natural curls were behaving themselves in the cooler temperatures of the evening.

She could see Rafael standing outside the restaurant. He looked divine. He was wearing a pale blue granddad collared linen shirt and beige linen trousers. On his feet were tan coloured thong sandals. His thick dark hair was swept from his face in waves, and his bearded face greeted her with a warm smile. He had the most stunning blue eyes, the colour of the sea.

He leaned in and kissed her on both cheeks. "Hola, hermosa."

"Hola, guapo." Rafael smiled. Clearly he liked being called handsome.

"I have reserve a table so we eat now, si?" He gestured for her to walk ahead of him.

They were greeted by his uncle, who informed her that her beauty was beyond measure. *I could get used to this.* They were presented with a bottle of the finest red wine on offer, which was made at a local vineyard. Lily unabashedly ordered Paella – predictable but it was her favourite. The food was wonderful and Rafael kept her entertained with stories from the time he had spent travelling. They had that in common, and she told him all about Australia, a place he claimed he was desperate to visit.

"So, you are a journalist now, si?"

"That's right. I'm here to do a piece about tourism."

Rafael nodded thoughtfully. "It is…erm…how do I say? Less tourists now. The money is not…erm…easy…you understand?"

Bless him. He insisted on speaking in English even though Lily had informed him numerous times that she was fluent in Spanish. She found it endearing. "Yes, you're quite right. Money is tighter and people don't have enough to spend on luxuries such as holidays. It's okay for me. I get to travel for work." She smiled. "I see lots of places."

He stared at her mouth as she spoke. His eyes snapped up to hers. "Lo siento…I get distract by your accent…it is very beautiful."

She sipped her wine and looked everywhere except into his eyes. She feared she might fall in and drown. She was already feeling the familiar effects of lust coursing through her veins, and she knew very well where this evening was heading. Well at least she *hoped* she knew.

"I may please walk you back to your hotel?" Rafael broke her away from the road her thoughts had decided to travel and she placed her glass down.

"Look…Rafael…I think you're very sweet…very handsome too, but I…I'm not looking for a relationship. I thought I ought to point that out right away. I'm only here for a week and—

He reached over and took her hand, halting her words. "I know this…I know I am not someone you want to keep. But I desire you and I hope that you desire also me. Perhaps we walk a little?" His eyes were tinged with sadness. He was truly stunning. Young but mature in his outlook. If she was staying for any length of time, she could see herself falling into those eyes regularly.

"Si, let's walk, Rafael."

He linked her fingers with his own as they strolled along the seafront. Every so often he would glance over and smile at her. Suddenly, he stopped and turned to face her. His expression had become serious, and he stepped into her, sliding one arm around her waist as the other cupped her face. "Lily, I know this is…lo siento…I am not thinking of the words. I know what you say about relationships…" She could see that he was struggling. "Quiero hacer el amor contigo…this is how I mean. Me entiendes?"

Lily's breath caught. Being told by an incredibly sexy Spaniard that he wants to make love to you was not an everyday occurrence, but it was one she liked…very much. "Sí entiendo." Of course she understood. Even if the verbal language had evaded her, the body language hadn't.

"And what is your answer to this, Lily?" His warm breath caressed her lips as he leaned in so that his were almost touching hers. Instead of using verbal language, she responded by pulling him down into a long, wet, lingering kiss. She stroked her tongue over his, and a low growl emanated from his chest. Electric shocks fired throughout her body and she was ready to rip his clothes off there and then, but managed to restrain herself.

When she pulled away and looked into his eyes, her own lust was reflected back at her. He smiled and stroked her cheek. "I take you to my home." He grabbed her hand with urgency and began to lead her along the road. *Oh good grief…I'm such a tart*, she thought as she followed him willingly.

Eventually, they arrived at a small apartment block, and he stopped and turned to her. "Lily, are you sure? I am not a crazy man. I swear this… But…how can I say… Usted me no conoce… You understand? You…um…know me not, and I don't want to ask this if—"

Lily stopped his mouth with a kiss. She had to stop him from talking her out of this. She wanted him even if it was only for tonight. She needed to feel something other than her woes over Adam.

Over the years sex had become her distraction of choice and it was working well, for the most part. To hell with the consequences. He grinned against her mouth and led her up a whitewashed stone staircase to the second floor. When he opened the door, she was pleasantly surprised. She had expected an untidy sham of a room. Something akin to a crash pad belonging to a student. Instead, white walls in an open plan living, kitchen, and dining area greeted her. The walls were adorned with his own stunning artwork. Glancing down she noted a tiled floor, which she surmised would be cool underfoot in the scorching temperatures. A leather sofa and a log burner in the corner provided a cosy and homely feeling to the bright, modern space. A small balcony looked out over a communal garden.

"It is a small apartment. I have it from my uncle. He lets me to live here."

"It's lovely Rafael," she said as she admired his beautiful artwork.

He sauntered slowly toward her. "I like how I hear you say my name." Coming to a halt before her he stroked a finger down her arm, sending shivers through her body that settled in her core. "I need to feel you. Por favour, Lily?"

"Si, Rafael."

He covered her mouth with his and fisted a hand in her hair. His arousal pressed into her as his other hand grasped her bottom and pulled her into him. He broke away and pulled her by the hand through a door to the left. Another white room. This one had a large black wrought iron bed in the centre. He let go of her hand and pulled his shirt off over his head, revealing his muscular chest with the dark smattering of hair Lily had enjoyed looking at the day before. She gasped at the sight of him, stepped forward, and lightly dragged her finger nails down his torso. He closed his eyes and inhaled through his teeth.

He turned her around and slid the zipper of her dress down her back, pushing the shoulder straps down her arms and letting the dress fall to the floor. She stepped out of it and turned to face him in just her white lace panties.

He groaned. "Hermoso pechos...Lily...you have beautiful breasts." His eyes were filled with lust as he stepped toward her and cupped one breast running his thumb over the tight bud.

Lily moaned and let her head roll back. She heard a zipper and opened her eyes to see him standing before her in all his naked glory. His arousal strong and ready to take her. He pulled her to him and together they tumbled onto the bed. He caressed her breasts and took each nipple into his mouth for a lingering wet kiss. Pleasure rocketed through her body, resting at her core as she grasped and tugged at his thick hair.

He slid his hand into the front of her panties and stroked her slowly and languidly. Once he had touched her for a few moments and almost sent her soaring, he slipped her panties down her legs, kissing her stomach, and mumbling incoherently in Spanish. She didn't much care what he was saying. Placing himself between her thighs, he sheathed himself before hovering over her and gazing longingly into her eyes. She could tell he wanted confirmation that this was okay once again, but he had given up on words. She simply nodded and pulled him toward her body. He entered her on a slow thrust.

He caressed her body with his mouth and fingers while he feathered her skin with kisses. He continued his Spanish words of passion telling her how incredible her body felt around his and how he could stay like this forever. They rolled around the large bed, their sweat covered bodies sliding together as their breathing became one combined staccato rhythm. His biceps flexed and stretched as he held himself over her, and she wrapped her legs around his waist. They both cried out in unison and collapsed in a tangled heap of racing heartbeats and entwined fingers.

Rafael was a skilled lover and brought her to orgasm several more times that night. Afterwards as they lay in bed, she told him that on completion of the brief research trip she was heading back to the UK to be with a friend for an important anniversary—she didn't explain about Adam or the fact that it was his wife who had died a year ago—and that she would return shortly afterwards to film the piece she had been working on. He asked if he could see her again and she agreed. The sex, after all, had been pretty amazing. But yet again, she was very much aware, on her part, that it was *just* sex. There was no emotional connection. There never would be.

Chapter Twenty-Five

Owner of a Lonely Heart (Yes)
July 2010

Lily had been gone almost a week and was due back in a couple of days. The anniversary of Eve's death was looming, and Adam was relieved to know that she'd be back with him to help him get through it. She was only home for a few days, however, and was getting straight on another flight to cover yet another story in yet another foreign country. That was the nature of their friendship. One needed the other and there they were. No questions asked. Except it seemed to be Adam doing all the needing these days.

Thankfully the anniversary fell in the school holidays, meaning he could take his time to wallow in his misery and reminisce about the happy times in his life when everything actually worked and he smiled frequently. The times when his world revolved around Eve and things were all about the future. Not the past. These days everything was about the past.

Lily arrived on his doorstep at eleven o'clock on the dreaded day. He hadn't been sleeping and it was evident, he knew from looking in the mirror, thanks to the dark circles around his eyes and the five o'clock shadow covering his square jaw.

"Come on, Adders, I've got junk food, beer, and Monty Python. We'll get through this," she said as she stepped over the threshold.

Just seeing her had his lip quivering. "A year, Lil…a fucking year. How does time go so fucking fast?" His voice broke.

Dropping the bags, she wrapped her arms around him as he sobbed. Eventually she pulled away. "Come on, you big cry-baby." She smiled sadly. "You're getting snot all over my best coat." She reached up and wiped tears from his cheeks with her thumbs.

He sobbed out a laugh. "Whoops...sorry 'bout that." He attempted to wipe the wet patches away.

Giggling, Lily slapped his hand away. "Oy, just because you're grieving doesn't mean you can cop a feel."

With a smile tugging at his lips, he shook his head and rolled his eyes. She always managed to cheer him up. Even if she did make light of the most serious of situations. He knew that this was how she handled him. She was the only one who could get away with it, that's for sure.

♥♥♥

After more tears and quite a few beers, they were both comfortably tipsy and stuffed full of cheese loaded food.

Lily nudged him. "So what did you decide about that Sapphire woman? Did you go out with her?"

Adam shook his head slowly. "Not been back in touch yet."

"Oh? Why's that? If you like the sound of her, you should meet her." Lily suggested, not really knowing why she was encouraging him.

"D'you think so? I mean...she can't be any worse than pig lady, can she?"

Lily smirked as she remembered that whole situation. "Exactly. She might be just what you need. Maybe you just need sex, Adders." She shrugged. "You're a man after all. Men *need* sex." She wagged a finger in his face. He started laughing but she had no clue why. "Oy, why're you fucking laughing at me, pee pants?" She poked his arm with her bottle.

He leaned close to her with a wide smile. "You just make me laugh. Men *need* sex. You make it sound like we can't function without it. Well, I can tell you that *I* have for a year and I'm still alive."

She swallowed hard. He was so close to her that his warm breath tickled her nose. It made her nervous. Not because she was afraid of him. But because she was afraid of herself. The urge to grab him and kiss him was coiled deep within her. She couldn't throw a jibe back. Nothing sprang to mind. She was rendered speechless just by his close proximity.

His face became serious. "And what about women?" he whispered.

"W-what *about* women?" she croaked, her eyelids fluttering.

"Don't they *need* sex?" His voice was low and gruff and he emphasised the word *need* making her core clench.

She swallowed again. "I…I s-suppose *some* do."

He reached and tucked a curl behind her ear. His voice still a whisper, he asked, "Do you *need* sex, Lil?"

She pulled her brow into a frown. "I'm sorry?"

He leaned closer still so that his nose was almost touching hers. "Are you one of those women who *need* sex?" *What the fuck?* Lily had no clue what was making him behave like this. She blamed the alcohol. She desperately wanted this to be the *real* Adam, but deep down she knew that just wasn't the case.

Suddenly feeling very sober, Lily smiled. Trying to alleviate the tension that had descended between them, she pushed his chest and chuckled. "Why? Are you offering your services?"

He didn't move for a long moment. He cleared his throat. "What would you say if I was?"

A needful heat pooled between her thighs as she struggled for what to say in answer to him. Her eyelids fluttered. "Erm…erm…I—"

He sat bolt upright and rubbed his hand over his face. "Ha ha! Your face! Your face was so serious!" He pulled himself to his feet. "I need to go pee." He left the room quickly and she sat there reeling from what had just happened. What *had* just happened? Was he kidding around? Or was he seriously asking her for sex? *Shittyshittyfuck! What. The. Hell?*

When Adam returned to the room, he sat in the chair opposite where she remained in stunned silence on the floor. "Lil, sorry about that. I…I was messing… I've had too much beer. You must have been scared to death that I meant it. Well I was jesting, okay?"

Tears stabbed her eyes. "You shit," was all she could say.

He ran his hands through his hair. "Oh hey, come on. I didn't mean to offend you. It was stupid. I'm sorry."

She clambered to her feet. Her legs wobbled. "I'm off to bed…*alone*."

She made her way up to the spare room and after collapsing on the bed, she cried herself to sleep.

♥♥♥

Adam awoke to a banging headache. He thought back to the events of last night. *What a prick.* He was very much aware he had almost lost his best friend after nearly making a drunken pass at her. *Fucking, knobbing idiot. That's what talking about sex when you haven't had any for so long does to you. Stupid, stupid tit.* Alcohol, Lily, grief, and talking about sex were clearly not a good combination for him. Huh, go figure. *Good job she knows me and knows I can be a complete arsehole.*

He made his way downstairs and set a pot of fresh coffee brewing. Ten minutes later whilst he sat at the tiny table at one end of the kitchen, Lily walked in.

He nervously stood. "Hey…Lil…look I'm sorry about my behaviour last night. I'm so ashamed. I know I was a complete wanker. You need to know that I respect you, and you really didn't deserve that."

Her cheeks coloured. "What?"

"You know…what happened…what I…erm…said to you…you know about…sex."

She shrugged her shoulders and snorted. "Oh that? You tit, it was just a bit of messing about."

He huffed a huge sigh of relief. "Thank fuck. I was terrified I'd crossed a line. I'm so, so sorry. I was drunk and being a tosser."

She smirked. "Clearly not enough of one if you were still coming on to me!"

He felt heat rising in his cheeks. "Shit, Lil. What you must think of me. You're my best friend in the world, for fuck's sake." He ran his hand through his hair.

"Oh give up, you nutter. Just forget it. I have." And just like that the matter was brushed under the carpet.

Lily left for Spain again the next day.

Arriving back in Spain was a relief for Lily. At least she would have that temporary distance she needed to get her head on straight again. She met with Rafael and had a couple of nights of mind-blowing sex.

Saying goodbye to Rafael was not the easiest thing she had ever done. He had asked for her number saying he wanted to keep in touch. But Lily convinced him what they had shared was something they shouldn't taint by dragging things out. She knew the inevitable would happen, and Adam would crawl into her brain to stop her from falling in love. It was pointless allowing herself to get close. Rafael had been reluctant. He insisted they could see how things progressed and that the distance wasn't so great. But her final answer had been *no*. Her final answer was always no.

♥♥♥

After what had happened when Lily was at his house, Adam had taken the plunge and arranged a date with Sapphire. He regretted it immediately. Lily wasn't there to help him figure out what to wear or where to take her. He hadn't dated in so long he felt like a complete novice. At least with Lily here it felt more do-able.

He was meeting Sapphire in Melrose where she lived. They had arranged their rendezvous at seven thirty outside a little bistro that served Mediterranean food. Sapphire was slightly younger than him at twenty-six. She sounded very sweet when he talked to her on the phone but nerves were getting the better of him. He dressed in black jeans and a white shirt.

When he addressed himself in the mirror, he shook his head. "You look like a fucking waiter." It was too late to change completely, and so he swapped his black jacket for the slate grey one. He still felt too dressed up and wished he had washed the ketchup mark off his blue jeans in time. He huffed and made his way out to the car.

As he climbed into the driver's seat, he felt his phone vibrate in his pocket. He pulled it out and opened the text from Lily.

L: Good luck, Adders. Hope she is the 1

Yeah right. He didn't even really want to look for *the one*. He'd had her and lost her thanks to some drunken dickhead. He was shaking and struggled to get his key into the ignition. If he didn't have a conscience, he would have texted Sapphire and cancelled. But unlucky for him he did have a conscience, and it wouldn't let him leave her stranded.

He arrived and hung around outside the restaurant for a while. There was no sign of a woman fitting Sapphire's description. He paced up and down a little and checked his watch a few times. Still no sign. He checked for his phone and realised he had left it in the dashboard tray in his car. After waiting for twenty minutes past the time they were due to meet, he jogged back to the car. His phone was reading three missed calls. There was no voice mail but there was a text message.

He clicked to open the message.

S: Adam, you seemed very sweet on the phone and I hate to do this but I can't go through with it. My ex has been in touch and wants to meet to talk things through. We were together for five years and I think I owe it to both of us to hear him out. I'm so sorry. Please don't think too poorly of me. All the best, Sapphire.

He ran his hands through his hair as a mixture of relief and disappointment washed over him. *Dumped by a fucking text. Great. It gets better, eh?*

He sent a simple message back that told her not to worry and that he wished her well. He drove home, stopping at the off license to pick up some crisps and a bottle of beer. *Oh what a pitiful life I lead.*

As he flicked through the channels on the TV, he decided he needed to hear Lily's voice, and so he located her in his mobile phones address book and clicked call. She answered within a couple of rings.

"Why are you ringing me?" she snapped.

"Hello to you too, *best friend*. Lovely to speak to you," he grumbled at her response.

"Sorry, Adders…but again…why are you ringing me? Shouldn't you be out with Sapphire? Oh God, don't tell me she was a snorter too?"

"I wouldn't know."

Lily sighed. "Oh Adders, don't tell me you chickened out."

"No...*I* didn't. *She* did. She texted...bloody late too...to say that she'd had a change of heart about meeting me. I waited for her for twenty minutes, Lil. I feel like a total prick."

"Oh heck. I'm sorry to hear that, and you're not a prick." She was silent for a few minutes. "There *will* be someone out there, Adam. I know there will."

"I'm not even sure I *want* someone. I feel like I've had my shot at true love. Maybe you only get one chance to have it so good."

"Now you don't really believe that do you, Adders? I think there's more than one someone out there for everyone. I don't think we're just destined for one individual. How unfair would it be if that were true?"

He rubbed his hand over his face. "When are you home?"

"Middle of next week. We got the footage we needed. Oh and...I met someone."

He sat up. "Did you?" He tried to sound enthusiastic but ended up sounding surprised instead. He cringed.

She huffed. "Yes, thanks for making that sound like an impossible feat. I'm not completely repulsive to the opposite sex, you know." She sounded pissed off and he didn't blame her.

"Sorry, I didn't mean it to come out like that. So...who is he? I take it he was a *he*?" He sniggered.

"Very funny, shit head. Yes, he was a very sexy Spanish *he*. Rafael Gaspar. He was amazing in bed."

He gasped. "Lily! You have to learn to say *no*."

"Why? He was hot and I fancied him."

"So are you seeing him again?"

"No, it was pointless. It wouldn't have gone anywhere."

"I suppose not with him in Spain and you...well, wherever work takes you I guess, eh?"

"Exactly. Anyway, sod off, will you? I'm exhausted and I want to sleep."

"Charming. Well, I'll see you when you get back. Bye."

"Bye, pee pants." She hung up before he could respond.

Chapter Twenty-Six

Something I can Never Have (Nine Inch Nails)
August 2010

Having Lily back in Scotland made Adam feel more settled. What *didn't* make him feel settled was the fact his profile on the dating site was getting a lot of attention. He was being bombarded with emails and had no real clue why.

"Errr, hello…anybody in there?" Lily knocked on his forehead with her knuckles.

He swiped her hand away. "Fuck off!"

"Well, come on and get with the bloody programme, will you, you tit."

He scrunched his face at her. "What are you going on about?"

She gazed up at the ceiling momentarily and shook her head, clearly feeling exasperated at his complete and utter obliviousness. "Good grief. Do I have to spell it out to you? Really?"

"I just don't see it myself. I mean I look in the mirror and I just see…*me*… I think you over exaggerated when you wrote that fucking profile. Any woman who meets me is just going to be disappointed." He slumped backward on her sofa, rubbing his hands though his hair. She was putting the finishing touches to her make-up after convincing him to go out for a few drinks in town.

She paused and turned to him, sighing. "Adam, you are *most* women's bloody dream man."

He scrunched his face at her again until she stood, hands on hips, staring at him incredulously. *Most women?*

Shaking her head, she began to count off on her fingers. "Okay, you're tall, you're dark, you're muscular, you're handsome…you know…if you *like* that kind of look—"

"Charming, thanks, I feel so much better."

"I haven't finished."

"Oh, I apologise. Do continue. This is helping me to no end."

"Shut up. You have a noble profession—"

"*Do* I?"

"Durrr…Adam, you're a teacher. *Some* women find that sexy as hell."

He snorted. "Again, thanks."

"You own your own home, you earn a decent wage, and you have a nice smile—"

He grinned. "I do?"

Her cheeks coloured. "According to the women I know, you do."

"You don't know that many women. You only know two that I'm aware of and they're both old enough to be my Gran."

She rolled her eyes. "Do you know what? Fuck off and I won't try to help you then."

Adam sniggered. "No, please do carry on. I'm sorry."

"You have what they call the complete package, Adders."

He felt the heat in his cheeks rise, and he placed his hands over his groin. "What do you know about my package?"

She blushed. "Not *that* package, you idiot! You *are* the complete package! I wasn't talking about what's in your trousers!" She shook her head. "I mean you have the full gambit. You know…the full monty—"

"There you go again talking about me getting my package out!"

She threw her arms up. "Not the Full Monty as in the male strippers, you tit!"

He pondered things for a moment. "So you think I have a lot to offer a woman and that's why I'm getting a good response?"

She burst out laughing. "Finally, the penny has dropped. God, you can be dense sometimes."

♥♥♥

The club was already heaving when they arrived. Bodies gyrated on the dance floor and the lights pulsed along with the beat. Adam felt out of place.

"Lil, why did we have to come here? I'm sure I've just seen two girls from my S5 class."

She slapped his chest. "Oh shut up moaning. Just don't hit on them and you'll be fine."

She was already quite drunk when they left the last pub. A club was not really on Adam's *to-do* list.

He gasped in disgust. "I have *no* intention of hitting on *anyone*, never mind kids from my school who are clearly drinking under age. What if they see me in here?"

"Oooh, it'll add to the rumours that you actually have a life. Won't that be terrible?" she responded sarcastically.

"One drink and then I'm off. You can come with me or you can make your own way home." He knew very well he was stuck here for as long as she wanted to stay. There was no way he would leave her to make her own way home.

"You're a boring old fart," she grumbled.

"Oy! Less of the *old*."

They made their way to the bar and after what felt like an age, he managed to get the bartender's attention. "Two bottles of whatever beer you've got."

The bartender placed two bottles in front of him. "Ten eighty."

His eyes widened. "I only asked for two! I'm not buying for the whole fucking club!"

"Aye and like I said…ten eighty." The burly looking man behind the bar stared him down.

Reluctantly, Adam handed over his cash and passed a bottle to Lily. "Savour it coz it's all you're getting at that price."

She rolled her eyes. "Boring *and* tight with your money. Forget what I said at home about you having the whole package."

They sat on the only two stools available at the bar. He glanced around the room and caught the eye of a dark-haired woman leaning up against a pillar by the dance floor. She smiled. He looked behind him to check who she was looking at. She laughed and bit her bottom lip seductively. *Shit, she really is eyeing me up.*

Lily glanced over in the direction of his gaze. She leaned into Adam and spoke directly into his ear, no doubt so she could be heard over the noise. "I think you're in with a chance there, Adders." She pulled away and looked into his eyes.

He smiled and bending forward, shouted into Lily's ear. "You think so?"

She just nodded. He glanced back over and the dark haired woman was still watching him. Lily leaned in again. "The more I lean into you, the more she licks her lips and stares. I'm making her jealous, which is making her want you more."

He scrunched his nose. "Eh?"

Lily giggled. "Women usually want either what they *can't* have…or what another woman *has*." She fought the urge to just kiss him, consequences be damned. What would he do?

"Really? Fucking hell, Lil. You're like a font of knowledge for all things female."

She gaped at him. "You make that sound like a shocking thing! I am a bloody woman, you know."

"Yeah...yeah...you are... I know, sorry."

"I'm off to go pee." She huffed and stormed off.

Shit, I've pissed her off again. This is becoming a habit. He sat there drinking his beer and minding his own business when someone touched his leg.

"Hi...is this seat taken?" He swung his head around and locked gazes with the dark-haired woman from earlier.

"I...erm...well." *Smooth Adam, very smooth.*

"Did you upset your girlfriend or will she be re-joining you?" The woman had a sultry smile.

He shook his head. "Erm...no...Lily's not my girlfriend."

"Oh good, I'll sit then. I'm Gina." She held out her hand.

He shook it a bit too firmly, like he would grasp the hand of a male colleague. "I'm Adam."

"Good to meet you, Adam."

She was quite pretty close up. Slim and petite with black hair in a very short style, a little bit like a Pixie. Her hair just covered her ears and he had to fight his semi-drunken urge to check to see if they were pointy. Her eyes were almond shaped and he couldn't really tell how old she was.

"Erm, good to meet you too. Can I get you a drink?" *Please say no.*

She held up her glass. "No thanks, I'm good...just got one."

"So...erm."

"Gina."

"So, Gina...what do you do?"

"I'm a hotel receptionist at the West Sentinel. You?"

"Teacher...high school."

"Oh wow, a brain-box then?"

He rubbed the back of his neck feeling heat rise in his cheeks. "I wouldn't say that."

"Are you kidding me? Teachers are hot." *Okay, so Lil may have had a point.*

He smiled. "Well…thanks."

Gina narrowed her eyes at him. "Are you sure that girl you were with before wasn't your girlfriend?"

He laughed. "No…she's my best friend."

She licked her lips. "Hmmm, best friend with benefits I bet."

He raised his eyebrows. "Erm…what do you mean? That we…have *sex*?"

She giggled. "Exactly. I saw how she was pawing you. She had *fuck-buddy* written all over her face. She was all possessive like."

He chuckled a little and shook his head. "Nah, it's not like that with us. I don't see her that way. We don't see *each other* that way. She's just my friend, that's all. Nothing more."

♥♥♥

No one else was in the ladies' room when Lily pushed through the door. She breathed a sigh of relief. Why was being close to him so hard tonight? She berated herself for suggesting a night out. Seeing other women flirting with him was hard. This thought lead to her next point. Why the *fuck* was she trying to set him up with other women anyway? Had she developed some kind of masochistic streak since falling in love with him? Gazing at her reflection in the mirror, Lily tried to remember a time when she hadn't loved Adam. Realising that the exercise was futile, she took a deep breath and made her way back to tell him she wanted to go home. Enough was enough tonight.

The woman who had been flirting with Adam was sitting on her bar stool when Lily arrived near to where she had been sitting. She slowed down and stood close enough to hear Adam refer to her as *just his friend and nothing more*. Her eyes stung with unshed tears. He had no clue. And even if he did, it would make no difference at all. Biting her lip and taking a deep breath, she walked over to him.

Tapping him on the shoulder, she said, "Hey, Adders, I'm shooting off. I'm shattered, so I'll grab a cab. See you later."

He swung around. "Wait, what? No, don't go. I've just met…erm…Gina. Gina this is my friend Lily."

Gina held out her hand. "Nice to meet you, Lily."

She grasped Gina's hand brusquely. "Yeah, likewise. Look Adders, I'm going. You stay and have a bit of fun. See you tomorrow maybe." She leaned in and kissed his cheek. His delicious cologne infused her alcohol fuelled senses. Her heart did a little skip and then immediately sank when she remembered he wasn't going home with her.

He started to get up. "Look, I'll come with—"

"Adam, I said I'm fine," she snapped and walked away.

The chilly evening air helped to sober her completely as she stood at the taxi rank with her arms folded around her body. Her flimsy skirt fluttered around her legs like a trapped butterfly, and her visible breath came in quick puffs as she tried to calm herself down. *What's the point in being upset, you stupid cow?* She stepped from foot to foot as her teeth chattered. *Gaawd, it's bloody freezing considering it's August. Where were all the taxis in this town when you really needed one?*

She felt warmness envelop her and she turned quickly, feeling a little panicked. "Fuck! Adders, you scared the shit out of me." She slapped his arm as he placed his jacket around her shoulders.

"Well, I was hardly going to let you go home by yourself, was I?" He rubbed his arms rapidly up and down Lily's to warm her up.

"I told you I'd be fine," she snapped, immediately regretting her tone.

"Bloody hell, Lil. Did I do something drastically wrong to you tonight? You've been like a bear with a fucking hangover ever since I started chatting to..." His eyes looked upward.

"I believe her name was Gina." Lily snorted derisively.

"I know that, thank you." He stared at her, his jaw clenching. "That's the fucking problem, isn't it?"

She huffed. "What are you going on about?"

"You're pissed off coz I was chatting to that...that woman." He gestured back in the direction of the club.

"*Gina.*"

"I. Fucking. Know," he said through clenched teeth.

"No, you're wrong, actually." Lily felt panicked again. *Shit, he's seen through me. Shit, shit, shitty-shit.*

He wagged his finger. "I know what your fucking problem is." He was nodding now. *Oh nooo.* She braced herself for a frank discussion. "Yeah, you're all bent out of shape coz you didn't bloody pick her off one of your dating sites. Yeah, that's what it is, you fucking control freak."

Oh...right. "Don't be ridiculous. God, you're a moron, Adders."

"Don't try to deny it. I know you. I know your bloody game."

Humph, don't know me that well then, do you? "Oooh, you got me, Adam. Ooh, you must let me pick out the girl of your dreams because I've got nothing better going on in my life." She turned away from him. "And for an English teacher, you do seem to have a limited vocabulary," she muttered.

He growled. "What's that supposed to mean?"

"All that effing this and effing that. It's not attractive, Adam."

"Good job I'm not trying to attract *you* then, eh?"

Ouch. She didn't outwardly respond. How could she? He had no idea how much his words had hurt her.

A taxi pulled up and she took off Adam's jacket and threw it at him. "Go back and find *Gina*, Adam. I'm going home," she said feeling defeated and hurt. Clambering into the taxi she tried to slam the door, but Adam grabbed it and climbed in after her. She rolled her eyes. "Can't you just piss off? I can't be bothered now. I'm tired and I've got a headache. I just want to go home."

"Yeah, well, we may as well share a taxi coz I'm going home too." He folded his arms over his chest. "Ten fucking eighty." He shook his head.

She sighed and leaned her head on the window.

Chapter Twenty-Seven

Waiting For a Girl Like You (Foreigner)

The next morning, Lily came downstairs to find Adam asleep on the couch. He had followed her out of the taxi and tried to talk to her, but she had just walked up the stairs, slammed her bedroom door, and gone to bed. Instead of sleeping in her spare room as he usually did, he had crashed on the sofa. She had no clue why. Rubbing her eyes and yawning, she began to make a pot of fresh coffee. When she turned around, he was leaning against the doorframe in his T-shirt and boxers. His arms were folded across his broad chest, his hair was all over the place, and he had fresh stubble around his jaw line. She paused for a moment and wondered what the stubble would feel like against her soft skin, what it would be like to see him like this every morning. She shook her head and turned away when she realised she was staring.

"Morning," he croaked.

"Morning," she replied, carrying on with the coffee preparation.

"Look, I've been thinking, Lil…"

She turned toward him and mirrored his stance. Her arms crossed over her chest. "Oh?"

"Yeah…look… I know why you didn't want me hooking up with that Nina woman."

"Gina."

He threw his arms up. "*Fuck…Gina…* God what's wrong with me?"

A wry smile pulled at her lips. "You were saying?"

"Right…yes… I think that maybe you thought I shouldn't go for the type of woman who picks up men in bars. Am I right?" He cringed. Her heart squeezed, he looked so adorable. She wanted to throw her arms around him and declare her undying love. Luckily she managed to restrain the urge.

She cleared her throat as she saw her get out. "Yes…yes, that's exactly it, Adders. She was obviously on the lookout for a one-night shag and you're worth more than that. You deserve the real thing, Adders. Not some desperate tart out for a quick fondle."

He walked over and encased her in his arms. "I'm sorry for being an arse. I knew it… I lay awake for ages last night just trying to figure out why you were so pissed off and then it dawned on me. I'm sorry for pissing you off. You've done a lot to try and help me, and I do appreciate it. I just feel a bit like a fish out of water, you know?" He smelled all manly and his body was hard and warm against her softness. She blinked up at him. His nose was an inch away from hers…all it would take was…

She snapped herself back to Earth and pulled away. "Yeah, well, that's what friends are for, eh?" she said as jovially as she could.

"Aye, Lil. And you're the best."

"And don't you forget it." She smiled as sadness tugged at her heart.

❤❤❤

After they had sat and eaten a cooked breakfast together courtesy of Adam using whatever he could find in Lily's fridge, the friends stood at the sink washing up.

He flicked soapsuds at her. "You should join the twenty first century and buy a bloody dishwasher you know."

"There's only one of me and I don't produce enough washing up to warrant adding to the hole in the ozone layer, actually."

He stood silently for a while. "Lil?"

"Yes?"

"Can we go through some of the profiles together? Will you help me?"

"What...*now*?"

"Why not?"

She swallowed hard. "Well, because it's Sunday, and I've got many things to be doing with my time today."

He scrunched his face. "Like what?"

She shrugged. "Stuff...things...you know." She tried her best to sound convincing.

"Come on, Lil. Please?" He fluttered his long dark lashes at her.

"Fuck off, Adders, you can't get around me like that." Who was she trying to kid?

"Please, Lilington McPretty Pants. I'll be your very bestest friend in the world. *Please?*"

She pursed her lips, trying not to laugh. "Oh for goodness sake, Adders, you really are a big girl...and a pain in the arse."

"Seriously though, who knows me better than you?"

She shook her head. "Oooh, I don't know...your mum?"

"Oh no, she doesn't. *You* know me best of all. And do you honestly think I would ask *twin-set and pearls* for relationship advice? The most significant relationship she's had outside of Dad is with her tomato plants."

Lily sniggered. "Well they say that they grow better if you talk to them." She pulled her lips in, trying to stifle a full-blown laugh.

"*Exactly*...so please will you help me? Just to go through them?"

She rolled her eyes for what felt like the millionth time. "Oh, go get my bloody laptop will you?"

♥♥♥

Adam logged into his profile and nervously clicked on his matches. He tapped his fingers as he waited for the list to load up. Thirty-five matches.

Lily's eyes widened. "Fuck! Adders! Aren't *you* mister popular?"

He grinned at her with pink cheeks. "I know. I couldn't believe it."

"Okay, let's go through them, one by one."

"Okay…here goes…" He clicked on the first profile. She read aloud from the description. "Thirty-four-year old busty, brunette. Loves cats—"

"Nope…next."

"But, Adam—"

"I'm allergic, next." He slurped at the mug of coffee he was holding.

She scrunched her face. She had totally forgotten about the time they had visited her aunt in Coldstream who had four cats. By the end of the visit, Adam was covered in purple blotches and was wheezing like a heavy smoker. It was *not* pretty. "Oh shit, yeah, of course."

He clicked the next one. "How about this one…Dark-haired, sexy, adventurous woman, willing to try new things—"

She gasped. "Ooh God, no."

He looked confused. "What? Why?" He took another slurp.

"Means she's a bit kinky."

He almost spat coffee all over the keyboard. "What? It could mean she'd be willing to try white water rafting, or windsurfing…or something."

"Yeah, white water rafting or wind surfing with a strap-on attached, probably."

"Eh? Strap-on?"

She shook her head. "A strap on? A fake penis, Adam…good grief."

"Well it didn't look to me like there was any mention of strap on penises…penae…penisae… What *is* the plural for penis anyway?" Adam gazed up at the ceiling with his brow furrowed. "As an English teacher, you'd think I would know that."

"Adam, concentrate."

"Sorry, Lil…okay, next."

"Right…ooh this one sounds okay…curvaceous, strawberry blonde, with a passion for skin art…and metal work…ooh you like curves, Adders."

"You kidding? She's a tattooed, pierced, fat, ginger bird. I don't think so. Next."

"There's nothing wrong with red heads, Adders."

"Oh fuck, yes… I never thought of that. Maybe she just has a tattooed red head…no hair." He shivered and made a *bluegh* noise.

"Well, I think you're just being too bloody picky now."

"Says you who discounted the adventurous water skier."

"Feel free to give her a call, Adders. But don't come crying to me when she's tried to tie you to her bed and whip your arse from here to next week."

He shrugged. "Fair point…okay…next."

"Okay…Brunette…curves…loves Monty Python…loves Snow Patrol, loves Alanis Morissette… Owns her own business… Ooh this is a good one. I think I'd date her!" She laughed.

He turned to her with raised eyebrows. "Are you *really* sure you're not a lesbian?" He teased. She punched his arm…*very* hard. "Fuck! Ow that hurt!"

"Good. It was meant to. Now what about this woman? She sounds great."

♥♥♥

After following all the necessary protocol required by the dating site, Adam had the email address of Mallory Westerman. She lived around three hours away in Leeds and sounded rather lovely. With Lily hovering in the background, but banned from reading over his shoulder, and with hope in his heart, he began to type.

Dear Mallory

I viewed your profile on the Made For Each Other website where you and I were seen to be a match. We seem to have quite a lot in common judging by our interests. I'm a huge Monty Python fan and have seen Snow Patrol live in concert several times. I find the music of Alanis Morissette can be very aggressive sometimes but she sure has a talent even if she does scare me a bit.

I live just over the border in Scotland, which I know seems like a long way but I was wondering if maybe you would like to meet in Leeds for coffee some time? I'm happy to come to you one weekend.

I should tell you about myself I suppose. I'm almost thirty-one and I teach English to delightful high school kids. I say delightful because I suppose I have to make myself <u>sound</u> like I like kids! Actually I'm only kidding. I <u>do</u> like kids. I think you have to like kids to be a teacher. That or you have to be a sadist...or a masochist... And I can assure you I'm neither!

I'm widowed. My wonderful wife was killed by an idiot drunk driver just over a year ago and whilst I'm still trying to get over this, I also realise that I'm young and need to get on with my life. I'm worried I'm sounding a little morose so if I am please forgive me. I'm actually quite funny most of the time. Although my best friend, Lily, wouldn't agree. She thinks my jokes are crap! Am I allowed to say crap in a first email? Oh well, it's out there now! I don't swear much normally. Okay that last sentence was a lie, I do swear but only usually when something shocks me! I'm sure I will swear a lot when I read this email back after I have clicked send. But I'm going to just keep typing and try not to think about it too much. Do I use too many *exclamation marks? As an English teacher I maybe should address that! << That one was meant as a joke* ☺

I sense that, even without reading back, I'm rambling so I'll close now. It would be lovely to hear from you. I like your photo. You're very pretty and have stunning eyes. I hope that's not too creepy or forward.

Bye for now
Adam

He hit send and then debated whether to read back what he had sent. Lily came over and sat on the sofa beside him.

"What did you say then?"

He shook his head and let out a long huff of air that puffed out his cheeks. "Not a fucking clue. I just typed. Oh shit, Lil." He rubbed his hands over his face. "I think I may have sworn and talked about masochism!"

She gasped. "Oh...Adders." She slapped her hand on her forehead. "Give it here. Let me read it." She made a grab for the laptop but he gripped it tighter.

"Fuck off! No way, Lil. I've sent it now so it's too late." A struggle ensued.

"Adam! It's my laptop!"

"Yes and I'm still logged in so let me log out and you can have it back!"

She pulled at the laptop again. "Adam! Give...me...it...now!"

He leaned back on the sofa and held the laptop above his head. She scrambled over his body and reached for it.

"Lil...as much as we're close, will you please get your tits out of my face. I'm a man after all."

She gasped in horror and fell to the floor. Her cheeks were bright red. "For goodness sake, Adders." She crossed her arms over her chest while he howled with laughter at her embarrassment.

She pouted and remained crossed-legged under where Adam lay on the sofa. He huffed again. "Oh for fuck's sake…here…read it… Tell me what an utter-fucking-moron I am…go on!" He thrust the laptop in her face. She grabbed it grinning widely and opened the lid eagerly.

After what felt like an eternity, she closed the laptop lid and turned to him. She was biting her lip. He couldn't tell whether or not that was a good sign. "Well?"

A wide smile took over her face. "I think you were, completely and utterly, one hundred per cent Adam Langton. If she doesn't adore you from that, then *she's* a lesbian…or head over heels in love with someone else." She patted his leg and stood.

A sense of relief washed over him and he breathed out of the O formed by his mouth. *Thank goodness for that.*

He followed Lily into the kitchen. "So what do I do now?"

She shrugged. "You wait. In the meantime, maybe you look at a few more profiles? You know…just in case."

He pulled his face into a frown. "But…but I only liked the sound of her. I didn't fancy any of the others." He sounded like a sulking child.

"Adam, unfortunately it's out of your hands now…but I'm sure she'll email back."

❤❤❤

Adam went home to finish off some marking and get ready for school the next day. Lily's words had really given him a boost. She really was the best. He wondered what would come of his email. Would she reply? Would it be right away? Who knew? He logged onto his email on the off chance, and his breath caught in his throat. *Shit! A reply! Already! Now this can either be a really good thing or a really bad thing…shiiit!* Nervously he clicked on read.

Dear Adam

Thank you for your lovely email. It really made me chuckle. I think your friend, Lily, is wrong. You sound like a complete hoot. And we really do have such a lot in common. The thing is, my best friend, Josie, who is a sweet person but doesn't know when to stop interfering, set me up on the dating site quite a while ago and I never really got anything from it. She did it without my permission, and I was so annoyed when I found out. Anyway, when nothing really came of it I put it to the back of my mind. Getting your email came as quite a surprise. A nice one though!

I'm so sorry to hear about your wife. I can't imagine the pain you must have experienced…still be experiencing, and I really do hope that time heals your wounds. You sound like such a lovely man.

I am sorry to have to tell you this…as you do seem really lovely…but last month I got engaged to my Canadian man. He proposed to me on holiday in Canada while we were visiting his family. I won't go into lots of detail, as it's neither fair nor relevant but just really wanted to inform you that I'm no longer looking for the love of my life. I have found him.

All I can say, Adam, is that I met Sam at the strangest time and in the strangest circumstances, and I know that this will happen to you too. Love will find you again when you least expect it. I honestly think you should stop looking and let it happen. You sound like the kind of person who is funny, warm, and kind, with a good heart. And yes I got all of that from one email. So some girl somewhere will get that from one meeting, Adam. I really believe that.

I wish you all the very best but I do feel love will find you. I just hope that it's soon.

Take care

Mallory

Adam closed the lid on his laptop. *Ah…head over heels in love with someone else it is then.*

Chapter Twenty-Eight

Meet Me In The City (The Black Keys)
September 2010

Adam hadn't bothered to look through any more of the profiles from the dating site, despite Lily's insistence that someone out there could be *the one*. Once again he was plagued with thoughts that he'd had his one shot. Everything had been perfect and wonderful for a while. Eve had been the real love of his life. His other half. She had been the central star in his sky. And now…if there was a heaven…she was up there shining brightly for everyone to see.

August melded into September and work was tiring but still rewarding. Coming home was still the hardest part, especially when his best friend was overseas so much. Lily loved her job passionately. She effervesced whenever she talked about it, and she was really making a name for herself. He thought it felt rather surreal seeing her on TV when she was so far away, off reporting something or other. But he was so proud of her. She had succeeded in her chosen field. He just missed her. Whenever she was away he didn't really see anyone. He would pop over to his parents' every so often to be the dutiful son but as for friends…well…they all had their own lives that didn't usually involve him. Lily was the only one who made the effort.

Her latest trip had taken her to Germany. He had no clue what the piece was that she was working on, but her hours were long and she was travelling around from place to place. They were communicating via email mostly, as he never seemed to catch her when he called and if he did she always had to end the call quickly.

Friday afternoon rolled around once again. The weekend. He sat on his sofa drumming his fingers on his thighs. Boredom had already set in and it was only six o'clock. He had marking that needed to be done but just couldn't be bothered. Grabbing his laptop he lifted the lid and logged into the dating site. *God, this is the epitome of boredom and desperation.* He loaded up the profiles and began to flick through.

"Too old…too young…eugh! Too skinny…sounds boring…looks like my mum…good grief is it my mum?" Adam looked closer at the screen. "No…*not* my mum…phew! That was weird." He flicked through over a dozen profiles but none seemed to spark his interest.

He made the decision there and then that Internet dating was simply not for him. He grabbed the local paper and thumbed through it, not really taking any notice of anything. Nothing massively newsworthy ever happened where he lived. Although he smiled at the way the local reporters made news out of the smallest things. Stories such as *LOCAL ALLOTMENT OWNER, MALCOLM, STRIPPED OF ROSETTE FOR PRIZE TURNIP*— allegedly for using some banned fertiliser he'd bought online. And CAT BURGLAR TURNS OUT TO BE A REAL CAT!— a story about an old woman who'd had some steaks pinched from her kitchen only to discover a sneaky stray feline was the culprit.

He turned the page and paused. There was an ad for a singles night at a local pub. Maybe meeting someone face to face would work? There would be less of the *blind date* about it.

Immediately he logged onto his email and opened a new message to Lily.

Hi Cheesy

So what you been up to? I'm sitting here bored shitless on a Friday night. Couldn't think of a single thing to do so I decided to check out some more profiles seeing as you keep badgering me. Anyway, I have decided to abandon the Internet dating thing. But I've found an ad in the gazette about a singles night and thought that might be a good way to meet someone. You know, face to face. I'd like to know your opinion. It's tomorrow night at the Stewart Hotel. Get me being all brave and suggesting this! I hope you are suitably impressed.

Write me back asap so I know whether it's worth it.

Adders x

Around an hour later he got his reply.

Adders…I think you will find that my name is Lily and I refuse to respond to Cheesy.

He hit reply.

Hi Lil

Sincerely sorry…so what did you think?

Adders x

P.S. You know you love me really.

He got an immediate response.

Hi again

Love you? Hmmm, debatable. Anyway…yes it sounds like a good plan if you ask me…which you did! And as they say, Nothing ventured, nothing gained.

Anyway got to dash as I am very busy and you seem to keep forgetting how extremely important I am, so stop bothering me.

Bye Pee Pants

Lily xx

Adam sniggered at her reply and the sly dig it contained. So she thought it was a good idea, eh? *Right. That's settled then. I'll be a big boy and will venture out alone tomorrow to see if the future love of my life is waiting for me at the Stewart Hotel. Hmmm. We'll see, I guess.*

With his resolve set he grabbed his jacket deciding to call to the local shop and buy beer and chocolate to give him a boost. He would have a Monty Python marathon…again. *Yay…I know how to live, me.*

He sighed as he walked back with his little stripy carrier bag. It was a fairly warm September Friday evening and the smell of barbeque was in the air. He and Eve used to have some fab barbecues. Inhaling deeply he smiled as the smell brought memories flooding back, making tears sting the backs of his eyes. *God I miss you, Evie.*

♥♥♥

Saturday evening came around at lightning speed and before he knew it Adam was showering and shaving ready for his date with destiny. Well, ready for his night out at the Stewart Hotel anyway. He buttoned up his favourite pale green shirt and pulled on his dark blue jeans. His palms were sweaty and he was thankful his jeans were dark enough to hide the moisture he wiped down his legs. The pub was only a short walk away, and he decided to go sans jacket, thinking the cool evening air would help his profuse nervous perspiring.

On arrival he was both shocked and pleased at the number of singles in attendance. Although a second glance informed him that the men outweighed the women at about a ratio of four to one. *Great.* He went to the bar and ordered a pint of beer, hoping an infusion of alcohol into his bloodstream might relax him a little. Suddenly the sound of someone clearing their throat into a microphone had everyone turning around toward the source of the noise.

"Good evening, ladies and gentleman. I'm Monica and I'd like to welcome you to Two's Company Singles Night here at the Stewart Hotel." She had a whiny, nasal voice that could be very irritating if listened to for any length of time. "Now these days many people are favouring online dating, but I say what better way is there to meet Mr. or Miss Right than face to face in a public place? Okay…so…you were all handed a little sticker on the way in, and you should've all written your names on them by now, so we'll be ready to go shortly." Adam had been tempted to write *Dolf* or *Arnie* on his sticker in case he met lots of weirdoes. But in the end he had caved and written his real name.

"Now, there are a few ground rules. Well, I say ground *rules*…I suppose they're more like ground *suggestions*." *Yeah coz that's a thing*, Adam snorted derisively to himself. "We prefer that if you connect with someone of interest that you swap email addresses or mobile numbers. We do *not* condone anyone pairing off and leaving together on the first meeting. Obviously, if you choose to do so Two's Company will accept no responsibility for any incident that occurs outside the premises." *Yeah, like if the person you cop off with turns out to be an axe-wielding maniac. Why am I even here?* "So, mingle, chat, and see where the night takes you. Enjoy and remember Two really is company." *As opposed to a threesome, eh?* Adam's negative subconscious was clearly in full flight tonight. It didn't bode well. Monica handed the microphone back to the bartender and began to walk around with a clipboard.

Adam stood there awkwardly contemplating ripping off his name badge and running for the hills, but that would mean the waste of a perfectly good pint of beer. He leaned against the post in the middle of the room and watched as everyone else seemed to make a beeline for someone. He cringed at how many medallions and hairy chests were on show and thought that perhaps a well-known manufacturer of hair product had gone into meltdown on account of having no stock left. Another scan of the room and his eyes fell on a pretty woman who seemed to be feeling as out of place as Adam. She stood there in the corner, chewing her lip and fiddling with the strap on her bag. She looked up and made eye contact, and her cheeks blushed crimson as a slow smile spread across her face. Taking a deep breath he made his way over to talk to her.

♥♥♥

He arrived home around an hour after chatting with Jessica. He decided that he felt too uncomfortable to be there and made excuses to leave but not before getting her email address. Once he arrived home he emailed Lily.

Hi, Lil

Well, I went to the singles night thing. Only stayed an hour though as I couldn't hack it. It was a bit like a meat market. I did meet someone though! She's called Jessica and she's a nursery nurse. She has long, wavy auburn hair and green eyes. Quite pretty really. She likes boy bands but I can let that go. She has a cat but only one! She's around five feet four and quite petite. I have her email address. What do you think? Should I give it a shot?

Write me back soon so I know what to do, eh?

Adders x

Around an hour later, after finishing off the huge bar of chocolate he'd bought the night before, he got a reply.

Hi Pee pants!

You did well to say you didn't stay long! She sounds normal. Not sure she is your type but hey, what do I know? Drop Polly Pocket an email and see where it goes from there.

Lily x

Okay, so for some reason Lily didn't think that this Jessica girl was his type. Well, he would email her anyway. What could it hurt? He opened up his email account and paused. He briefly considered doing a quick copy and paste of the email he had sent to Mallory but felt that Mallory was too nice to do that to. His email to her would remain unique. So he opened a new message.

Dear Jessica

It was very nice to meet you at the Stewart Hotel tonight. I'm so sorry for dashing off like that. I can only hope that you weren't swept off your feet by some other dashing hunk after I'd gone. That's not to say that I think I'm a dashing hunk. Nor do I intend to sound mean in hoping you didn't meet anyone else. Anyway I digress. You said that you are based on the outskirts of Edinburgh. That's quite handy as I'm near Jedburgh. Perhaps we could meet in Edinburgh for drinks or a meal?

Anyway, a little about myself, seeing as we didn't get much chance to chat. I am almost thirty-one and teach English in high school. I love my job and the kids are great. You obviously like kids too as you work in a nursery. I'll bet that can be exhausting but rewarding all at the same time.

Anyway, enough of my rambling. Do email back if you would like to meet up.

Cheers

Adam

He clicked send and then opened the message up to re-read it. *God I sound dull as fucking ditch water. Wouldn't blame her if she falls asleep before she gets through the first paragraph. Oh well. As Lil said, nothing ventured…blah, blah, blah.*

He watched TV for a while and had a bottle of beer. He bounced his knee up and down and kept glancing at his laptop as if Jessica would jump right out of it. After about forty minutes, impatience got the better of him, and he opened his email account again, just in case. There was a reply! Before he plucked up the courage to open it, he went to the kitchen and put a frozen pizza in the oven. Then, deciding he could put it off no longer he opened up the message.

Dear Adam

Thank you for your email. It was a pleasant surprise to receive it and it was nice to meet you too. I am on the outskirts of Edinburgh, so perhaps we could meet at a restaurant at Straiton? It would be nice to meet you properly. I left not long after you did, as I felt very much like a fish out of water, if the truth be told.

Are you free tomorrow evening? I know it's short notice, but I am due to go on a girl's holiday next weekend and will be spending next week preparing, getting a spray tan, packing, etc.

Shall we say half seven outside Benito's? It shouldn't be too busy on a Sunday evening. Hopefully I will recognise you from our brief meeting. Unless I was tipsier than I realised and you really are in actual fact a fat, balding sixty year old! Gosh…I hope I remembered you correctly!

Anyway, I will await your next email and I will see you tomorrow hopefully.

Jess x

A smell of burning wafted through the air, and he dashed into the kitchen to check his pizza. Realising that the burning smell was just some dripped cheese, he took a large swig of his beer. *Shit! That's quick! Tomorrow? Better email Lil.* He dashed back into the lounge and clicked to open a new message.

Hi Lil

Guess what? She replied! The Jessica one I mean. She wants to meet tomorrow! Aarrgh! What should I do? Should I go? If so, what do you think I should wear? She has suggested Benito's at Straiton, so it's casual dress normally. Shit, I wish you were here to advise me. Not sure I can do this without your help, Lil!

Adders xx

He knew she wouldn't respond right away and it bothered him. He couldn't leave Jessica hanging in the air wondering if he wanted to meet. He reread her email and decided to take the plunge.

Hi Jess

Thanks for getting back to me so quick. I would love to meet you at Benito's tomorrow night, yes. Seven thirty it is. I'll be the short fat balding man ;-) Only kidding.

See you tomorrow.

Adam

Nervously munching on his pizza, he slipped in Monty Python's *Life of Brian* and sat back on the sofa. He couldn't concentrate. He kept glancing at the laptop screen waiting for at least one of the girls to reply to his email. Lil was probably out getting drunk with Mack the camera man and Jess…well maybe Jess was picking outfits for her girl's holiday. His email pinged to tell him a new message had arrived.

Lily.

Adders

Just bloody email her and set it up! You dufus! You don't need me there to do this, Adam. You are a grown up! Accept it and embrace it. She sounds nice. Wear your jeans and your navy shirt with a white T-shirt underneath. You always look nice in that outfit. But seriously you will be fine! BTW try to remember her name!

Lily xx

Next came a confirmation from Jessica. She would be there. Seven thirty. Tomorrow. Adam wondered if he had made the right decision. *Only time will tell, I guess.*

♥♥♥

On Sunday evening, he donned the outfit Lily had suggested and set off. He arrived at Straiton ten minutes early and sat in the car feeling rather conspicuous. People walked past him whilst he drummed his fingers on the steering wheel and kept checking his watch. One of these days, he would replace the dashboard clock. He glanced over at Benito's and saw a small-framed woman standing outside. *That's her.* He remembered thinking she was pretty the night before, but twenty-four hours was a long time. He couldn't tell a lot from where he was, but his stomach lurched at the thought of the night being crap and not having Lily here to rescue him. He should've arranged for her to ring him with a get out. But then again, she was busy in Germany.

He climbed out of his car and made his way toward the woman. She was rather tiny, he'd forgotten just how tiny.

She smiled when she saw him approaching and pointed at him questioningly. "Adam?"

He smiled at her as warmly as he could manage. "Jessica."

She held out her hand to him. "Please…call me Jess. All my friends do."

He shook her hand. "You can still call me Adam…my friends call me it because well…it's quite hard to shorten Adam… I'll stop talking now." Heat rushed his cheeks. *Fucking knob.* Jessica seemed to be trying her best not to giggle at him. She was very pretty. He liked her instantly.

Clearing his throat, he opened the door for her. "So, are we eating or just having coffee or something, seeing as we're both driving?"

"Well, I'm starving, so food is good."

He smiled. *She must not find me repugnant then. Good start.* "Great. I'm hungry, too. I only had a pastry for lunch."

"At least you had lunch! I only managed a cup of coffee."

They stood in the doorway waiting to be seated. "How come?"

"Oh, I've been helping my sister move into a flat with her boyfriend today."

"Right…right…how old is your sister?"

"She's twenty-one. But they were childhood sweethearts so…"

They were shown to a secluded, romantic table toward the back of the restaurant. He pulled out her chair and she thanked him, smiling sweetly. The waiter came over and reeled off a list of specials and handed them menus and a wine list. They both shook their heads at the wine list. Adam liked that.

Chapter Twenty-Nine

She's My Best Friend (Lou Reed)

Once their food was ordered, Adam and Jessica sat in a shy silence. He glanced up and met with a curious gaze.

Jessica blushed when he caught her watching him. She leaned forward. "Can I ask you a very straight forward question?"

He cringed and fiddled with his napkin. "Hmmm, if I say no you'll think I'm an arse but if I say yes I may not want to answer...tricky...go on then." He held his breath.

"Why did you attend the singles night?" *Okay that was direct.*

He cleared his throat. "Erm, my friend, Lily...my best friend actually, signed me up to an online dating website, but I didn't feel right doing things that way. It's like that woman said last night...better to meet people face to face straight off."

Jessica narrowed her eyes. "You have a female best friend?"

He chuckled. "Why does everyone seem so surprised by that?"

She tilted her head to one side. "Do you and she have history?"

"Well, considering I've known her since primary school, yes, we have a hell of a lot...why do you ask?"

She shook her head. "No, I mean a history in the romantic sense not just *history*-history."

He began to feel uncomfortable and fidgeted in his seat. "No...and don't take this the wrong way, but why is that in any way relevant? It's not really any of your business."

She blushed again. "I'm sorry...look...I'll tell you why, Adam. My last boyfriend was supposedly in love with me. We went out for four years, but I still found him in bed with his female *best friend*." She made air quotes with her fingers. "Suffice it to say I'm not a big fan of the whole female best friends thing."

He puffed out his cheeks on a huff of air. "Well, maybe I'm wasting your time here, Jessica." He rubbed the back of his neck. "Lily and I are very close. She's my best friend and she helped me through a very rough time last year." He glanced up to see Jessica listening intently. Perhaps explaining things would help her to understand *why* he needed Lily in his life. "My...my wife was killed in a...she was... A drunk driver hit her and she was killed instantly." He struggled to get the words out. It was a long time since he'd had to explain.

Jessica gasped and her hand went to her mouth. "Oh, Adam, I am *so* sorry, that's terrible. How...awful." He saw tears forming in her eyes.

"Yes...yes it was." He swallowed his own emotions down along with the lump that had become lodged in his throat. "Lily was there through the whole thing. When I needed consoling, she was there. When I needed a shoulder, she was there. When I needed a kick up the arse, she delivered the blow. She's the one who's been encouraging me to meet someone and get on with my life. And as hard as that is, I'm young and I can't live in the past. If it wasn't for Lily, I would probably have jumped from a cliff by now."

Jessica nodded. "How come you and Lily didn't get together then? You know...instead of you going to singles nights. She sounds amazing."

He smiled affectionately as he thought about Lily. "She *is* amazing...but she doesn't think of me that way."

"And you?"

Adam narrowed his eyes. "And me what?"

"Do you think of *her* that way?"

He paused for a few moments as he considered her question. "There was a time back before university when I felt...*something*...but it was fleeting and it was clear that she didn't feel the same, and so I got over it. We both moved on and now we're family to each other."

"So you told her how you felt back then? And she said she didn't feel the same?"

He was getting increasingly frustrated and felt like he was under interrogation. "No... I never mentioned it. I didn't need to. Look, Jessica, I don't mean to be rude, but I feel under scrutiny here, or like you're psychoanalysing me. I don't understand."

"Please, just humour me. I'm fragile and uneasy knowing any potential boyfriend... God that sounds so immature...any possible love interest... God that's even worse... Okay, let's just say that I'm uncomfortable with your relationship with Lily, and until I feel comfortable I don't feel able to move forward with you even though I like you. I'm trying to be honest."

He rubbed his brow again. "But don't you think this is all a bit intense for a first meeting?"

She sighed. "Yes...yes I do...but I think maybe you and I could get on well, and I need to be honest with you."

He pulled his lips in between his teeth. "Look, there is nothing other than a strong family bond between me and Lily. I care deeply about her. But I'm not *in love* with her. If that's not something you can deal with, then perhaps we shouldn't take this any further." He frowned.

She took a deep breath. "No...no I think you've made it clear that it's just friendship, but now you probably don't want to see me again after this." She looked down at her lap. Just then the waiter brought their meals to the table.

When the waiter left, Jessica slowly lifted her gaze to meet Adams. "I'm right, aren't I?"

He closed his eyes and inhaled deeply, then opened his eyes and smiled. "I can understand your trepidation, but I do like you, so can we just start over?"

A pretty smile spread across her face and she sighed. "Sure. I'd really like that."

♥♥♥

Adam arrived home at half eleven. He was exhausted. Jessica was lovely but she came with baggage. But then again so did he.

He flopped onto the sofa and flicked on the laptop, which sat on the coffee table. No emails. He thought about it for a moment, but then decided against telling Lily the ins and outs of the date. It would feel strange telling her that he was grilled about his relationship with her. And no doubt Lily would tell him to get rid of the nosey woman.

At the end of the evening Adam and Jessica, or Jess as she had asked him to call her, exchanged phone numbers with a view to seeing each other after her girl's holiday. Lily would be home the following Saturday, so no doubt he would have plenty to tell her. His phone chirped in his pocket. Opening the message, he smiled to himself.

J: Hi Adam, it's Jess. Wanted to apologise again for the Spanish Inquisition. Even though I discovered this evening that you are a Monty Python fan, I'm not sure you expected it ;-) See you next week. Xx

He chuckled to himself. Okay…pretty…sweet…matching baggage and a sense of humour, too. This felt rather good.

♥♥♥

Jessica spent a week away on her girl's holiday but kept in touch with Adam the whole time. They had some long conversations by text message, and he wondered what on earth her friends must think as she lay there on a sun lounger with her phone permanently clutched in her hand.

A: Don't they think it's strange that you keep texting me? Isn't it spoiling your holiday? Adam enquired.

J: Not at all. They are rather intrigued about the man who has finally captured my attention ☺

A: I'll bet they are. What have you told them? He was rather intrigued to know. There was a long pause until he received her reply. He had almost given up hope of an answer when his phone chirped.

J: I have told them that I think perhaps this could be something special. Is that too much info?

Adam's breath caught. That wasn't really what he was expecting to hear. He didn't really know what he thought or felt about her. Their first meeting had been quite intense, and whilst he did find her very attractive, he hadn't really considered where it was going. But he had asked the question after all, so only he was to blame for opening that can of worms. He hit reply.

A: No that's fine. Look I have to go out. He lied. *Will text you later. Try to have some fun with your friends!*

Okay, time to let this thing breathe. Too much, too soon, perhaps. He threw his phone on the sofa and switched on the TV. She would be back at the weekend, but it would be too late for them to meet up, and so the next possible time for him to see Jess would be over a week from now. Plenty of time to let her think about the implications of what she had said. Plenty of time for him to get his head around the idea that she clearly thought this was going somewhere. *No pressure. None. None at all. Hmmm.*

Chapter Thirty

Achilles Heel (Toploader)
October 2010

Jess had contacted Adam on the Monday after she had arrived back in the UK from her girl's holiday. She seemed keen to meet up with him again and they arranged a second date. Adam invited her to come for dinner. He had always enjoyed cooking and had wowed Eve on more than one occasion with his culinary delights. He felt confident that cooking Jess a nice meal was a good plan. Also he felt that being on his own turf might ease the anxiety he felt at seeing her again.

He really liked Jess. She was pretty and had a nice enough figure, if a little thin. She was intelligent and they seemed to have a fair bit in common. The only stumbling block seemed to be Lily. Jess asked a lot of questions about her, and his reassurances, whilst they seemed to work initially, had been failing a little in the build-up to the second date. Her questions had been less subtle and more frequent. Hence the anxiety. He didn't feel like explaining his relationship with Lily to this woman every time they met. If a relationship became such hard work, then surely it wasn't worth pursuing.

Everything was prepared. Jess would be here at seven thirty, and so Adam ran up the stairs to shower and dress for her arrival. It felt strange inviting a woman here. It was something he hadn't envisaged himself doing, but it felt like the best thing to do. He felt like he needed to be at home. Perhaps Eve would be there, in spirit, to give him strength.

He stopped, mid scrub, as that particular errant thought preyed on his mind. What *would* Eve think of all this? Of course it was a moot point really, but what if she *was* still able to watch over him? Would she be angry? Upset?

Would she feel betrayed that he was trying to move on with his life after only just over a year? Sometimes he swore he could smell her perfume wafting by him, and he would close his eyes to do his best to capture the moment, to try to feel her presence. But these moments were fleeting. Clinging to a ghost was not how he wanted to spend his life. Eve was gone. He *had* to start to accept it.

Just after seven thirty, there was the anticipated knock at the door. He checked his reflection in the mirror over the fireplace. His hair was getting a little long and unruly but he kind of liked it. He had shaved and dressed in a grey T-shirt and jeans as Lily had suggested.

"You have to look more relaxed, Adders, she's coming to your home. Let her see you as *you* in your own environment." Lily's words rang in his head. She talked as though he was some kind of study and she was David Attenborough or something. He laughed and shook his head. *As long as she doesn't jump out of the under-stairs cupboard speaking in hushed tones with a camera crew in tow.* Although knowing Lily, anything was possible and she actually did have access to the camera crew. He made his way to the front door and tentatively opened it.

"Hey, Jess, come on in." He stepped aside to allow her to pass.

"Hi Adam." She leaned up to kiss his cheek, placing her hand on his chest. He helped her off with her coat and hung it on the peg at the bottom of the stairs. She too had dressed more casually in black trousers and a lilac v-neck sweater. It reminded him of something Eve would wear. A pang of sadness stabbed his heart. He'd begun to feel guilty for bringing Jess here.

She handed him a bottle of wine. "I thought maybe I could get a taxi home…if that's okay with you?" She looked concerned.

He did his best to smile. "Oh…yeah, sure." *But you* will *be going home!* He took the wine through to the tiny kitchen with its table for two neatly set out at one end.

"Something smells wonderful, Adam. What have you made?" She closed her eyes as she inhaled.

He reached for a couple of glasses. "I made beef in a red wine sauce. Is that okay?" *Shit, I never even checked if she eats beef. Shitty shit.*

"Mmmm, sounds wonderful." The sound she made was almost erotic and Adam swallowed hard. *Phew.*

"So you had a good holiday then?" He tried to keep his voice breezy and failed miserably considering she had just orgasmed over the smell of bloody beef in red wine.

"It was good. But I was glad to be home." She sidled over to where he was draining a pan of vegetables.

"Oh? Why's…why's that?"

She was touching his arm now. "Oh, Adam…because I was looking forward to seeing you again." She took the colander from his trembling hands and placed it on the drainer beside the sink. Reaching up onto her tiptoes, she pressed her mouth against his, flicking her tongue out to taste his bottom lip. He stood frozen to the spot. "Adam…it's okay…you can kiss me back now," she whispered against his lips.

Forgetting himself for a moment, his hands snaked around her waist, and he kissed her back, sliding his tongue between her parted lips. She groaned quietly as their tongues joined in a mutual dance. The kiss became deeper and more passionate as Jess ran her hands through his hair and he slid his hands down to her bottom. She moaned again. *Shit, what am I doing?* He suddenly pulled away. This was a little too much, too soon in the home he shared with Eve. It felt wrong.

He stepped back. "Erm, I'd better serve the food up or it'll be ruined," he stuttered. Jess smiled and took her seat at the tiny café style table.

"You're really sweet, Adam." She giggled as he served the food onto plates and placed them on the table.

He felt the heat in his cheeks rise. "It's just a little hard for me...this...here." He gestured around the room.

"Why's that?" Her brow creased and she tilted her head.

She should have figured that out for herself. "You're the first woman I've invited back here...since Eve passed."

Her face dropped and her cheeks coloured. "Oh gosh, of course, I'm so sorry... I should have realised what you meant. I feel foolish for kissing you like that."

He shook his head. "No...no it's fine. It was a...a nice kiss."

She looked up at him from under her long lashes. "Well I thought so."

♥♥♥

Adam's phone began to ring. The ringtone that Lily had programmed in under the nickname *Cheesy* was Queen's *Your My Best Friend,* and it was calling to him from the lounge. He placed his knife and fork down.

Jess watched him. "Can you just ignore it?"

"Oh...yes, yes sure." He didn't like ignoring Lily, but she would understand. Hopefully. The ringing stopped and Jess sighed with what Adam surmised was relief. Two seconds later it started again. He placed his cutlery down again.

Jess's eyes darted to his. "Adam?"

"Look Jess, it's Lily's ringtone—"

She huffed. "I guessed as much. Can't she leave you alone for *one night*?"

"Jess, I've told you it's not like that with Lil and me. But she knew you were coming for dinner tonight so—"

"So no doubt she thought she would spoil it for us!" Jess slammed her cutlery down.

He stood, pulling his brow inward. "Take it easy, Jess. God, I was going to say that she wouldn't ring unless it was important. I have to answer it." He began to walk over to the lounge when the ringing stopped. He paused but the house phone began to ring.

He vaulted over the sofa and grabbed the receiver. "Lil?" He heard sobbing from the other end of the phone. "Fuck, Lily what's wrong? Where are you?"

"I'm at the hospital, Adam…"

His heart thundered in his chest. "Shit, Lily what's happened? Are you okay?"

"I'm sorry to bother you, Adam, I know you've got—"

"Lily? Tell me what's wrong, please?"

"It's my dad. He's…he's had a heart attack." She sobbed down the line.

"I'll be right there. Hang tight, Lil, I'm coming." He hung up and ran his hands through his hair. He turned to find Jess standing, arms folded in the doorway with a sour look fixed in place.

She shook her head. "So you're going to her then?"

He scrunched his face at her incredulous question. "Of course I'm *going* to her. Her dad's had a heart attack, Jess. Surely you can't begrudge me going to her for that?"

Her cheeks coloured. "Doesn't she have other friends? Or family?"

Anger bubbled inside him, and he did his best to keep his tone calm. "No, she doesn't. She has her mum and me…that's it. So excuse me for wanting to be by my best friend's side when she's going through this. She was there for me all through losing Eve."

Jess snorted derisively. "So you feel you owe her, do you? When all she wants is to keep you away from me!"

He gaped open mouthed for a few seconds as he tried to process Jess's accusations. She was acting like some scorned lover. It was their second date, for goodness sake. Eventually, through gritted teeth, he managed to speak. "I think you need to leave, Jessica. I owe Lily everything. But this is *not* obligation. This is what real friends do. And regardless of what fucking mixed up, twisted idea you have in your head, this heart attack was not a fucking conspiracy! Now, please leave so that I can go to my best fucking friend when she needs me!" His voice became louder as his anger rose.

She grabbed her bag from the sofa and stormed to the bottom of the stairs to get her coat. "I'm not going to compete with her, Adam." She smiled sardonically. "So your Achilles heel wins out. I won't be seeing you again. This is your last chance!"

His laugh was humourless. "You think I would *want* to see you again? After this? Sorry, lady, but Achilles heel or not, I'd choose Lily *every* time…no competition."

Jessica slammed the door behind her. Adam stood, chest heaving. *How dare she? She has no fucking clue!*

♥♥♥

Thirty minutes later, Adam ran down the hospital corridor toward the Intensive Care Unit. He asked at the nurses' station and was pointed to the family room. He burst through the door and saw Lily in a crumpled heap on a corner sofa. She looked so small. So young and fragile. Immediately he went to her side and pulled her into his lap. She latched onto his neck and let out a pain filled groan.

Adam stroked her hair. "Hey…shhh…I'm here…it's okay…shhh." He rocked her gently as she poured her anguish out onto him, clinging on for dear life. Eventually when her sobs had subsided, she looked up into his eyes. He was doing his best not to let his own tears fall, but seeing Lily like this was too much to bear. A tear escaped and he rubbed his cheek on his upper arm.

She held his face in her hands. "Thank you…thank you so much for coming. I know you were—"

He rested his forehead on hers. "Shhh. It doesn't matter what I was doing, Lil. It never matters what I'm doing. I'll always come to you when you need me. You know that."

She closed her eyes, forcing more tears to trail down her face. She pressed her mouth to his. "Thank you…thank you. I don't know what I would do without you."

He felt a jolt of electricity when her lips touched his, which startled him. Trying not to show it, he pulled away and looked into her bloodshot eyes. "Hey, you don't have to worry about that, Lil, coz it's never going to happen." He buried his face in her hair as her tears came again.

♥♥♥

Having Adam near was such a comfort for Lily. She clung to him and he let her. He hadn't flinched even when she had stupidly planted a kiss right on his mouth. *What the hell was I thinking? Actually, that's the problem…I wasn't thinking. Mind you, why should he flinch? It wasn't as if it would have had any effect on him. Friends kiss friends.* And anyway, that was irrelevant right now. She felt so guilty at interrupting his date with Jess.

She vowed to herself that she would make it up to Jess in some way, especially if Adam really liked her. She would have to try to be friends with the woman. Even though she had the very thing that Lily wanted more than anything. No…no…right at this moment what she wanted more than anything was for her dad to be okay and for him to come out of this alive. It had been a huge shock.

As she sat curled up on Adam's lap, her mind whirred around with a million different things. Most of them silly. It was strange how, as a child she had always thought of her dad as a hero. He hadn't fought in wars or defended the helpless. He was just a normal man. But he was a good man, a strong man, and a wonderful father and husband. He had always put Lily and her mother first before everything else. Their happiness was paramount. That alone made him a hero. But she had always thought of him as invincible. It was only now, as an adult, that she realised how fragile he was. Just like everyone else. He was no hero. Not in the true indestructible sense of the word. What he *was* was irreplaceable. Suddenly, a thought occurred to her. Faced with her dad's mortality, she suddenly realised something.

She pulled away and looked straight into Adam's dark brown, troubled eyes. "Adam...I'm so sorry."

He looked confused. "For what?"

She took a deep breath and searched for the courage to continue. "For trying to get you to move on."

"Sorry? I don't get—"

"The dating site, Adam. I can't believe I was so stupid."

He still looked confused. "Lily, help me out here coz I'm not sure—"

"Eve can't be replaced, Adam. Just like my dad can't be replaced. Eve was an amazing friend, an amazing person, and I should *never* have interfered." Her lip began to tremble again.

Holding her face in his hands, he smiled at her. "Lil, you can't *make* me do something I don't want to do, so stop worrying, okay? I'm an adult, remember? And I'm not trying to replace her. She was one of a kind. We both know that. But you were right. I don't want to be alone. I know I have you but...well, one day...you'll meet someone...then you'll get married and I'll be all alone. I do want to meet someone. I do. And all of this has made me feel hope. But maybe I need to stop forcing it, eh? I think I'm done with dating websites and singles nights."

"Things not going well with Jessica?"

"Let's just say I won't be seeing her again and leave it at that, eh?"

❤❤❤

Lily's mum walked through the door, halting the conversation. She appeared broken. Lily climbed off of Adam's lap and enveloped her mum in her arms. The usually fiery and feisty woman was pale and drawn. Adam joined the mother and daughter as they sobbed together and clung to each other as if doing so would take away the pain they were feeling. With an arm around both women, Adam fought back his own tears.

"They asked me to leave, Lily. I don't know what is going on."

Adam had always loved to hear Lenora speak. Her Spanish accent had become tinged with a mild Scottish lilt as time had passed. It had always brought a smile to his face. Today, however, he hated to hear her so heartbroken when there was nothing he could do to ease her pain.

"It's probably just so they can check his vitals, Mama. Try not to worry, okay?"

"Tengo miedo…no puedo perder." Lenora sobbed. She had a tendency to revert to Spanish when she was upset.

"Mama, I know you're afraid. So am I. They're doing all they can so that we don't lose him. We have to stay positive." Lenora nodded but Adam could see that staying positive was something she was struggling to do.

Chapter Thirty-One

My Immortal (Evanescence)
November 2010
Lily watched as Adam walked into the kitchen of her mother's house. Another funeral over. She stood with her back against the work surface. The whole situation was painfully reminiscent of the previous year when Adam had buried his wife. She lifted her gaze to meet his with a sad smile.

"Hey," she whispered.

"Hey." He stood beside her. "How are you doing?"

"Funny, I was going to ask you the same thing." She nudged his shoulder.

Adam scrunched his brow. "Why?"

"Well because here we are at another bloody wake together. We really shouldn't make a habit of this, Adders."

He smiled and slipped his arm around her shoulders. "You're right. Let's make a pact, eh? The next function we go to together should be a wedding or a christening or something. Whaddya say?" He squeezed her and kissed her hair.

She snapped her gaze up to him and narrowed her eyes. "Why? Is there something you're not telling me?"

He huffed. "Absolutely not. I don't think I'll get married again if I'm honest, Lil. If and when I meet someone, I reckon I'll live in sin. I've had my happy marriage."

Her lip began to quiver. He pulled her into a hug. "Hey...hey I'm sorry. Did I say the wrong thing?"

She sniffed. "No...I'm just so sad, Adders. My poor lovely mum. She's heartbroken. Dad was her world. Apart from you and Eve, I've never seen two people more in love than they were."

Adam kissed the top of her head. Her words made his heart ache. "I know. I'm so sorry, Lily. Nothing I say can make things better. But just know that I'm here, okay?"

She nodded into his chest. "I know…thank you."

"I honestly wouldn't have got through losing Eve if you hadn't been there. You were my rock, do you know that?"

"I don't feel very rock-like right now. I feel more like a big pile of mush."

He breathed in the scent of her coconut shampoo. "I know you do right now. But we'll get through this…you and me…we can get through anything."

♥♥♥

The mourners, apart from Adam, had all gone. He kissed Lily's cheek and hugged her again, hard, reminding her he was there if and when she needed him.

"I can stay at your house, Lil. You might need me. I'm happy to stay and look after you."

She clung on to him. "No, honestly it's fine. You really need your sleep. And Mum needs me here. I'm going to help her clean up, and then I'll sleep in my old room. You should go."

"I'm just worried about you, Lil. You're my best friend. I'm bound to worry," he said as he gazed into her eyes, her sadness reflected back at her.

"I know and it means so much to know that you're there for me…really it does. I just think maybe I need to be here tonight."

"Okay, well I'll keep my phone on…you know…in case you need me in the night."

She smiled at the sweet gesture being made by this wonderful man. She wanted to thank him again but instead could only manage a nod of her head as emotion erupted from her body once again.

"Oh, Lil, I'm so sorry. I'm just so, so sorry." He squeezed her to him as she sobbed into his black suit jacket. The same suit jacket he had worn at Eve's funeral. Lily clung to him and poured out her grief for her father and for her unspoken heartache at loving the man before her so very, very much. She was filled with so many *if-onlys* that her heart felt like it would never mend. Ever.

Lenora looked on with a sad smile.

❤❤❤

Lily dried the last of the dishes and placed them back in the cupboard. Lenora poured them both a glass of wine and sat down at the dining table. Sighing, Lily placed the dishtowel on the drainer and joined her mother.

Lenora reached across and squeezed Lily's hand. "So when are you going to tell him, mi querida?" Her little touch of Spanish made Lily smile. No matter how much her accent had changed, her terms of endearment remained in her mother tongue.

Lily took a gulp of her wine and scrunched her brow. "Tell who what, Mama?"

Lenora gave Lily the look that told she was on to her. "Oh, Lily…come on, Mija, I think you know what I mean."

Lily shook her head. "Mama, I really haven't got a clue what you're talking about."

Lenora sighed and patted her hand. "You are my only daughter, Lily, and I want you to be happy."

"I know that, Mama…of course I do, but what are you trying to say exactly?"

Lenora pulled her lips into a line and frowned. "Mija, you have loved that boy since you were tiny. Am I wrong?"

Lily feigned ignorance but her eyes dropped to the floor, a telltale giveaway. "Who are you talking about, Mama?"

Lenora laughed as she rolled her eyes. "Oh goodness me. I really can't believe you are being so stubborn, Mija!" She shook her head. "Adam of course. You have loved him for so very long. Do you think it may be time to tell him so?"

Lily's eyes snapped up. "I certainly do *not*, Mama!" She swallowed hard. "And...and how long have you known?" she whispered.

"Lily, I have known since you were five years old. You and he were inseparable. Me and Gwen always said you would one day marry, but then he met Eve and I sat by and watched your heart break. I cannot tell you how hard this was for me and your papa."

Lily's lip quivered. "Oh, Mama, I *can't* tell him. There would be no point. He thinks of me as family...like a sister. It makes no difference how I feel."

Lenora squeezed Lily's hand again. "But, darling, how do you know this? You have never given him a chance to think about how he feels. All you have tried to do is match him to another. This has not been a good thing."

Lily fiddled with the stem of her glass. "I really can't tell him. What would I do if I told him and then he confirmed that he really *doesn't* feel the same? I'd lose my best friend in the world, Mama. I can't risk that."

"But what if he has felt the same all this time? What then?" Lenora looked at Lily with pleading eyes. "Surely he deserves to know."

"Mama, please... We're just not meant to be."

Lenora smiled. "You know, when I met your father I thought the same. There I was, a Spanish waitress working hard to get money for my family and in walked the most handsome man I have ever seen. He looked older, but I was so taken by him." Her eyes became glassy. "I was the only one who could speak English and my English was not so good, but I went over to the group of young men and could hardly speak when he looked at me. I was with another boy at the time. I thought I loved *him*. But the way I felt the first time I saw your father, Lily, words cannot describe it. I just…*knew*. The way you know about Adam. My parents were so angry. They forbid me to come to Scotland, but I love him so much I do it anyway. And I never look back, Mija. I never regret a day." Her voice wavered and a tear escaped. She quickly wiped it away. "I fear that you will never fall in love with another until you know how Adam feels about you. This is why I say you should tell him. You should never have regrets, Lily…*never*."

Tears cascaded down Lily's face as she listened to her mother talk about her father. She understood fully what her mother was saying but still she felt trapped by her own feelings. "Mama, I can't risk losing him from my life. If I told him, he could wind up feeling awkward around me. I couldn't bear that. He is the most important man in my life with papa gone. I…I love him so much that I'm prepared to watch him fall in love again just so that I keep him in my life. If he's happy then I'll be happy. If I lost him, Mama…" A sob escaped her throat and her mother leapt to her feet.

Coming around the table, Lenora wrapped her arms around Lily. "Please don't cry, darling, I do understand…really I do…I just wish things could be different…maybe if I speak—"

"No!" Lily gasped and widened her eyes. "No, please don't say anything…*please*. I need you to promise me that you'll keep this secret safe for me…*please*." She gripped her mother's arms as she pleaded.

Lenora cupped her cheek and nodded. "Okay…okay. I will say nothing, but please promise me if you get the *slightest* feeling that he feels something, you will tell him, si?"

"Mama, if *ever* things change, and I get the *slightest* inclination that he is in love with me…believe me…I *will* tell him. Just don't go getting your hopes up, okay? It won't happen." She kissed her mother's cheek.

Her mother kissed Lily's forehead. "I'm not so certain, Mija."

Chapter Thirty-Two

Lonely Pup In a Christmas Shop (Adam Faith)
December 2010

"I've got it!" Lily exclaimed as she and Adam sat in their favourite coffee shop.

"Oh shit…is it contagious because if it is I'm fucking out of here." Adam pretended to get up.

"Oooh, aren't we the funny one?" She pursed her lips and slapped his arm.

"Ouch! Oy! Okay, what *have* you *got* exactly?" He was filled with trepidation. And there was no wonder considering the last *great idea* that Lily had saw him registered, unbeknownst to him until later, with a dating website.

"Instead of a woman…you need…a pet!" she announced with a dramatic flourish of her arms.

"Are you fucking having a giraffe?" Adam laughed.

"No…but you could! Well not an actual *giraffe* obviously. Maybe something a bit smaller? A cat perhaps?"

He shook his head in disgust. "A cat? Seriously, Lil? I think you've had a temporary lapse in sanity. I'm allergic, *remember*?"

She scrunched her face. "Oh yeah, why do I keep forgetting that?"

He leaned toward her. "Erm…it's obvious… Did you hear what I said about the temporary lapse in sanity?" He leaned back again. "Although I'm beginning to think it's not so temporary," he mumbled.

She narrowed her eyes and pointed at him. "You think you're funny, Adders, but me and the rest of the world, we know differently." She gestured around them.

"Gee thanks… Anyway, I couldn't have a cat even if I *wasn't* allergic."

She cocked her head to one side. "Oh yeah? Why's that?"

His turn to roll his eyes. "Because I'm not a lonely old woman."

"Ha! You could've fooled me." She snorted.

"Fuck off."

"Honestly, Adders, you're sometimes more like an old woman than any old woman I know."

"Yeah…well… You're…you…oh fuck off."

She began to laugh hysterically. "Brilliant come back, Adders, as always so very quick witted." She guffawed slapping her leg.

He folded his arms and sulked as she wiped at her eyes. It was actually good to see her laugh, even if it was at *his* expense. Again. "Yeah, I can just see it now… Kids running past my house not daring to slow down in case *weirdo-stinky-cat-man* comes out and chases them. Great idea, Lil. *Great*." He couldn't help but laugh himself at the image.

"I can just imagine you in your dirty string vest surrounded by cats and smelling of wee." She threw her head back and howled again.

He held up his hands. "Right…right…I think we've established that me getting a cat is a *bad* idea, Lil."

She calmed herself down and dabbed at her eyes with a paper napkin. "Okay, so not a cat then. What about a dog?"

He thought for a few moments and raised his eyebrows. "Dogs *are* really good company." He spoke his thoughts aloud.

"They *are*. They love unconditionally. So even though *I* know your jokes are shit, it wouldn't matter to *Rover*. He would love you *in spite* of that fact."

"Again, Lil, fuck off…and who calls their dog *Rover?*"

She continued, ignoring his question. "I could imagine you with a dog, Adders. Let's face it. You're a teacher so you only work part time. It'd be perfect."

His mouth dropped wide open. "Part time? You *are* having a giraffe! Have you seen how many hours I put into marking…and planning…and…and…marking."

"You already said marking."

He folded his arms across his chest. "Yeah well, I put a hell of a lot of hours in, thank you." His tone was indignant even though he knew Lily was winding him up.

She laughed some more. "You're sooo easy to wind up. It's just like shooting fish in a barrel."

"A fish! Now there's a good pet," he said matter-of-factly.

"A *fish*? *Now* who's having a momentary lapse in sanity?"

"Yes but a fish doesn't need walking or feeding expensive food or—"

"Or loving or cuddling. Fish are shit pets and you know it. A fish is a lazy-man's pet. Fish have no feelings."

"I beg to differ. My Gran had a goldfish that used to know its name, and it used to come to the surface when it was feeding time."

Lily shook her head and crossed her arms. "Adam, the fish was called *Bob*. Every fish thinks it's name is Bob, you idiot. And you can't *train* a fish."

"But a dog is so tying. I mean, okay, so my mum would *love* to come around and look after a dog and walk it whilst I'm at work, seeing as Dad won't have one at home, but…they're tying."

"And, pray tell, what would a dog be keeping you from *exactly*?"

He looked to the ceiling in the hope of finding the answers scrawled up there. Clearly he was losing this argument. In fact, he was actually considering this ridiculous idea. "Stuff that I have going on…you know…in my life and shit."

"Ahem…Adders, when you're not…how did you put it? Oh yes, *marking and planning and erm, marking a bit more and shit*," she mocked him in a fake deep voice. "You sit at home watching Monty Python, eating crisps, and annoying the hell out of *me*. You could do all of that with a dog. And more. You could go for nice long walks in the Cheviots. You could snuggle up on the sofa and cry into its fur when you watch *Love Actually*—"

"Hey, that film is sad! It's got unrequited love and…and a guy who's a widower like me…and…and that little kid who loves that little girl singer…it's *really* sad, Lil."

She reached across and patted his arm condescendingly. "Of course it is, Adders. Well, maybe the first three times you watch it. Then even *you* should know what to expect after that."

He sat in quiet contemplation for a few minutes. "So I should get a dog then?"

"I think so. We could go and look at the weekend! They have to come and check your house over to make sure it's big enough, and you have to show that you're a responsible adult…" She pursed her lips. "Maybe I should be there when they come around…you know, so that there *is* a responsible adult there."

"Ha ha…very droll."

Following Lily's crazy, hair-brained suggestion and Adam's subsequent acquiescence, a team from Animal Welfare came out to assess Adam's home and living situation. After proving that a dog wouldn't be left unattended for long periods of time and that he could take care of a pet, Adam received approval. He wasn't sure who was the most excited about this situation, Lily or himself.

The day of reckoning arrived. Adam picked Lily up and

they made their way to the kennels to choose a furry friend. She was acting like a teenager and he couldn't help but smile.

"Oooh, I wonder who'll pick you, Adders!" she said as she bounced up and down in the passenger seat.

He scrunched his face and eyed her cautiously as if she was some kind of escaped lunatic. "Erm…hang on… *I'm* picking *it*…not the other way around."

She snorted. "Good grief, it's obvious you've never owned a dog in your life."

He chuckled and shook his head as he glanced over again at his hyperactive friend. "What are you on about, Lil?"

"Just wait and all will become clear, Adders."

♥♥♥

They arrived to a cacophony of barks and yelps as the rescue home manager showed them through to where the animals were cared for. The greetings from the friendly canines became louder as they began to walk down the aisles.

A lump lodged in Adam's throat as he looked at the dogs, all of which needed good, caring homes. "Oh God, Lil, how do I choose? I'm going to feel like such a shit not taking them all." He ran a hand through his hair.

She squeezed his arm. "Don't worry…you'll know. Trust me."

As they passed by each kennel, dogs lurched up vying for their attention, tails wagging frantically, each trying to bark the loudest. Suddenly, Adam stopped and stared down at a scrawny looking black dog with a big head. The dog sat there, tail swishing along the floor, head cocked to one side. He was what was known as a Heinz 57. Basically, no one knew what breed he was supposed to be. His ears were pricked up and his big brown eyes gazed up at Adam. He

had a white patch of fur on his chest and was almost
smiling, if that were possible for a dog.

Adam was besotted. He couldn't tear his eyes away.

The manager came to stop beside Adam. "Ahhh, this is
Monty. He hasn't been with us long. His owner moved
away to work on the oilrigs, and he couldn't find anyone
else to take care of him. He was heartbroken, poor guy.
Monty's been fretting a little and so he's lost weight. We
think he's a Labrador-Staffy cross breed, but it's hard to tell
really."

Adam nodded, swallowing past the lump in his throat,
his eyes glassy. Lily squeezed his arm again, making him
turn toward her. "Why don't you take him out and say hello
properly, Adders?"

He turned to the manager and gestured toward the dog.
"Could I…"

"Sure. Go through the doors at the end and wait for
me. I'll bring him through."

Walking through the door the manager pointed at,
Adam and Lily found themselves in an enclosed grassed
area. Adam looked down at Lily. "I think you were right.
The way he just looked at me as if *he* knew. He was
so…sure of himself sitting there. He didn't bark like the
others. I…I think *he* picked *me*." Adam said biting back the
emotion that had sprung from nowhere.

♥♥♥

Lily bit her lip, seeing the effect the black mongrel had
on him. "I'd say I told you so, but I'm not like that." She
winked.

Suddenly, the rescue centre manager brought the black
dog through the door on an extender lead. Adam crouched
down and the dog lurched forward to him, knocking him
onto his back. The dog proceeded to bathe Adam in saliva
as it greeted him like a long lost friend. Lily stood by and

laughed hysterically as the adoring animal mauled him.

"Erm, I think we can safely say that he likes you, Mr. Langton." The rescue home manager laughed.

"And, Adders, he's called Monty! How cool is that? You being a humongous Monty Python fan and all. Quite apt, don't you think?"

He somehow managed to get the giddy dog to calm down and roll on his back for a belly rub with his tongue hanging out—the dog that is, not Adam. Lily looked on with a smile on her face, which was mirrored in the one that beamed on her best friend's face. It was a beautiful sight, Adam smiling. It took her breath away. This was far better than playing match maker to him and another woman. This was safer. Lily's heart could share Adam with a dog. She could most certainly cope with this match.

Monty accompanied Adam to his new home. He was supposed to make the journey in the back of the car but after only five minutes of the journey had made his way onto Lily's lap and proceeded to wag his tail in her face or lick her from chin to forehead. Adam laughed, as Lily struggled to keep the dog off of his lap whilst he drove.

Chapter Thirty-Three

Sharp Dressed Man (ZZ Top)
January 2011

Christmas and New Year were over quicker than you could say Frosty the Snowman. Lily and Adam made regular trips out to walk Monty even though there was a thick covering of snow blanketing the ground and dulling every noise, like soundproofing. It was ridiculously cold and Monty had discovered a real affection for snow. Adam and Lily laughed hysterically when they saw the confused expression on the dog's face as he tried to eat some and it melted as soon as it made contact with his long floppy tongue. The canine was nothing if not tenacious. By the time they got back to the car he was soaked and the odour of wet dog permeated every fibre of their clothing.

"Bloody hell, Monty, you need a bath," Lily informed the soggy black dog whose tail was still wagging frantically.

"Now *that* will be an experience." Adam laughed.

"Yeah well, it's an experience you'll be having without *me.*"

"Lil, you're a spoilsport! I might need your help."

She snorted. "Not a chance!"

Once they were ensconced at Adam's house, back in the warm, Adam made hot chocolate. Monty was towelled off and Adam laid him by the radiator to finish drying his fur.

Handing Lily a steaming mug, Adam hesitantly spoke. "Sooo, I've got a favour to ask, Lil."

She frowned. "Oooh that sounds ominous. Be warned I may tell you to eff off."

He cringed. "You may, but I'm *really* hoping you don't."

She huffed impatiently. "Just spit it out, Adders. I have things to be getting on with, you know."

"Okay, here goes... Would you come with me to my work's Christmas party?"

She scrunched her face again. "Oh, either they're *really* organised at your school and they are having it *way* early or they seem to have forgotten that Christmas has been and gone quite recently."

"Neither. The venue the principal likes was booked up too far in advance, and she insisted there was nowhere else she deemed good enough...soooo...it was booked for January."

She started laughing. "That's what you call commitment. Anyway, can't you go alone?"

He ran his hands through his hair. "Yeah, I could. But I really don't want to. It's a dinner dance. If I go alone I'll look like...like..." His words trailed off and she immediately regretted her suggestion.

"Okay, of course I'll go with you. Silly arse."

He scooted up the sofa and hugged her. "Thank you, thank you, thank you. You won't regret it. Well, you *might* regret it...it might be as dull as ditch water...last year the food was okay but not fantastic...you may hate it...but if you do I'll owe you big time."

"You're selling this very well. I can't wait," she said sarcastically.

"Anyway...it's next Saturday. You need to wear a kind of evening dress type thing...if you have one."

"Of course, I've got one. You'd be surprised what I have in my wardrobe."

He wiggled his eyebrows suggestively. "Hmm, I'll bet, you saucy minx."

She smacked his arm. "Clothing, Adders...I just meant clothing."

♥♥♥

Adam arrived at Lily's place at seven fifteen in a taxi. It was the night of the not-so-Christmas party. Knowing Lil, she would probably be nowhere near ready. He tried the front door but it was locked, so he resorted to dinging the doorbell over and over until he received a response from the rather pissed off Lily who opened the door in her robe.

He closed his eyes for a couple of seconds and ran his hand through his hair. "Oh for fuck's sake, Lil, you're not even dressed!"

With a smirk, she began to unfasten her long, fluffy robe very slowly. Adam felt he should look away but couldn't. He wondered if he was about to see her in her underwear right there in the hallway of her house and wasn't sure why that caught his attention so much. He gulped as she opened and dropped the robe to the floor.

"Ha ha!! Your face was a picture! Hilarious! I've been ready for ages, you nutter."

He huffed out a breath he didn't realise he was holding in. "Funny, Lil. *Very* funny."

She gathered up her robe and flung it over the banister. Turning, she walked back toward him. He swallowed hard. She did a twirl. "Will I do? It's more of a cocktail dress than an evening gown, but I really like it and never get to wear it. It's designer you know." She winked. Adam stared. "Oh God…say something will you? Should I go change?" Her cheeks coloured, which drew Adam's gaze up from the figure hugging black velvet, off shoulder dress to her made up face. He had never really seen her wear make-up before. She was more of an *au naturel* type usually. But here she stood all smoky eyes and glossy lips. Quite different. Quite, *quite* different.

He shook his head to dislodge the confusing thoughts he was having about his best friend. "You…erm…you…look…erm…"

She sighed and stamped her foot like a spoiled child. "Right. That's it. I'm changing. We'll be late now."

"No!" He lurched forward toward her but didn't make contact. "No...no don't change. You look...erm, *great*. And anyway, there's no time, like you said."

She folded her arms across her chest. This didn't help Adam. All it did was push her breasts upward, creating more cleavage. "Well thanks, I *think*. Don't overdo the enthusiasm or anything. I'm only doing you a huge fucking favour, Adders." She looked really pissed off.

He closed his mouth briefly, feeling a little confused. "Lily, I'm *very* sorry. What I meant to say was you look...stunning."

A smile spread across her face... Lily's quite beautiful face. *Shit, stop that right now, dickhead. It's Lily. Remember? Lily who you've known your whole life? Get a fucking grip.*

Trying to rid himself of whatever the hell this feeling was, he gestured toward the taxi. "Come on, Cheesy, or we'll be late." He turned and made for the car as quick as his legs would carry him. He heard Lily cursing and locking her door.

♥♥♥

Drinks were being served when they arrived. Adam quickly made his way to the bar and ordered a double Jack. Lily opted for a more sophisticated glass of red wine. He felt unreasonably nervous. But then again, he was up for promotion to Head of English and at such a young age everything he did from now would create a certain impression. He had to get that job.

"Go steady, Adders. You'll be in no fit state to dance at this rate!" Lily snorted as he downed the bourbon almost in one go. "Look, I'm off to the ladies', seeing as you rushed me out the door. Try not to get pissed in the five minutes I'm gone, okay?"

He nodded. "Yeah…okay." He watched her walk away, hips swaying in the dress that accentuated every curve he'd never really noticed before. He groaned. *What the hell is wrong with me? I seriously need to get laid. That's it. It must be. If I'm ogling my best friend then it must be desperation point.*

He noticed Jaz—real name Jared as if that wasn't fucking cool enough on its own— Malone across the room. The new *American* music teacher. He was every teenage girl's fantasy and had caused quite a stir amongst the females at the school in the short time he had been working there. He was all male-model good looks, messy dark hair, muscles, and coolness. He had tattoos too, apparently. He had heard one of the younger female members of staff telling another in the staff room, *"He has…you can see them when he wears his white shirt. They look all…tribal. Oh what I wouldn't do to get a proper look."* The two women had swooned.

Adam secretly rolled his eyes when the image of male perfection came and stood next to him, beer bottle in hand.

"Langton." He nodded as he spoke in his American drawl.

"Malone." Adam nodded in return. God he was the epitome of fucking cool. It made Adam sick. *He even makes a bloody penguin suit look good.*

"Your…wife is smoking hot, man," Jaz informed Adam as he too watched Lily sashay toward the ladies'.

"She's not my wife," Adam said plainly, regretting it immediately.

Jaz's eyes lit up. "So, what then…fiancée? Girlfriend?"

Adam took a swig of the depleted contents of his glass. "Best friend."

Jaz nodded. "So…is she single?"

Adam snapped his face toward Jaz. "Erm, no. She's in a relationship with some Spanish guy. I think it's pretty serious." *Whaaat? What am I saying?*

A look of disappointment clouded Jaz's features. "Oh…right. Yeah that figures, I guess. Damn shame though, man. I bet you wished she was more than a friend, huh? With looks and a body like that, maaan, that's what you call a sweet piece of ass, right there." Jaz grinned as he shook his head.

Adam felt offended and affronted at Jaz's observations of Lily. Suddenly, feeling the urge to smack him or defend her honour, he slammed his glass down and went for the latter. "Actually, Lily and I have been friends since we were kids, so I don't appreciate hearing her being referred to as a piece of anything. Let alone a piece of *ass*. She's a person, for fuck's sake, Malone. And she is off limits, got it?"

Jaz held his hands up in surrender. "Okay, my man. Sorry if I offended you. I can see you've got it bad, dude. I apologise."

Before Adam could make further comment, Lily rejoined them at the bar. "Hey, Adders, who's your friend?"

Jaz held out his hand to her. "Jaz Malone, music teacher at the fine institution your *best friend* here works at." Jaz emphasised the words *best friend* as if trying to get under Adam's skin. It worked.

Lily blushed as she shook his hand. "Nice to meet you, Jaz. You're of the American persuasion, I take it?"

"Sure am. Seattle born and raised."

Lily bit her bottom lip.

Adam's gaze darted between Lily and Jaz. *Great. She fucking fancies him. The womanising fucking yank. Typical.*

"So, Jaz…what brought you here to Scotland?" she asked.

"I came over for a study break during my time at U-Dub and fell in love with the place. My girlfriend and I decided to try and get work here so when study was over we hopped on a plane." Adam saw disappointment flood Lily's face.

"So is she here tonight? Your girlfriend?"

Jaz dropped his gaze momentarily. *Oh for fuck's sake, now he's going to play the heartbreak card.* When Jaz looked up into Lily's face, his expression had changed. "Nah...me and Esther broke up not long after we arrived. I guess it wasn't meant to be. And I'm hoping that maybe one day I'll meet the right girl...maybe a Scottish girl. I love the accent." His mouth lifted in a sexy half smile.

"Yours isn't so bad." Lily fluttered her eyelids at him. Adam suddenly felt nauseated.

Jaz lifted his chin at her. "So where's your guy tonight?" *Whoops...dammit!*

Lily scrunched her brows. "My guy?"

"Yeah... your Spanish love?" Jaz chuckled.

"Rafael? Oh he and I aren't an item. We just...erm...enjoyed each other for a while. We're not in a relationship." Her eyes shot to Adam. She was clearly pissed off.

Jaz licked his bottom lip. "Oh? Well, maybe you and I could dance later?" He gave her one of his all American, handsome-as-all-get-out smiles.

"That would be lovely. I'll look forward to it, Jaz."

The host announced dinner was to be served and asked for everyone to find their seats.

"Why did you tell Jaz I was in a relationship with a Spanish man?" Lily spat as they sat side-by-side at the table.

"Because he's a womaniser, and I didn't want you being a notch on his bed post. That's why."

"Adam, I'm an adult. I can make my own decisions about who I do or do not sleep with. And looking at him I would *certainly* sleep with him, so do me a favour and stop the bloody big brother act for one minute so I can breathe, will you?"

"Well, excuse me for caring."

"I excuse you for *caring,* but I don't excuse you for meddling. And how do you know that he and I might not hit it off and actually have a relationship?"

He lowered his head and spoke in a harsh whisper. "Because you, Lily, don't *do* relationships. You do shagging men and then leaving them. You never fall in love. It's just not in your nature." He growled. "And neither does he, so you would end up as fuck buddies and nothing more. But if you did happen to *miraculously* fall for him, you'd get hurt."

Lily sat there agape. He regretted his unforgiving words. She was his best friend and in his own roundabout way he *was* trying to protect her. Wasn't he? She opened and closed her mouth like a fish out of water. Just before she turned away from him, he saw tears welling in her eyes. *Shit.*

He leaned across to her. "Lil, I'm sorry, okay? That was mean and unnecessary. Please forgive me?" She didn't respond at first. "Lily…please…I'm really sorry."

She slowly turned to him with glassy eyes. "I have never been made to feel so cheap, Adam. I can't believe you could be so cruel. And you already know that I *have* been in love. But I got my heart broken…no…smashed to smithereens. So excuse me if I'm not willing to give my fragile heart out to the first man who says he loves me. And there is nothing wrong with enjoying sex. If I were a man, you'd be patting me on the back. Now I suggest you just don't speak to me at all for the rest of the evening, and then when this is over, I would like you to leave me alone for a while, please." She stood from the table, pushed her chair back, and excused herself.

He felt like he'd been winded. He'd really hurt her. She had never spoken to him with such venom. They'd had plenty of fights, sure. But this one felt different. It felt real, and he hated himself for the things he had said.

For the rest of the evening, he watched Lily and Jaz getting to know one another on the dance floor and off. She left with him at the end of the evening, and Adam felt sure she did it out of spite but he couldn't say a word. He had practically pushed her into it.

Adam went home alone and feeling like a cruel and heartless idiot.

Chapter Thirty-Four

In My Life (The Beatles)

March 2011

Adam had respected Lily's wishes and left her alone. It had been one of the hardest things he'd ever had to do. He missed her like crazy. He'd lost count of how many times he had dialled her number only to hang up, or how many times he'd half typed a text message only to hit cancel. As a last ditch attempt to check she was okay, he had reluctantly spoken to Jaz, albeit briefly.

They were in the staff room during lunchtime one day, and Adam had finally plucked up the courage to ask the question.

He stood by Jaz and waited for him to finish his conversation with Elodie, the French teacher. Once the pretty brunette walked away, Adam cleared his throat. "Alright, Malone?"

Jaz narrowed his eyes. "Yeah, fine thanks…s'up?"

"I was just…erm…wondering if you'd seen Lily at all?"

"Oh right…yeah a little…but not for a couple weeks, why?"

Adam fidgeted with his empty coffee mug. "Oh, nothing. Just wondered how she was."

"You guys still not speaking, huh?" Jaz looked a little amused and it really pissed Adam off.

He flared his nostrils. "No thanks to you."

Jaz shook his head. "You two make me laugh."

Adam scrunched his brow. "Why's that?"

Jaz drained his mug. "She kept on asking about you the whole time we were together."

Adam brightened at the news. "Yeah? What's she been up to? Are you two…you know…"

Jaz dropped his gaze to the floor for a moment. "She's been out of the country a lot lately. We went on a few dates, but she decided that we weren't working out so..." Jaz looked quite solemn about the fact.

"Oh, right. You okay about that?" Adam was surprised at his own question. Why should he care?

"Yeah, yeah I'm okay. I really liked her though. She's fun and sexy and..." He shook his head. "Man, I can't believe you didn't get together with her. You clearly have the hots for her, dude."

Adam snorted. "Jaz, I've known her since we were in primary school. We used to make mud pies together and play cops and robbers. She's like my sister."

"Yeah? Maybe once, but it sure as hell seems to me like there's something more there."

Adam scrunched his brow. "Why? Did...did Lily say something?"

Jaz laughed. "Nope...not a single thing. But looking at the way *you* are right now? That speaks volumes, Langton." Jaz patted his shoulder and walked out of the staff room. Adam watched him leave. His mouth was agape. *What the f...?*

He took Jaz's comments with a pinch of salt. He did feel a little lost without her. But why wouldn't he? She was his best friend. They had gone periods of time without talking before, but *this* hurt. It hurt because his words had caused it. She was right of course. Enjoying sex didn't make her a slut. It made her human. She didn't deserve his judgment. His comments about her being unable to fall in love were just plain cruel. He knew she'd been in love once. It had affected her so badly she couldn't even tell *him* about it and she usually told him everything.

Sex was important to Lily. He knew this. Hell, he enjoyed sex himself. He just couldn't seem to get any.

Correction, he didn't *just* want to have *sex*. If he was completely honest with himself, he wanted love again. He wanted to feel that connection you feel when you *make love* to someone and they give themselves to you in the most intimate way, wholeheartedly. He wanted to get to know someone's body again.

♥♥♥

It was a cold Saturday afternoon and Adam was reading a book, sprawled out on his couch. Monty was laid beside him on the floor, on his back with his tongue lolling out, fast asleep. There was a knock on the door, which made Monty jump up and begin barking and bouncing around. Slowly, Adam dragged himself to his feet and placed his book on the coffee table. He made his way to the front of the house, trying to avoid a collision with his giddy dog. Bleary eyed he opened the door.

"Get the kettle on, Adders, I'm gasping for a cup of tea."

Adam stood open mouthed. "Lily?"

"Erm...last time I checked, yes. Can I come in or what?"

He stepped aside, feeling bemused at the way she had just waltzed back into his life as if nothing had happened. He followed her into the lounge. She flopped down onto the sofa.

He stood over her in his jeans and T-shirt with bare feet. "Is everything okay?"

She inhaled a long deep breath. "Look, Adders, you hurt me, okay? Don't do it again. I didn't like you very much for a while, but you *are* my best friend, and I didn't *like* that I didn't like you. Look, I'm sure you get my drift, so can we just get back to being *us* again?"

He leaned down and grabbed her hand, pulling her to a standing position. Wrapping his arms around her, he mumbled, "I've missed you, Cheesy."

She hugged him back. "Well, yes. I'm sure you have. After all you can't function without me in your life. How have you managed to get dressed and stuff?"

"With great difficulty."

"I can imagine."

"Look, Lil…I'm so sorry for the things I said. I was a complete shit."

She looked up into his eyes. "Yes…you were."

"I didn't mean to hurt you, you know?"

"Well you did. But I forgive you now. So let's just drop it, okay?"

He made a pot of tea and brought it through to where she sat. It was good to see her sitting on the sofa in his house again. He laughed at the sight before him. Monty had clearly missed her, too. He had climbed up and spread himself across her lap. He had filled out quite a lot and was far too big to be a lap dog. But Lily was happily scratching him behind the ears and he was loving it. His tongue was hanging out again and every so often he licked her from chin to brow.

"Ah, I see I've been replaced, eh?" He gestured towards the contented canine.

"I think you have. This one doesn't give me half as much grief. And I'm sure he can manage to dress himself when he goes out on a date."

Adam grinned. "Funny. I've missed being insulted constantly."

She giggled. "Ah well, don't you worry. I've been saving up and I have a couple of months to catch up on, so brace yourself!"

Chapter Thirty-Five

Crazy (Cee Lo Green)
June 2011

Supermarket shopping was the bane of Adam's life. Eve used to make it more bearable and even fun. These days he favoured shopping later in the evening when it was quieter. Thursday night. Shopping night. The supermarket was a little busier than he was used to and it irritated him. He was standing in the tinned food aisle trying to decide between a tinned chicken pie or a tin of chicken curry for dinner when suddenly a trolley crashed into his legs sending him careening across the aisle and onto his side. Expletives flew from his mouth as the air pretty much turned blue around him.

"Oh my God! I'm so sorry!"

Adam looked up, pursed-lipped into the face of a very pretty young woman. She had beautiful red hair that fell in long waves around her shoulders. Her eyes were a vivid green and filled with a look of horror.

He clambered to his feet. "What the hell were you doing? You obviously weren't watching where you were going!" he snapped.

The young woman's bottom lip began to quiver and her verdant eyes welled with tears. "I'm really very sorry. I was…I was texting my mum, and no, I wasn't looking. I'm sorry."

His frown softened at the poor woman's expression. "It's okay. I'll live," he chuntered, feeling rather guilty.

"I bet you'll have a bruise there tomorrow." The woman cringed.

"Yeah, probably…look, don't worry…I'm fine."

The woman sniffed and wiped her eyes. His chest clenched. She looked really upset as she stood there clearly not daring to walk away. Finally he smiled. "I'm Adam Langton by the way," he informed her, but unsure why that was even relevant.

She smiled back and a look of relief washed over her. She breathed out a huff of air that she must have been holding in. "I'm Petra...Petra Millar," she said with a shaky voice.

"Look, Petra, you seem really shaken up. Can I buy you a coffee over in the cafe?" He gestured toward the back of the store where the little coffee shop was situated. He hoped it was still open.

"Erm...erm..."

"Sorry, sorry...I'm a stranger and it was creepy of me to ask. I just feel really bad about...you know...the poor impression of a footballer diving after a wee tackle." He nodded to the floor.

Petra laughed. "Coffee would be great, thank you."

They wheeled their trolleys toward the coffee shop and parked them up at the edge in the trolley park. Adam ordered two lattes and carried them over to where Petra sat fiddling with her fingernails.

After handing her drink over, he sat opposite her. "Are you okay now?" he asked.

"Oh, shouldn't I be asking you that question? After all it was me that pole axed you with a shopping trolley." She pursed her lips and her eyes pulled into a frown.

"Oh, I'm fine. I'll speak to my lawyers tomorrow."

Petra's face drained of all colour. "Oh God, you're going to sue me?"

He frowned. "Oh hell, no I was kidding." He shook his head slowly.

"But you might change your mind...when you get home and your leg is all bruised...you'll sue me, won't you?" Her eyes were wide.

He held his hands up in a surrendering motion. "Honestly, Petra, I'm kidding. I'm *not* going to sue you."

She narrowed her eyes. "Are you sure?"

He chuckled. "I'm *very* sure. I was kidding."

"Okay…okay…that's fine then." She was a very nervous person judging by the way her hands were juddering.

"So, Petra, what do you do?"

"I…erm…I work in the whole foods shop in town."

"You work in *Nutty As*?" He smiled.

She nodded. "Yes…that's me."

He grinned. "But your trolley was full of junk food." He remembered noticing the large amount of chocolate, wine, and crisps in the trolley, not to mention the ready meals and pizzas.

Her cheeks coloured and she cringed. "Guilty. I work with pulses and oats and tofu all day. All I fancy when I get home is a burger and chips or sweet stuff." She bit her lip as a smile spread across her face.

Adam laughed. "Clearly use of the products is not a requirement of the job."

She shook her head with a wide smile on her face. After a pause she asked, "So Adam Langton, what do *you* do?"

"I'm an English teacher. High school." He took a sip of his coffee.

"Oh gosh. Teachers were never that good looking when I was at school." She slapped her hand over her mouth as soon as the words had finished leaving it. "Oh God, I shouldn't be allowed out in public, should I?" she said as she covered her eyes and the pink in her cheeks became a vibrant red.

"Don't worry about it. It's a nice compliment. And to be honest most of the ones I work with are ugly as sin, but don't tell them I said so." He winked.

She giggled as she sipped her coffee. "So…are you married, Adam?" she eventually asked.

"Yes…well…no…widowed actually." He winced at his mixed up answer.

"Oh that's sad. I thought you must be married. All the good looking ones are." She pulled her lips in, closed her eyes, and hit herself on the head. "Stop putting foot in mouth, Petra."

"I'll take that as a compliment too, eh?"

They chatted for a while about the whole food shop and some of the interesting characters Petra encountered on a daily basis, and Adam regaled her with stories of his own unhealthy diet.

Eventually, Petra took a deep breath. "Look…Adam…I know this is quite forward of me, but as you can see my brain-to-mouth filter is malfunctioning today anyway. Why stop now I say. Anyway, can we swap numbers? You know, in case you decide you might want to meet up again? You seem really nice, and well, most of the guys I meet are either married, old, boring, or gay…so…"

He reached into his inside pocket and pulled out a scrap of paper and a chewed biro, probably one he had found on the classroom floor. He proceeded to scribble down his number and hand it to her. "Here you go. You have mine. You know, in case you decide you don't want to hear from me. That way it's up to you if you contact me or not."

She took the number and put it in her bag. "Thanks. Look, I should go really. I have to get home to feed Grunewald."

He was the one to narrows his eyes this time. "And Grunewald would be…?"

She shrugged. "He's my parrot. I get quite a good deal on seeds," she stated as if that was the sole reason one had a pet bird.

"Ah, of course." He nodded.

The two new acquaintances parted company with an awkward handshake. She said she would call and arrange coffee maybe. As he walked away he surmised giving her his number was possibly a stupid thing to have done. She seemed a bit flaky after all. She was pretty, but that was maybe where things ended. As he put his items through the self-check-out, he decided she probably wouldn't call him anyway. She'd seemed very nervous. He put thoughts of Petra from his mind and left the supermarket.

❤❤❤

The following day was draining. Chaucer and a group of disaffected fifteen-year-olds was a combination set for disaster. The language was neither easy to pick up nor did they feel—as they informed him on a regular basis—that it held any relevance to them whatsoever. Adam had tried every which way to get through to them, but they were behaving very badly and were testing his already stretched patience. Thank goodness, it was Friday at last.

After running a whole class detention, Adam arrived back to his car. The car park was all but empty, and he had a cold beer waiting at home with his name on it. Well, it quite possibly had Mr. Bud Weiser's name on it, but he was going to drink it regardless. As he was throwing his bag of exercise books for grading into the back of the car, he spotted something moving out of the corner of his eye. He glanced up to see Petra's face disappearing behind the wall. *What the—?*

He slammed the door. "Hi, Petra? What are you doing here?" he called as he approached where she was trying to hide. He heard her cursing and she slowly walked out from where she was badly secreted.

Her cheeks were flushed. "Oh…erm… Hi, Adam. I…I just…erm…wanted to check your leg was okay," she stuttered and fiddled with her hair as she spoke.

"A simple call or text message would have sufficed, you know. You have my number, after all. You didn't have to come all the way out here, and I didn't actually say where I worked, did I?" He asked the question more of himself.

She shook her head. "No, you didn't say where, but well…I figured it out really…and I had the day off from work…so…" She continued to fidget.

"Oh…right…well, that's nice, but really you didn't have to come and wait for me on your day off."

She shrugged. "Oh, no it's okay. I took the day off especially."

A sense of unease settled in the pit of his stomach. "You took the day off especially so you could come to my place of work to check on my leg? Oh…" He tried to sound breezy. "Well…well, as you can see I'm upright and fine, so you can go home and stop worrying now."

"Are you free tonight?" she blurted out.

"I'm sorry…no, I'm going out with my friend for her birthday."

A look of horror spread across her face. "You said you were *single*."

He shook his head and narrowed his eyes. "No, no, I said I was *widowed*, but really, Petra, I only met you yesterday. What's all this about?"

She shrugged again and looked at the floor. "I like you…a lot."

He puffed his cheeks out. "Thank you, that's sweet and everything, but you can't just go turning up at my place of work. It's not the done thing. It's not exactly healthy, Petra." He glanced around to see if anyone was bearing witness to the conversation, suddenly desperate not to be alone with her.

She jerked her head up. "Are you saying I'm crazy or something?"

Oh so, she's a mind reader, eh? He couldn't help but laugh. "I never said that. I just think that taking a day off just so you can follow me to work is…well…just not healthy, that's all."

"Okay, I won't do it again. So when are you coming around?"

"Sorry? Coming around?" *When did I say I was going around?* He racked his brains but came up blank.

"Yes, when are you going to come around to mine… When are we seeing each other again?" She continued to fiddle with her hair rather like a sulking toddler.

He pulled his features into a confused frown. "Erm…I…erm." He shook his head as he struggled to process everything. "I'm sorry, Petra, but we didn't actually arrange to meet up again. That was why you took my number, remember?"

"I know but I'm asking you now instead, seeing as I'm here and everything. I think we were meant to meet. Yesterday I mean. I think it's the universe telling us something, don't you?" She lurched toward him and he stepped back.

Oh great…someone forgot to take their crazy pills this morning. He smiled and spoke as calmly as he could manage. "Petra, I think the universe is saying it's time for me to go home. I've had a rough day, and I'm just not in the mood for this…this…whatever this is. I think once you've had time to think this all through you'll realise that I'm not for you." He stepped back again. "I'm not really ready for a relationship, and I think you're maybe looking for something that just isn't here. I met you in a supermarket. We had coffee. That's all."

"You led me on!" she cried out.

"No, what I did was give you my number, which was maybe an error of judgement on my part. If that was misleading then I apologise, but really I'm not looking for a relationship. Friendship maybe, but to be honest, you've freaked me out a little bit, and so maybe we should just rethink the whole thing."

"I've told my mother about you!" she said accusingly, hands on hips.

He was feeling exasperated now. "We've met *once*, Petra, *once*. You know nothing about me. Nothing at all!"

She frowned and looked at him from under her lashes. "Yes and we *both* felt a connection, Adam. I know you felt it, too."

"What I felt was agonising pain when you rammed me with your bloody trolley!" he raised his voice without meaning to.

Suddenly, she burst into tears. "This *always* happens! Men *always* treat me like this."

He felt guilty and more than a little disturbed at the same time. "Petra, don't take this the wrong way, but maybe you're just a little bit too intense. Maybe following someone to work is not the best way to try to start any relationship, eh? Just slow up a little. You'll scare people off."

She slowly lifted her head. "Do you think so?"

He nodded. "I do yes. I'm sorry to say that, but just think about how you've behaved after only meeting me once."

"I know...I know...but...you seem so...normal. I *want* normal, Adam. I want a man like you. But men like you think I'm stupid."

"No, that's not true. Intense, maybe. Stupid, no." *A complete and utter fruitbat, absolutely*. He cringed at his errant thought.

"Okay." She nodded as she sniffed. "Okay, I won't come here again. I apologise. But can I still call you? Could we still go out on a date?"

Shitty-shit fuck, what do I say now? "I don't think *I'm* what you need. You seem like a nice girl who needs a man who can offer a relationship. I can't do that. I don't mean to be cruel. But perhaps you and I should just…you know…be friends maybe…leave it there?" *Friends who never speak and never, ever acknowledge each other preferably, you crazy stalker person. Think it's time to change my number.*

She nodded resignedly. "Yes…yes I think I spoiled it. I always do." She turned and walked away with her head hung. Adam breathed a huge sigh of relief at her absence. He almost ran to his car, praying she didn't follow him home. Visions of the movie *Fatal Attraction* flashed through his bewildered mind.

❤❤❤

Later that night, Adam sat in the restaurant with Lily and filled her in on the parrot owning, creepy, stalker-type he had met at the supermarket the day before and how she had turned up acting all bizarre at school.

Lily, of course, thought it was hilarious.

She listened, wide eyed but with a huge grin on her face. When he had finished telling her the story, she leaned forward. "Oh no, Adders, I bet you were *Petra-fied* of her! Get it? *Petra*-fied!" She burst into fits of hysterical laughter and guffawed as tears streamed down her face.

He scrunched his eyes and crossed his arms over his chest. He was not amused. "Very funny, Lil. I'm telling you, she *was* scary. I'm talking major bunny boiler material. I feared for my life for a wee while there."

Lily held up her hands. "I'm sorry, Adders, I'm sorry, seriously… Did you…did you have to repeat things to her *parrot-fashion* for her to listen?" She slapped her thigh as her voice reached a kind of strangled, high-pitched squeak, and she was unable to contain her mirth.

Other diners were beginning to look at them.

He leaned across the table and spoke in a low voice. "Lily Macrae, will you bloody calm yourself down and get a fucking grip?"

She pursed her lips and it was clear that she was trying to hold back her laughter. "Sorry…sorry…you're right though…she did sound *seedy*! Ha ha! Seedy! I'm so good at this." She dabbed at her eyes. "And when you think about it, she does work at *Nutty As,* so you should have known she was a few oats short of a granola bar."

His face finally broke into a wide grin. Shaking his head he raised his glass at his watery-eyed best friend. "Okay…I give up. I'm glad I made your day. Happy Birthday, Cheesy."

Chapter Thirty-Six

Leaving On A Jet Plane (John Denver)
August 2011

"Are you the only bloody reporter they've got, Lil?" Adam was in a huff again about Lily's latest trip to the United States.

"Obviously not, you numpty, but they think I'm good at what I do. And believe it or not I actually *like* the travelling."

The pair sat on his sofa eating pizza and drinking a nice bottle of Shiraz whilst Monty waited for the crusts. They'd been having yet another Monty Python film marathon, which had lasted from Friday night through to lunchtime Saturday. Lunchtime drinking was never a good idea, and Lily had said she felt sure she would regret it when she had to get to the airport later that night. Luckily a car was being sent for her and so the alcohol didn't cause her any issues.

"You're never fucking here," he grumbled.

She nudged his shoulder. "Oh shut up your bloody moaning. You should be relieved I'm going. At least when I'm away I'm not trying to set you up on dates."

He grinned. "Yeah, you've got a point." He munched on his slice of pepperoni thoughtfully. "So where are they sending you this time? And what's it about?"

"I'm heading off for sunny Florida to do a piece on beach front businesses."

He huffed. "Do they just make stuff up to send you on holiday?"

"Don't care if they do." She laughed. "I'll go and do my job and bloody well enjoy myself. Might even catch some rays on Daytona beach."

"Yeah well, no more tattoos, okay?"

"Ha! You haven't even seen my tattoo! So you can't judge. You're just too chicken to get one."

"Ahhh, that's where you're wrong!" he slurred, sloshing his drink as he pointed his finger at her. "I *have* seen it...a few times in fact, when you've been crouching! I haven't a clue what it says though, and anyway, the word you're looking for is *sensible*, Lil." He pursed his lips at her. "I don't like needles, so why would I want someone sticking one in me repeatedly?"

"Yeah...true...you'd probably just pee your pants anyway." She burst into fits of laughter whilst he sat open-mouthed searching his alcohol-addled brain for a witty retort but none came.

"Oh fuck off, cheese head."

His response made her laugh harder until tears were streaming down her face. "Sorry...but...you're so immature...I can't...breathe." Her voice came out as a strangled squeak.

He gaped at her incredulously. "*I'm* immature?"

The heat was intense as Lily sat on the balcony of her hotel room eating breakfast. The film crew would be arriving soon and they had been instructed to get their footage and get out. A hurricane had been forecast just after she had arrived the day before. It was a little bit disconcerting and had set her nerves jangling.

Whilst she sat there, her cell phone vibrated, notifying her of a text.

Adam.

A: Lil, just seen on news that a hurricane is heading for Florida. You shd come home.

She sighed and hit reply.

L: S'ok Adders, will be out of here before it hits anywhere near. Stop worrying!

Ten seconds later.

A: Lil it sounded bad. Please come home.

She didn't respond. She had learned that the more she pandered to Adam, the more he worried. It was best to ignore him when he got scared. Eventually, he would calm down when he realised she was on her plane journey home.

The film crew arrived on time, which filled her with a sense of relief. *Surely the impending storm can't be that bad if people are still travelling in.* She met the guys in the hotel bar.

"So how bad is it supposed to get?" Mack asked. He was the best camera operative she had the pleasure to work with. He was Glaswegian with a wicked sense of humour and was usually filling them in on his latest practical joke or drunken weekend exploits, but today he was seriousness personified, which set Lily on edge.

"Pretty bad." Kyle was the only American on the team. He was in charge of sound. He would control the boom and mix at the same time, which was awe-inspiring in itself. He was incredibly handsome for an older guy. She guessed he was in his late forties but had never asked his actual age. Usually unshaven, with shaggy, sandy brown hair, he had a look of Kevin Bacon and sounded a little like him, too.

Of course she was a huge fan and constantly had to remind herself that he was in fact *Kyle*...not *Kevin*. Suffice it to say she always found working with him distracting on account of the Kevin Bacon issue mainly but also for the fact he had some intricate ink-work covering his left hand that disappeared up his sleeve. It was the hand that held the boom right in her face. She'd often meant to ask him about it, but had never got around to it. Kyle and Mack were like a double act. The best of friends despite the distance that sometimes lay between them. Their friendship had been set in stone a long time ago.

Kyle rubbed his tattooed hand over his face. "They're starting to board up windows and remove any freestanding heavy items from the beach front. It's looking pretty serious out there, guys."

She snorted and the men turned to look at her. "Sorry, but it can't be that serious. I was sitting out on my balcony eating breakfast just this morning. I mean, people are here on holiday. There are kids all over the place."

Kyle turned and gave her a warm smile. "Yeah, and that's why the precautions are being taken, honey. Nature doesn't tend to discriminate by age. As long as we do what we're asked to do, we'll be fine." Kyle patted her arm in a patronising way that made her blood boil.

She clenched her jaw. "We need to get on a plane. There's no point in staying here when we're not going to get what we came to film," she snapped.

Kyle shook his head. "That's not going to happen, Lily." He looked worried, which didn't help her rising fear. "The weather front is moving in pretty damn fast. No one is leaving and no one is getting in. Flights in are being diverted and all flights out are grounded." He glanced over to the window. She followed his gaze and saw that the palm trees outside were swaying dramatically, almost doubling over in the increasingly strong tempest. The previously blue sky was now a dark, ominous shade of grey. A stray piece of newspaper flew toward the window and stuck there for a few seconds before flying off and continuing its frantic journey to an unknown destination.

She gulped and let out a nervous laugh. "But they're used to this kind of thing, aren't they? I mean…it happens a lot, right?"

The men looked at each other before Kyle cleared his throat. "Oh…yeah…sure, sure. We'll be fine…fine…totally fine." His brow was scrunched. It was not a convincing performance.

The crew agreed to stay put in the resort hotel—not that they had any choice in the matter. Lily went to her room, closed the drapes, and switched on the TV. Every channel in the local area was reporting the devastating effect Hurricane Irene was having on the east coast of the United States and in the Caribbean. Lives had already been lost. Trees had been ripped up and homes destroyed. Lily stared open mouthed and suddenly felt very, very homesick. Her phone vibrated in her bag.

A: Lil, please tell me you are okay. This hurricane is doing a major number on the part of USA where you are. I'm terrified for you.

Lily took a calming breath and hit reply.

L: All is fine here, Adders. Not as bad as it sounds on the news - she lied – *Don't think we will get footage we need so prob comin home early xx*

No reply came. Lily wondered if her message had even gone. There was a good chance that networks were down locally. Lily went to the window and pulled back the drapes. She gasped, her hands reaching for her face. The scene below was one of utter devastation. In a very short period of time since she had closed the drapes, the palm trees she had been watching earlier were now bent double and staying there. Some looked on the verge of being torn from the ground at any second. Garbage swirled a rhythm less, chaotic dance around the parking lot of the hotel. Several cars were already damaged and the rain hammered down relentlessly. The wind whirred eerily through the invisible gaps in the windows, creating a creepy whistling sound, and she swore she could see the glass bowing inward. She stepped away, just in case. There was a knock on her door and she dashed over to open it.

"Miss Macrae, you must come down to the hotel restaurant immediately, please. We need to clear every floor above ground level." The young bellhop's face was pale and his tone urgent.

She nodded, nervously, the weight of the situation finally sinking in. "Yes, yes sure. Let me just grab a few of my belongings."

His eyes widened and he held up his hands to her. "Miss there isn't time, please." She was already inside the room grabbing her phone and handbag. Everything else would have to wait.

Once on the ground floor, she gave her name and room number to a gaunt-looking woman who wore the hotel's uniform. Her name badge read *Sindy Mason, Head Receptionist*. She had clearly been given the job of completing a roll call. Lily glanced down as Sindy ticked her name off the list. She noticed that there were still a number of names not marked off. Her heart rate increased. Walking past Sindy, Lily was surrounded by people dashing around frantically. The restaurant had been turned into some kind of refuge centre. She felt like she had walked onto the set of a disaster movie. There were people wrapped in blankets, some with injuries.

Many of the male staff were already outside wrestling with large sheets of what looked like marine plywood for boarding up the windows. Some of the male guests were making their way outside to help, too. Lily rushed to the exit and stepped outside just as a large metal object came hurtling toward her. She screamed and jumped back just in the nick of time as the mail box hit the ground in front of her and twisted into a heap at her feet, gouging a chunk out of the asphalt. Her hair swirled around her as if it had a mind of its own. With her heart pounding, she retreated back inside, feeling shaken after her brush with death.

She watched as the men outside tried hard to keep the boarding in place whilst dodging debris flying through the air. It all seemed too little too late as one window blew inward showering Lily and a group of people with shards of glass. People screamed and ducked down or ran. An older lady cried out in pain and a female member of staff rushed over with a medical box in hand. The poor woman was covered in blood. The wind howled through the open space left by the implosion and people rushed to the aid of those who had been hit, while men outside tried their best to cover the window. Each panel of boarding that was fixed in place darkened the already dimly lit room a little more.

Lily's heart pounded in her chest. It was like a war zone. She remembered being offered a post reporting in Afghanistan but had turned it down feeling unable to cope with what may have been presented to her there. She felt sure it could have almost resembled this horrid situation she found herself in. Looking around at the fear-filled expressions that surrounded her, something suddenly clicked in her mind, and she rushed into action making her way over to help an elderly gentleman who was also covered in blood and hobbling away from the large group that had gathered.

She managed to grab some swabs and antiseptic from one of the staff and helped the old man to sit down in a chair at the opposite side of the large room.

A faint scream could be heard coming from outside, and a piece of the boarding at one of the windows was whipped away by the ferocious storm. She rushed to the direction of the noise and caught sight of a crumpled, lifeless body just through the opening. Her stomach lurched. *This can't be happening. It just can't. It has to be a nightmare. Wake up, Lily…please wake up.*

On shaking limbs and with adrenaline coursing through her veins, she made her way back over to the old man and began to clean his wounded arms. Someone grabbed her shoulder from behind. She swung around.

"Lily, have you seen Kyle anywhere?" Mack was pale and his face was scratched and grazed.

"No…no, Mack I haven't," she stuttered. "Some of the men have gone outside to help. What happened to your face?"

"Got hit by flying glass when my room windows blew in. I'm okay though." He squeezed her shoulder.

"Oh no, I can clean it for you if you—"

"No, it's fine, honestly. I want to find Kyle." He patted her arm and headed out of the door which led into the corridor in search of his friend. She turned back to the elderly gent.

"Not what you signed up for, huh, honey?" the man said as Lily dabbed at the cuts on his arm.

"No…no…not at all. Sorry if I'm hurting you." She winced.

"I'm Abe. And don't worry, honey, I'm a tough old guy. Fought in my fair share of battles."

"I'm Lily, nice to meet you…although I wish it had been in better circumstances." She shook his hand lightly.

"Hmmm, not the best way to spend the holiday, is it?"

She laughed nervously. "No, you got that right." More screams and shouting could be heard from outside, making her flinch and whip her head around.

"Anyone dumb enough to still be out there is pretty much a goner I'd say." Abe's voice was croaky as he spoke. She turned back to see his eyes filled with emotion. She swallowed down the lump lodged in her throat.

"Abe…Abe! Where are you, Abe?" A frantic woman was coming toward them, her eyes scanning the room. The round faced, well made up lady caught sight of Lily and Abe and came dashing over. "Oh thank goodness, thank goodness." She grabbed Abe and pulled him tight into her large chest. "What would I have done, darling?"

"You got Lily here to thank, Audrey. She's been looking after me." He winked up at Lily as the woman turned and grabbed her.

Audrey pulled her in for a bear hug and almost squeezed her last breath out of her body. "Oh sweetheart, thank you...thank you. Fifty-five years married and this happens. It's the last time I suggest we go away for our anniversary." She dabbed at her teary eyes and then turned her focus back on her husband.

♥♥♥

Night fell and the temperature dropped even further. The storm still battered the building relentlessly. Staff had handed out as many blankets as they could find, and people tried their best to sleep, but the cramped conditions were not conducive to relaxing and neither was the tense atmosphere. Mack hadn't returned and there had been no sign of Kyle. Lily's phone had died, but no one seemed to have a signal anyway. The landlines were all down as well. It was as though they were completely cut off from the outside world in their own little corner of hell.

Just before midnight, the power went out, and an audible gasp traversed the room as the place was plunged into an eerie darkness. Sadness washed over Lily, replacing some of the fear she had been feeling up to this point. Almost everyone else was on holiday and had family or friends to hold onto as the violent storm raged around their safe haven. She was quickly reminded that she had no one. Even at home she was alone.

Really alone.

Tears stung her eyes as she pulled herself into a foetal position and shivered beneath her thin blanket. She had foregone a thicker one in the selfless hope that someone who had sustained injury during the ordeal would benefit instead. Every so often crashes could be heard outside. No one rushed to find out what the noises were anymore, probably feared what they would see. *Ignorance is bliss, as they say.*

The night seemed endless, and she fought against her tiredness, fearing that she would never wake up again if she gave in to sleep. As she lay huddled in a ball, she could hear quiet sobs and sniffs from somewhere within the room as the reality of what was happening continued to sink in. Adam's face sprang into her mind. Tears stung her own eyes as she thought about his handsome face and thick, dark hair. His smiling eyes could see through her most of the time. He could cheer her up simply with a quirk of his mouth. And what a mouth. What she would give to taste his kiss once and have him kiss her back. Suddenly fear struck her, as she imagined never seeing him again. And what the hell would he do if he lost her, too? He'd been through so much. She had to stay safe and alive. She *had* to. A sob escaped her as Adam's grieving expression filled her mind. Her chest ached as she tried to stifle her cries in the flimsy blanket.

"Are you alright, sweetie?" She looked up into the twinkling eyes of an older lady whose features she could barely make out in the darkness.

"Y-yes…thank you so much for asking. Just feeling homesick and a little scared," she admitted.

"Oh, honey, you'll be fine, you'll see…it will all be over soon." The kind lady reached for Lily's hand and squeezed it. "Hold onto me, sweetie. If it helps."

She sniffed, feeling overcome by the stranger's kindness. "Thank you, it does."

♥♥♥

At around eleven the following morning, the power suddenly brought everything back to life. Lights came on, the TV began rotating images of sheer devastation, and a member of hotel staff announced that hot food was being prepared. A short while later another person came in and announced the storm had moved on. An audible sigh traversed the room followed by tears, whoops, and lots of hugging.

The older lady who had held Lily's hand hugged her tight, and Lily's eyes welled with moisture once again. "See, sweetie, we made it…we made it." Lily clung onto her and sobbed into her striped T-shirt, which was adorned with gold shimmering images of anchors and shells. Pulling away, the lady wiped Lily's tears with her calloused thumbs. She had kind eyes and pinky-red hair. The fake rinsed colour that old ladies seemed to favour. "I'm Maud, by the way."

"Thank you so much for everything, Maud. I can't tell you what it meant to me to not feel alone through the night…I'm Lily."

"Well, Lily, if you need a hug anytime soon, you be sure to come find me." She patted Lily's shoulder and turned back to fold her blanket.

♥♥♥

Several people made their way toward the outside of the hotel. Lily followed behind, scanning the area for any sign of Kyle or Mack.

The scene outside still resembled a war zone. Fallen trees, broken glass, crushed cars, and shattered windows were all that could be seen for many hundreds of metres.

Paramedics and other people wearing bright fluorescent coats picked through piles of debris.

Lily's next sight would remain etched on her brain for all eternity. She rounded the corner and saw a row of bodies with blankets covering all the way from just above their feet right up and over their faces. Her hand came to her mouth and her stomach lurched as nausea washed over her. People really were *dead*? She felt the colour drain from her cheeks.

Walking toward the macabre scene and shaking like a leaf, her breath caught and a convulsive sob burst forth from her chest. Poking out of one of the blankets was a tattooed left hand.

Kyle.

She screamed and trembled as tears over-spilled her eyes and she dropped to her knees. "No! Kyle...no. Oh please no."

One of the paramedics dashed over to her and placed his arm around her shoulders. "Miss, you shouldn't be out here. Come on, let's get you back inside...come on now." He helped her to her feet and walked her back into the restaurant as her legs shook and she wretched, her empty stomach aching with the spasms. After placing her in a chair, someone, she didn't see who, handed her a steaming mug of tea. She could smell the sugar.

Someone squatted beside her. "Lily." She lifted her head and looked into Mack's distraught face. "Oh God, Lily, Kyle's dead." He sobbed.

Lily nodded. "I know...I can't believe this has happened." Tears escaped from her eyes once again. He removed the hot drink from her grasp, placed it down on a nearby table, and enveloped her in his arms. They both clung to each other and succumbed to their mutual grief.

Chapter Thirty-Seven

If I Lost You (Travis Tritt)
August 2011
Lily arrived back in the UK four days after the devastating hurricane had almost taken her life and had succeeded in taking her friend's. Adam picked her up from the airport and clung to her in the arrivals lounge whilst she sobbed into his chest. Her relief was immense. He held her up as her legs weakened, then grabbed her suitcase and helped her to his car. Once they were both seated, she glanced over to him. His head was back and his eyes were closed.

He gulped and opened his red-rimmed eyes. "I thought I'd lost you, Lil," he croaked as he reached over and squeezed her hand. "I don't know what I would've done."

She forced a smile as she squeezed his hand back. "Shhh, it's okay. I'm here. You can't get rid of me that easily."

"You're so important to me, Lil. You do know that, don't you? I can't lose you, too. I can't."

"Stop it or you'll make me cry again." She sniffed.

"No, I mean it. I hope you know how much you mean to me... What your *friendship* means to me." His eyes were intense as they bored into her. She desperately searched for something hidden in there. A tiny shred of hope that maybe something good would come of all this. That he had realised he loved her.

He inhaled deeply. "You're my family, Lil...you're my family. Me and you against the world." Her heart sank. *Family.* "I'm so glad you're back and that you're okay." Squeezing her hand one last time, he smiled and then turned to start the engine.

Once she was deposited back in her own home, he rushed around making tea and taking her case upstairs. He eventually worked off his nervous energy and sat at the opposite end of the sofa, holding his steaming mug.

She cleared her throat. "So…what have you been up to while I've been away?"

He scratched his chin. "Erm…well I went on a date but I don't think it went too well."

She frowned. "A date? Really? Who with? I thought you were giving up on the dating sites."

"Yeah…yeah I have. I met her through Diane at work. She's a friend of a friend."

"Oh? What's she like?" She feigned interest.

He huffed. "She's really pretty, Lil. Blonde hair, green eyes, slim. She's called Emily. She's…really nice. I'm supposed to be seeing her again."

She snorted. "Can't have been that bad if she's agreed to see you again."

He pursed his lips and his forehead creased. "I suppose not."

She leaned forward. "What made you feel it wasn't a success last time?"

"I was…a little distracted." He dropped his gaze.

"How come?"

"Well, you'd gone to Florida and the hurricane had hit. I couldn't rest. I was really out of my mind with worry. I explained, and she said we should call the night off early so I could get home and wait for news. She offered to come with me, but I didn't think it was fair, so we agreed to see each other tomorrow instead."

"Oh…tomorrow? Well, that's…promising then. You'll be fine." She did her best to encourage him.

"Yeah…yeah, probably. Just wasn't that sure."

"Look, I'm here and I'm fine. Normal services can now resume. Your wardrobe assistant is back." She held up her hands and smiled breezily, but inside her stomach was knotted.

A stunning grin appeared on his face. "Lily, you're the best."

"And don't you forget it."

♥♥♥

Lily had yet another restless, nightmare-filled night following her arrival back in Scotland. Adam texted regularly, but she had assured him she was completely fine and that he shouldn't worry.

It was the morning after his second date with Emily. Lily had showered and decided to make the most of the compassionate leave that had been thrust upon her by her superiors. She had spent a little time pottering in the garden and then had been to the local newsagents to buy the Sunday papers. After brewing a fresh pot of coffee, she had the newspapers spread across the kitchen table and was reading all about the further devastation caused by the hurricane in the south of the United States as it had continued to move on wreaking havoc whenever and wherever it hit land.

She paused when she heard *Bring Me to Life* by Evanescence on the radio. The song stirred emotions inside her and sent shivers down her spine as she absorbed the lyrics. The powerful love story told within the song was something she'd hoped would have happened to her and Adam. She longed for him to feel that way about her. To have his eyes opened in that way. When she felt her eyes stinging, she reached over and turned the radio off.

The doorbell rang, snapping her back to reality. She could see the tall shape through the glass panel and in daylight it was obvious who it was.

"Adders, to what do I owe this unexpected displeasure?" she teased as she opened the door.

He huffed. "Sod you, then. Last time I bring you a bloody cream cake." He turned to walk away.

"Adders, I was kidding!" she shouted after him, feeling panicked.

He turned back to her with a wide grin on his face. He pointed at her. "Haaaa! Got you!"

"Shit head."

"Oh shut up and get the kettle on." He flicked her head as he walked past her.

"So mature, Adders, so mature." She made her way through to the kitchen and washed out the cafetiére.

"So…do you want to hear about my date?" he asked enthusiastically.

Nope…not in the slightest. Can't think of anything worse at the moment. "Sure…how'd it go?"

"Weeeell, I'm seeing her again."

She turned to face him and put a smile on her face. "Great…see…oh ye of little faith."

He ran a hand through his hair. "Yeah, yeah it's great. We had a lot to talk about, you know? No awkward silences. She flirted with me a lot and kept touching my leg… I think…I think she really *wants* me, Lil."

Placing two mugs of freshly brewed coffee on the table, she said, "Why do you sound so surprised?"

He pursed his lips. "Oh, I don't know. I think it's been so long since I've fancied a woman it's all a bit bizarre."

Fiddling with the edge of the newspaper, she asked, "So…you do fancy her, eh?"

He laughed. "Lil, there's nothing to *not* fancy. She's sexy, she's intelligent, and she laughs at my jokes."

She snorted. "Well then I'd ditch her immediately. Finding your jokes funny is a good reason to avoid her, I'd say." He threw a dishtowel at her. It landed on her head and he burst out laughing, almost falling backward off his chair. She pursed her lip. "Funny man." She tried her best not to laugh.

"Yeah, well, she loved the shirt you picked out. I've never liked stripes. That's why it still had the tags on, but she commented on it straight away. Said I looked very handsome."

"Ha! The woman is clearly delusional. She thinks you're handsome *and* laughs at your jokes. Poor, poor woman."

He raised his eyebrows. "Yeah, well, just you wait until I get my own back."

Her heart skipped a beat and her mouth dropped open. "Meaning what?" she asked, narrowing her eyes at him.

"Funnily enough I have access to the Internet and photos of you, too. I could always return the favour and set *you* up on a dating site, so be very, *very* careful, Lil."

She threw the dishtowel back at him. "Don't you bloody dare. It's different for me." Heat rose in her cheeks and she suddenly felt flustered.

He chuckled for a few moments. "Seriously though, Lil, you should date. In fact, remember Doug Jenkins from our Science Department?"

She pursed her lips. "Yesss?" she said cautiously.

"Weeeell, he always asks after you. He's asked me for your number before, but I never gave him it because you were always overseas when he asked. Now you're back for a while, you should go out. He's a really nice guy. And I'm told he's considered quite attractive."

She scrunched her face up. "He's…alright. But he's not my type, Adders."

He looked frustrated. "Why won't you allow yourself to be happy, Lily? And who the hell *is* your type? Does the thing even exist? Or is he some kind of mythical fucking creature? Coz I'll be damned if I can tell!"

Feeling insulted by his comment she folded her arms over her chest, the heat rising in her cheeks again. "That's a lot of questions, Adders. Not really necessary. And of course he exists...somewhere...but I'm not going to dive into a relationship with someone I don't fancy just because I'm lonely." She folded her arms over her chest.

"And what? You think that's what I'm doing?" Anger flashed across his features and his cheeks coloured.

She sighed. "Of course not, you pratt. I didn't say that, did I? I just want to find my *own* man. When *I'm* ready."

"Oh? But you couldn't leave *me* to do that?"

"What? Find your own man?" She stifled a giggle.

He pulled a face at her. "Funny. Come on, Lil. Why were you so hell bent on setting me up when you won't accept the same help? You've pretty much just admitted that you're lonely. So what's the problem?"

"For fuck's sake, it's like the Spanish Inquisition. Can we just change the subject?" she snapped.

After an uncomfortable silence, he asked. "So do I tell Doug *no* then?"

"You do."

Chapter Thirty-Eight

I Can't Make You Love Me (Bonnie Raitt)
September 2011
Being back in the UK was a strain. This permanent change did not sit well with Lily. Okay, so she was a little traumatised from the situation she had found herself in while she was in Florida, but what do they say? You have to get straight back on the horse. Unfortunately, that horse had been allocated a new rider. Her bosses just didn't feel she could cope with being out there again. Who were *they* to make such a life changing decision for her without consultation?

The only marginally good thing was that she got to spend more time with Adam. Sadly, that was a double-edged sword that might just finish her off better than the hurricane's attempts. She was tired of setting him up and helping him get ready for dates, emotionally drained in fact. Surely, he was capable of finding his own woman? She had started this whole thing off with the best intentions, but as always, her intentions had backfired.

This latest woman, however, was a tad different. She was, to all intents and purposes, *perfect* for him. Blonde (just his type), pretty (from the photo on his phone that he had shown her), intelligent (ran a business training school), and slim. This was his *third* date with her. Yes. *Third.* He was, as ever, nervous as hell, he told her on the phone. He had begged Lily to come over and help him get ready. Tonight, it was the last thing she wanted to do. He was a grown man for goodness sake.

She finished off the last dregs of her cold coffee and climbed into the shower. Having been for a jog to try and clear her head, the last thing she needed was to go around to Adam's stinking and give him yet another reason not to love her. No, this was it. This was the last time. She was thirty-one years old.

Time to let go.

She let the hot water cascade over her body and face as the tears came. She had spent so much of her life in love with this man. This wonderful, protective, handsome, sensitive, caring man. But she had to let go now. She had suffered in silence for far too long. Never having the right opportunity to tell him how she felt. Not that it would make any difference. She would always be Lil—the best friend. Family. Always the bridesmaid, never the bride.

Enough was enough.

Solemnly, she dressed in her favourite jeans and sweater. Applied a little makeup and did her best to tame her wild brunette curls. With a sigh, she climbed into the car and headed for Adam's house. The bare chested man opened the door before she had a chance to knock.

She stifled a gasp. His body never ceased to affect her. "Someone's eager." She tried to smile.

"Oh God, Lil, thank goodness you're here. I'm a wreck!" He panted as he stepped by to let her in. "I've tried on five different shirts and three different pairs of trousers." He ran his hand through his luscious, thick dark hair.

Her chest ached.

She forced a smile. "Good grief, you're such a girl, Adders."

"I am…I am, aren't I? Oh shit, Lil. She could be *the one* and I'm acting like a teenage fucking girl." He paced the room.

The one? "Look just calm down, okay? So she's perfect…but so are you." Lily bit her lip.

"Huh? Oh yeah, I'm perfect alright. I'm sweating like a pig, I have emotional baggage, and I crumble under pressure. *Perfect!*" He threw his hands up, clearly exasperated.

Sighing and rolling her eyes as she always did, she went over to the wardrobe door where all the shirts were waiting like washing hung untidily out to dry.

"This is your third date, Adders. You haven't put her off yet, so there's no reason you will now. Right, where are you going?"

"I'm taking her to Bella Roma. It's quite a nice place but not exactly posh as such." Lily had only been once with a date. It *was* rather lovely. She remembered the owner was a sweet Italian man called Arlo.

"Okay. You won't need a tie and you can wear jeans. These are the ones that make your backside look...I mean...erm...that...erm...these are the best ones." Stumbling over her words as her cheeks heated at her almost-slip-up, she held them out to him.

He scrunched his face and then shook his head. "Okay...okay...shirt?" He ragged his joggers off and stood there in just his boxers. She tried to avert her eyes. But God, he really *was* perfect. In every possible way. She gulped as she felt the sting in her eyes. She would have to tell him soon. Tell him that she could no longer do this. He was on his own. He had overcome his grief with her help, but he had to go it alone now. She bit the inside of her lip. "Lil? You okay?" She glanced up at the beautiful, half naked man who now looked very concerned and just nodded, unable to form words.

She breathed in a long, calming breath. "Right...shirt. Well, personally I've always liked the pale blue one with the button down collar. It's...you look...it makes you look...a little less repugnant." She teased in the way she always had but didn't really feel the joke.

"Gee thanks, Lil. With friends like you…" He grabbed the shirt and slipped it on his muscular torso. His sculpted back muscles flexing as he moved. She swallowed hard again and turned away.

"Okay…will I do?" He turned around on the spot in his bedroom. She couldn't help but smile. He looked stunning. This Emily woman would fall for him tonight, if she hadn't already, and that would be it. The end. Taking a deep breath she stood before him and put her hands on his arms.

"Adders, she would be crazy not to fall head over heels in love with you right then and there." Her voice was almost a whisper. He locked his gaze on hers and unreadable emotions flashed across his face. She dropped her arms still looking into his eyes, willing him to see the truth. But instead he shook his head as if to rid himself of some confusion or something.

He cleared his throat and said, "Awww, thanks, Lil. You're such a…wonderful friend."

She bit down harder on the inside of her lip. "And don't you forget it." Repeating her well-used phrase, she punched him lightly on the arm. She went back over to the bed and sat down.

He paced again. "I'm scared shitless though. Tonight might be…you know…*the* night." He chewed on his thumb. "She's made it very clear that she wants me. But…it's been so long, you know?"

Her heart sank. The last shred of hope left her body. Once he made love to Emily that was it. No going back. She wouldn't let him go and who could blame her.

Finding a little courage from somewhere, Lily took a deep breath. "Look, Adders…I need to tell you something… I may struggle to get the words out, so just let me speak, okay?"

He sat beside her, a look of concern on his face once again. "Sure…anything…what's up, Lil? Are you…are you alright?"

"I'm…yes I'm fine…it's just that… I can't do this anymore…this…this—" Adam's phone interrupted them.

He glanced at the caller ID. "Oh God, it's Emily. What if she's cancelling? I should take this." He looked apologetic but Lily just smiled and nodded. "Hey, Emily…how are you?... Yes…ahuh… oh right…that's fine…no problems… I'm looking forward to seeing you again, too." Lily stood. Feeling that the moment had passed, she walked toward the door. "One sec, Emily… Lily? Lily where're you going?"

She turned and smiled at him as breezily as she could. "Don't worry…we'll talk later. Have fun tonight…and…good luck, eh? Let's hope she's *the one*." She turned and walked down the stairs as she heard Adam continue his enthusiastic conversation.

By the time she reached the car, Lily's tears were relentless and she felt like someone had reached in and pulled out the very heart of her. Well, what was left of it anyway. There had been no closure like she'd hoped. But she had to make her own now. She *had* to let go. Finally. He would *never* love her back. Not in that way. Not in the way he had loved Eve. Not that she wanted to replace her friend in his affections. No, she just wanted him to love her in a way that wasn't *just* friendship. She took a deep breath and opened the car door. She wiped the tears from her eyes and stood for a moment with her head hung down, trying to compose her emotions and willing herself not to look back. She *couldn't* look back. She would just get into the car and go home, drawing a line under everything. He would get the message eventually.

♥♥♥

Adam finished his call to Emily. The plans had changed. She had asked if she could meet him at the restaurant instead. That was fine. He was ready now, thanks to Lily. *Oh God Lil, she had wanted to talk!* He rushed to the window and looked down into the street. Lily stood by her car looking at the ground and leaning on the open door. Her shoulders were shuddering. What was she laughing at? She wiped her eyes. No, she wasn't laughing. She was crying about something. He was about to go after her when without looking back she climbed into her car and drove away.

Lily never cried. Well not often. She was a tough cookie. Checking his watch, he realised he would have to set off and wouldn't have a chance to speak to her until probably tomorrow. After all, he would no doubt be back too late tonight if he came home at all.

He sat on his bed to pull his suede boots on. The conversation played over in his mind along with the images of her face. Her expression had been…lost…resigned even. But about what? It didn't make any sense. *What* could she not do anymore? Visit and help him pick out clothes? She'd always done that. Boost his confidence? She'd always done that. Help him find a woman to share his life with? It had been her idea…

He thought back through what had been said again, trying to decipher the clues, if there were any. *She sounds perfect…but so are you…she would be crazy not to fall in love with you right then and there…* He remembered back to other conversations they had shared. The look on her face when he had told her he was getting married to Eve; the way she always came running no matter what; that moment all those years ago when they had been playing tennis as teenagers. That had always stuck in his mind. He swallowed hard and rubbed his hands over his face.

Running his hands through his hair, he grabbed his jacket and keys and made his way down to the car.

Chapter Thirty-Nine

All I Want Is You (U2)

Emily was waiting outside the restaurant when he arrived. She smiled widely as he approached her. She really was attractive. Shoulder length blonde hair, green eyes, and a very nice figure. She was wearing a fitted black dress and grey jacket. *Very sophisticated.*

Adam kissed her on the cheek as they greeted each other. "It's good to see you again, Emily."

"Lovely to see you too, Adam. Although, it only feels like yesterday with all the phone calls." There had been several after each date since Diane, head of Science, had passed Emily's number on to him. "I don't know about you but I'm starving." She giggled.

"Me too…I could eat a horse."

Smiling and leaning into him, Emily whispered. "Um…I don't think they serve it here, but I know they do a very good steak."

He held the door open for her. "Awww…that'll have to do then." He chuckled.

The Maître d' showed them to a table for two by the window, and as soon as they were seated. a waiter brought a wine menu over and handed it to Adam.

"Any preferences?" he asked as he began to peruse the list of reds, whites, and roses available.

"Not really. You choose.'"

"Well I'm driving, so I'll be sticking to soft drinks…you choose."

"Oh, come on, one glass won't hurt…or are you trying to get me drunk?" A sultry smile played on her lips.

His jaw clenched. "I don't drink and drive…at all…ever."

She gulped and her cheeks coloured. "Oh gosh, of course…I'm so sorry."

He closed his eyes and gathered himself. Opening them, he smiled. "No, it's…it's fine. What should I order?"

Her cheeks were crimson as she replied, "Pinot Noir?"

"Sure thing."

He waved over the waiter and ordered the wine. Nodding his head, the Italian gentleman commented that it was an excellent choice and made off to fulfil the request.

After a few quiet minutes, Emily said, "Gosh everything sounds so delicious, Adam. What do you like the sound of?"

He was staring out the window, totally distracted by a woman with long, dark curly hair as she walked past with her head down, rummaging in her bag. She lifted her head just as she was parallel with the window. "Sorry? Oh erm… I think I'll have the steak." He stared blankly down at his menu, not really paying attention to the text.

"Are you having a starter? Maybe we could share one?" Emily asked

He snapped his head up. "Erm…sharing…yes…so what do you fancy?"

Looking at him from under her lashes, she smiled. "Other than you?" she asked seductively.

"Sorry? Oh…yes…ahem." He felt the heat rise in his cheeks. The waiter came to take their orders. When he had left them alone again, Adam cleared his throat. "So what have you been up to since I saw you last?" He took a sip of his sparkling water.

"Working mainly. I signed a big contract this week so this is a bit of a celebration for me. I like getting what I want." She kept her eyes locked on his.

He peered at her over his water glass. "And what is it that you want next, Emily?"

"I think maybe you know the answer to that." Her voice was a breathy whisper.

He curled one side of his mouth up, keeping his eyes focused on her. "Oh, I don't know. Tell me anyway."

Leaning forward and touching his hand, she answered, "You."

♥♥♥

Looking at the clock through the fog of her tears, Lily realised it was almost one a.m. She had cried non-stop since arriving home from Adam's. Letting go was so very hard. She had put her CD of *Adam songs* into the player and allowed herself to look back through all her old photo albums, telling herself this was the last time. They would go into storage tomorrow with some of her other belongings. They would remain there indefinitely. Then she would say goodbye to Jedburgh and head off to London. The offer of the news anchor's position had been a shock. She hadn't told Adam. Not yet. But she would take the job. She had to. She needed distance again. Things were always easier with distance. Not easy. But *easier*.

Her heart ached as she looked back through the box of wonderful memories. The difficult memories, too, like Adam's wedding. He had adored Eve so very much. But who wouldn't? She was a beautiful person. Lily was sure that deep down Eve knew about her feelings for Adam. There had been many knowing looks over the years. But Eve had never treated her differently. She had never gloated or shunned her. She had included her in their lives as if she knew how much being apart from Adam would hurt her. Eve knew she was no threat because Adam worshipped his wife. They'd had the kind of love that everyone aspires to. That *Lily* aspired to.

Eve was cruelly ripped from Adam, too young, by the idiot who thought driving whilst under the influence of alcohol was acceptable and safe. Lily would never forgive that foolish man who had caused her best friend so much pain and heartache. But now was the time to just admit defeat. She was young enough to meet a nice man and have children. Surely, she could love someone else now? Surely?

Just as the melancholia of U2's *All I Want Is You* washed over her and overtook her senses, she gathered all the photos back up into the box and closed the lid on her memories for the very last time. Wiping her eyes once more, she switched off the lamp and took her wine glass and empty bottle into the kitchen, letting the song resonate through her. The CD would have to go, too.

Suddenly, there was banging on the front door that made her jump. She pulled her robe tightly around her and gingerly walked to the front door to see if she could tell who it was. Stopping a few steps away, she squinted to try to make out the tall figure. The rain was coming down in torrents, which made the obscured glass panel in the centre even more opaque.

"Hello? Who is it?" she shouted as calmly as she could.

"Lil, it's me, Adam." He sounded out of breath.

"Adam? What the hell? It's gone midnight." She began to walk toward the door again.

"I know and it's fucking chucking it down, so can you please open the door?"

She unfastened the latch and pulled the door open. She inhaled sharply at the vision before her. Adam was standing there, drenched, rain sliding from his wet hair, down his face, and soaking through his shirt, which was now clinging to his chest. *So beautiful.* He wiped his hand down over his face and slicked his hair back, his chest heaving.

Coming to her senses, she gestured toward him. "Come in, you'll catch your death out there." She stepped aside and he passed her, stopping in the hallway and dripping all over her tiled floor. He turned toward her with a huge grin on his face.

"I'm sorry it's so late, Lil." He ran his hand through his hair once again. "I...I just had to come and tell you...you *are* my best friend after all. And I wanted you to be the first to know."

Her heart shattered into a million pieces and the tears that had been falling all evening began to dampen her face yet again. This was it. This was the news she didn't want to hear but knew was inevitable.

"Oh?" was all she could muster.

He stepped toward her. "It's happened, Lil." She forced a smile through her tears, not bothering any more to wipe them away. "I've found her...the *one*." He smiled the most beautiful smile. Happiness radiated from every pore. She took a deep breath and nodded. She wanted to be happy for him, but it was hard when her heart lay trampled beneath his feet. He stepped closer still. "It's an amazing feeling, Lil. Just the *best* feeling ever. I had to tell you."

She closed her eyes. They must have made love. He had such happiness in his eyes. She knew there would be no going back if that happened. *When* it happened. He had fallen for Emily. And Adam didn't give his heart away easily so it must be right. This was it. This was the end of her impossible dream. Biting the inside of her lip to stifle the sob that was building inside her, she opened her eyes again looking straight up into his melted chocolate gaze.

He took her face in his hands and brushed his thumbs over her cheeks to wipe away the tears. He rested his forehead on hers. His eyes were damp now, too. "Lily...please don't cry."

She couldn't help but set the sob free. "Sorry...but...I'm...I'm so happy for you."

He smiled that glorious smile again and whispered. "Thank you…I'm glad that you're happy for me. It's so important to me that you are. It's all so clear to me now. I've found *the one*, Lil…*the one*." She had heard him. He didn't need to keep saying it. Each time was like a dagger through the remains of her broken heart. She nodded; it was all she could manage to do.

He took a deep breath and with shimmering eyes and his lower lip quivering he spoke.

"Lily…I can't believe I've found the one I'm supposed to be with. I never thought I'd love anyone this way again. Not after…after Eve. But…this feeling…I'm awake again. It's like everything makes sense again. Like someone's switched the light back on. My heart's bursting and I just feel so…so happy. It's so incredible. I…I had to tell you first. I can't believe it…I've found *the one*, Lily."

Tears continued to make their escape from her eyes and she nodded. "Yes…yes you've said. I get it."

He shook his head. "No…no I don't think you do."

She frowned. "What do you mean?"

"Lily…the one…the one I'm supposed to be with forever…it's *you*."

She gasped as she looked deep into his eyes and saw it. That look.

Adoration.

He really meant it. He was in love with her. With one hand slipped around her waist and the other into her hair, he sealed his declaration with the kiss she had always longed for and her broken heart mended.

Epilogue

I Alone (Live)
Two Years Later

Lily awoke to an empty bed. Sunlight streamed in through the curtains, which were floating in the uncharacteristically warm Highland breeze. She sat up and curled her arms around her legs, resting her chin on them. She had always hated waking up alone.

There was a knock at the door, and she tiptoed across the smooth wooden floor of the luxurious log cabin to open it. There stood a young man with a large bouquet of flowers in his arms.

"Hello, Madam. I'm from McCaig's florist. Where would you like these flowers?" the smartly dressed young man asked with a polite smile.

She gazed first at the huge display and then back at him. "Oh wow, thank you, they're beautiful. Please, could you put them on the table by the window?"

"Yes, Madam…but…there are a few more to come." He gestured behind him where another three men stood equally as loaded down.

Her hand came to her mouth and tears welled in her eyes. "Oh…goodness…please, bring them in. They look heavy."

The man smiled. "Yes, as you can see I had to get extra help for this delivery."

Her heart skipped as her senses were bombarded with beautiful colours and scents. "Just place them wherever you can."

Following her instructions, the men placed vases filled with the most fragrant flowers she had ever smelled wherever there was an empty surface. Their sweet, heady perfume permeated the air around her. Once the deliverymen had gone, she stood in the centre of the room surrounded by vibrant colours. A calm serenity washed over her and a smile pulled at the corners of her mouth.

Walking out to the balcony that overlooked the mirror-like sea loch with the majestic mountains in the distance, she inhaled the fresh, clean summer air. As she stood there looking at the view out over the crystal-clear water, listening as it lapped at the shore beneath the cabin, arms slipped around her waist. Kisses were feathered from under her ear down her neck to her shoulder, sending shivers tingling down her spine.

She closed her eyes and sighed. "Hmmm, I wondered where you'd got to."

"Went out to get my beautiful girl a few flowers."

"A few? I think you bought all the flowers on the island." She giggled, enjoying the closeness of her man. She turned around and gazed into his eyes, slipping her arms around his neck. "Who would've thought that we'd end up here?"

"In the Highlands? It seemed the perfect place. It's ours. *Just* ours."

"Actually, I meant who would've thought we'd end up *together*."

"Well, I'm glad we did," he said as he rubbed his nose against hers.

Leaning up on her tiptoes, she kissed him gently on the lips. "Me too. I think there's a good chance that I'm the happiest woman on earth right now."

"Well that stands to reason, seeing as I'm definitely the happiest man." He removed his hands from her waist and laced his fingers in hers, pulling her back inside the plush log cabin.

She willingly followed him to the bed where he removed his linen shirt, khaki shorts, and boxers, never tearing his eyes from hers. Pulling her toward him, he slipped her white cotton nighty over her head. "God, I was right...you really are beautiful." He sighed as his eyes, filled with adoration, roamed her naked body.

She ran her hands over his toned stomach to his chest, caressing his tattoo. "I do love this," she said as she traced the script with her fingertips.

"I'm glad you do." He smiled. Sliding his hands into her hair, he pulled her into him and kissed her gently at first. She returned the kiss with tenderness until his tongue danced with hers and the kiss deepened, becoming more passionate and filled with need. She moaned as he slipped his hand down her jaw and over her collarbone to caress her breast. Her head rolled back as desire washed over her. The way he made her feel...

Tumbling backward, he pulled her on top of him on the huge bed, the crisp, soft, white linens billowing around them like the summer clouds above their romantic highland hideaway, his mouth still locked with hers. His fingers continued their sensual journey down her body, right to her core as his mouth moved over one of her tightened nipples. She stroked her hands down his muscular back, delighting in the feel of his muscles flexing under her touch. Rolling her onto her back, he laid atop her body resting on his elbows. "I love you so much," he whispered. His gaze locked onto hers as he slipped inside her, making her gasp as she revelled in the feeling of closeness.

Grasping him as he moved, she breathed, "I love you too...more than anything."

Their bodies moved together as they made love slowly and languorously, kissing and caressing each other and whispering loving, tender words. Suddenly, they were lost together out in the heavens, crying out each other's name and holding on tight. Lily was once again overwhelmed with emotion and tears escaped her eyes. She would never get enough of this feeling.

Never.

When they had calmed and she was resting her head on his chest, she traced the tattoo once again. She reached up and placed a kiss where it scarred him so beautifully. "I still can't believe you did it."

"What? The tattoo? Well, once I knew that yours was done all those years ago for me, I had to have one to match." He kissed her hair and stroked his fingers down her back. "I still can't believe you did that for *me*...before I even knew... I always wondered what it meant... Gaelic was never a language I understood, even though it really is beautiful."

She paused for a moment. "Well, the words are true... I *will* always love you."

He squeezed her closer to him. "Well, now you know the feeling is mutual and the words are there permanently...only for you...*forever.*"

She sighed as she continued to trace the script.

He tilted her chin up with his finger, so that their eyes met. "Happy honeymoon, *Mrs. Adam Langton*," he whispered as he lowered his mouth to hers once again.

The End

About the Author

© Craig Photography Studio 2013

Lisa is a happily married mum of one with two crazy dogs and a passion for writing. After relocating to Scotland from England and writing her first novel she gave up on running a craft business to do what she loves full time and is now putting the finishing touches to books four and five so watch this space.